Raves for *Amidst Traffic*

"Michel Sauret skillfully weaves a collection of twenty-two short stories, each an independent original creation brilliantly crafted into an interconnected melding of storylines... Sauret has created characters that elicit empathy, concern and hope in the midst of their anguish, and grief. These compelling stories will challenge you emotionally in a way that opens your heart... A unique collection of engaging symbolic poetic prose that challenges the reader to reflect on the potential impact of one life on another."

-Reader Views

"An ambitious collection of interwoven short stories about negotiating Christian values in a corrupt, violent world... There are bright spots of quirky but straightforward storytelling, as with 'The Problem With My Shoes,' which delightfully begins: 'I knew I was in trouble when my shoes started talking to me.'"

-Kirkus Reviews

"From an old man collecting drinking straws three at a time to a pair of Chicago drug addicts fairing poorly in their attempt to raise a child, nearly everyone involved in this collection of connected short stories cannot seem to shake the feeling that something bigger than themselves is going on... Readers interested in Christianity as it pertains to everyday people will find much to revel in."

-IndieReader

"Yes, this is a 5 star book... It's like a glimpse of what we see as opposed to what God sees. We see happy bits, sad bits, and bits of what doesn't make sense at times, but God sees it all as blending to one creative story He's putting together... Michel Sauret is a creative author, there's no denying it, and this book shows that creativity in abundance... Read it. I can't see how you'd be disappointed!"

-Christian Fiction Book Reviews

"Writer Michel Sauret is also a photographer, and the ability to capture brief yet rich instances applies to his fiction."

-Pittsburgh City Paper

"A lot of twists and turns that keep you reading story to story until the end."

-Janet Shawgo, author of "Look for Me" series

AMIDST
TRAFFIC

short
stories

Michel Sauret

AMIDST
TRAFFIC

Book design & publishing by
One Way Street Production,
Pittsburgh, PA

Cover photo by Matthew Kovalcik

ONE WAY STREET PRODUCTION
is a registered trademark in the U.S.A.

For information, contact:
onewaystreetproduction@gmail.com

Cover art and book design by One Way Street Production

www.onewaystreetproduction.com

RENEWED EDITION

Trade paperback ISBN: 978-0-9883784-0-7
Electronic book ISBN: 978-0-9883784-1-4

Categories:

FICTION - SHORT STORIES
FICTION - THEOLOGICAL
FICTION - LITERARY
FICTION - SUSPENSE

Printed in the United States of America

For Heather
My love, my life, my inspiration

CONTENTS

A Word to the Reader

When I first published "Amidst Traffic" my goal was to write gritty and compelling stories that conveyed the depravity of the world in which we live. We live in a world full of fear, violence, rebellion and chaos. Christians have to somehow weigh in that reality into an equation that involves a Just and Sovereign God.

As an effort to display that depravity, many of my characters indulged in some pretty graphic language. I created scenes involving Soldiers in Iraq and bank robbers in the middle of a heist. In the process, F-bombs were dropped along with a few other choice words.

It was a struggle for me to publish the first edition with that type of language inside. I originally justified the decision by reasoning that this is how the world really is. This is how people really talk.

So I published the book, but I constantly battled with that

decision.

This book was always intended to be literary first (with passages of poetic prose and story endings that left you wondering or figuring things out for yourself), and Theological second. I think both Christians and Atheists struggle with the emotions conveyed in this book. We are all human, after all, and we all suffer human pains. I wanted this to be a book that could bring Christians and Atheists to the table and provoke a conversation. This is not a book that bashes Atheists or proclaims Christians victorious.

This book is meant to make the reader reflect on how we are all connected. Our pains touch one another, even among complete strangers. It's a book that is meant to strip down our pretenses and our defenses, and force us to face our inner struggles, our fears and our doubts.

Most of these stories were inspired by philosophical questions.

What is our conscience? Why are some people crazy? What does it mean to be grateful? Who is God? Why do some people choose not to believe in Him? Why is there violence if He truly exists? If He is sovereign, are we free?

I think these are questions that everyone battles with in some form. It's only natural that we do so. Even when we stand at a point of conclusion, a point of certainty, we will always look back to the days when those questions troubled us.

But I realized that I was alienating fellow believers with language that was intentionally written to offend. How can you spark a conversation with someone if the language you use forces people not to listen?

So I asked myself, "Is the vulgar language really necessary? Is it vital? Would these stories cease to exist without it?"

I made efforts to rewrite dialogue and passages that would

portray a sense of vulgarity without actually being vulgar in doing so.

I slaughtered my own children, as they say in the creative writing world.

With that, I decided to release a Renewed Edition of "Amidst Traffic," which is the one you're holding in your hands right now. If you currently own the First Edition in paperback, and you simply find the language too offensive to get through, I would be happy to replace your copy with this edition. Just send an email to the address found in the copyright page, and we'll replace your First Edition with the Renewed Edition.

My hope is that these stories can still come across authentic as a result of these changes. My hope is that the dialogue still rings true to the ear.

In today's world of literary fiction there is already too much vulgarity, and I didn't want to add to it unnecessarily. Unfortunately, nowadays, redemption found in novels and movies relies on worldly solutions to worldly problems. That's like saying that gravity can help stop an avalanche. Not all of my characters get redeemed, unfortunately. But those who do get a chance to battle with deep, theological questions we too often dismiss in our society.

There are a lot of Christian themes underlying the stories in this collection, but I wouldn't say these stories are like your typical Christian novels seen today. Much of my writing is dark and sobering.

This will seem unusual to those who are familiar with my photography, which is often very bright and colorful. In my photography, I've had the pleasure of capturing the happiness of children laughing and of brides and grooms committing their love for one another in a covenant before God. Usually the images I produce with my wife, Heather, are bold with color and vibrant with energy.

Most of these stories are not so.

The majority of them are somber and complex.

They're intended to mirror the inner struggles we all battle with as human beings. Here is an opportunity to think, really think, about the world we live in.

Another theme found in this collection is that of voices we hear inside our heads.

Before you think that this author has gone crazy, I want to reassure you that I don't actually hear voices. Except, the stories we read in fiction books sometimes act like voices in our minds, especially for the author.

We all wonder where authors get their ideas. To be honest, we wonder that too, sometimes. There are moments when story ideas feel like they were whispered to me. It's hard to imagine they were always lodged in my brain from the beginning, from the day of my birth, only waiting to grow and mature so I could write them down and publish them.

The story, "A Tin Can Mind" addresses this question of inner voices and ponders their origin. If our mind is just a tin can, private and sealed off, then how do new ideas get inside?

I will admit that the "Duct Tape People" came to me while reading a newspaper article. Later that day, I was working at a pizzeria peeling garlic cloves when, suddenly, a vision for a scene came to me. From that, characters and dialogue erupted. Sometimes I was so afraid that I would forget those details, those words of dialogue, that I wrote down my thoughts on a napkin right then and there, before it all faded away.

How many times has that happened to you? Some great idea came to mind, and you thought you'd remember it later, except you couldn't. It was gone and you couldn't retrieve it again. This sense of urgency to save an idea before it fades away is reflected in the story, "Amidst Traffic."

That's how these stories were for me at times. Like I was in control of them, but only as a steward. At times I wanted my characters to do something, but as I wrote, they decided to do something else. Often, I expected to write a story with a specific ending, but that ending didn't happen. It changed on me. (That's why the metaphor unveiled in "Author" is not a perfect one. When talking about God and His sovereignty, our metaphors are often flawed. But still, I love that story.)

Soon, more stories spawned out of stories I had already written. Characters appeared again and again in my mind. Sometimes older. Sometimes a bit more mature. Sometimes a little more dangerous.

It was later I decided I wanted all of these stories to be interconnected. So I went back to writing. I changed or added details that would create a web.

In the end, I wouldn't say this collection is totally complete. There are still characters hanging out there. More stories need to be told. The web will likely spread as I write more fiction in the future. I've even thought about writing a whole novel about the "Duct Tape People." There is still a lot left to discover about the character named Adren Banner, for example, who is dark and mysterious, but also has a hero's heart.

I think the fact that this collection leaves off with these untied threads is a true representation of our own life.

In life, we constantly meet strangers who make an impact on

us in some way, and then we never see them again. We wonder about them, where these strangers have gone or disappeared to. We meet people we think will be in our lives forever, but they don't stay very long at all.

Other times we meet strangers we think have their lives all figured out and put together. Then, as we look a little closer, we realize their lives are just like ours. We all have unraveled seams somewhere.

This collection has many unraveled seams.

It's intended to feel a little chaotic at times. It's intended to make you feel surrounded by the traffic of stories going in different directions. Sometimes the vehicles of these stories will collide. Sometimes they will miss each other by just a hair. Other times, they travel on different roads completely.

But they all have the same thing in common.

Each of them poses a human question. A question about our minds. About our existence. About human desires. About addictions and obsessions. About the poetry of language. About love. About fear. Even about God.

And hopefully, you, as the reader, can help answer these questions.

Just don't get lost in the midst of all the traffic.

Enjoy.

—Michel Sauret

Three
Straws

The same dream kept coming for Eli, and it was terrible. The worst part about it was the faces of children who chased him through cobbled streets beneath dilapidated, stone-faced buildings of a foreign country. In the dream, he kept looking back over his shoulder as he ran. Their faces looked as if someone had taken a box cutter and carved at their lips, noses and eyelids. Tiny monstrous faces. Eyes wide and nostrils flared. Their cut-up lips revealed small, gnashing teeth.

They looked so much like his father's drawings.

Eli couldn't take another night of those faces. So he stood outside behind his trailer because he didn't know what else to do. He didn't want to go to sleep.

He stared at the dark forest for a while, but then he imagined those children hiding among the trees. So he looked up at the sky and stared a while longer at the stars. Time simply passed, but eventually even in the sky he could connect the dots and see those carved-up stares.

"Oh my God," he said, covering his face with his hands. "Let it stop."

Impulsively, he hurried to the shed. He needed to put his hands on something. The first thing he saw was a shovel, so he grabbed it. He walked a few hundred feet into the open stretch of land behind his trailer and stabbed the dull blade into the earth.

It felt good.

The blade went in. The ground was soft. So he pulled out a chunk of dirt and stabbed the earth again. The soil was moist and easy to dig. A few more of these, he thought, and he would be okay. He just needed to work it out. He just needed to release whatever demons plagued his mind. If any alcohol had been in the house he might have washed those demons away with booze, but he rarely drank and there were no liquor stores open this late for miles. Living out in the countryside of Oklahoma relaxed him, but even out here he couldn't hide.

Don't think of it. Keep digging. Keep working.

He dug and flung chunks of dirt across his body and over his shoulder. He thought that after a few shovelfuls, the labor would make him exhausted. Then it would be okay to sleep. Maybe if his body ached, he would pass out from exhaustion and there would be no dreams. He didn't know how this worked, but that seemed right.

After an hour, he had only built up momentum. Now he was consumed in his digging. Sweat formed a paste with the dirt and glued to his skin from the neck down. It wasn't until three in the morning that the pains finally caught up to him. In a few hours he had to start his morning shift at the diner. He finally paused, looked around and realized he had dug a hole as wide as a kiddy pool four feet into the ground.

"Good," he said, although it wasn't.

What would he do next; fill it back up?

"No," he said, "Leave it." He said this as though he needed to answer the question. Maybe I'll fill it later. It will give me something to do.

He slept for two hours that morning and dreamed nothing.

The diner was a few miles from the Texas border. When he showed up for his shift, his muscles felt like knotted ropes of twine. He grabbed an apron, tied it around his waist and stood at the grill in the kitchen. Food orders came immediately. He didn't realize how many muscles he used to simply grill breakfast orders until that moment. Pouring pancake mix with a ladle made his arm feel twisted against his will. Every step he took shot a flare of pain from his heels up.

He washed down a mix of pain pills he found in the first-aid kit and fueled his mind with coffee as the morning wore on. He regretted sleeping only two hours. In the midst of a breakfast rush, it became harder for him to focus on orders. Cynthia, one of the waitresses, had to send two plates back to him because the sausage was burnt on one and he forgot to include cheese in the omelet on the other.

"What in the hell's wrong with you this morning, Eli?" she asked him. "This ain't the time to be messin' up orders. It is too damn busy right now, okay? I ain't made tips since you came in, and haven't stopped apologizing to customers since."

After a week of this—mindless digging, no sleep, then coming to work half-dazed, feeling broken and sore—the diner's manager still had no heart to fire him. He was a good kid. Didn't talk much, but up until now had always been a good worker.

Instead she asked him, "Would it help to put you on night shift, honey? You'll have to work the counter, too, and you won't get no sleep until the morning risers come in, but it's 'tween that and lettin' you go."

"I'll switch," he said, and although his voice was a whisper, his eyes were desperate with relief. Anything to work through the night, he thought. Anything to avoid the faces.

Eli wasn't good with people. He could never get a hang of the small talk the other waitresses mastered so effortlessly. Most of the truckers who came through told stories of drunken hitchhikers, cross dressers and visitor centers no one should ever visit after dark. Eli listened, nodded on and served their midnight breakfast orders.

"Y'ain't gonna make no tips if all you do is bob that noggin' of yours. Gotta converse with the fellas," Rosie, the manager, whispered in Eli's ear as he grilled some hash.

"Not worried about tips all the much. 'Need just enough to get through."

It was true. He didn't need much. The land he lived on was paid for. So was the trailer. He had no girlfriend. No hobbies. No other desires. Wasn't a boy with many complexities. Just lived by himself in a single-wide big enough to feel like he was sleeping inside a box. The land was his after his father passed on.

At one point he had wanted to go to Bible college and become a preacher just like his daddy. But those felt like boyish thoughts now. He was twenty-two, and somehow that made him feel very old.

"Alright then," she said.

But then a man walked in with a strange aura about him. There was a tenderness to the man's walk. A careful step, as if he didn't want to disturb the air around him. He was an older gentleman with a glow to his face that provoked a feeling of friendliness in Eli. It was a strange, strange sensation.

"How are you doing young man?" he asked, but sounded as though he actually expected an answer.

"I'm quite fine, sir."

The old man's face held lines, but his eyes didn't sag.

"I'll take your finest roast. Straight black," he said.

Eli rushed to fill him a cup, wondering if this oil-resembling crud would satisfy the man. He brought over the mug, felt the need to introduce himself, but instead found the man joking around with Rosie, asking about the kids, complimenting her new hairdo.

Eli waited a while to see if the opportunity came up to interject. What in the hell's wrong with you, man? He's just some guy old enough to be your daddy's father. Just some customer with stories as any other.

The man might have been seventy, but he made gestures with his hands and spoke like he had the energy of a man half his age. He had a gentleman's face, that of someone who might never utter an insult at anyone. He wore a small red rose was pinned to his vest, like a corsage.

"Will there be anything else, Sir?" Eli asked after refilling his third coffee.

"Sure is. Could I kindly have three straws?"

"I'm sorry?"

"Straws. Three of them, please."

"Three?"

The man nodded.

"Straws?"

Nodded again.

"What for?"

"Just three straws, and I'll be on my way."

So he grabbed the straws and handed them to the man.

The man nodded, smiled and went on his way.

The sun rose during Eli's drive home. He expected to walk into his house dog-tired, fall into his bed, and succumb to a dreamless sleep. But his bones were restless. His body ached from a full week of digging, but now the shovel called him.

"No more dreams," he said. So he went on digging. By now the hole was six feet deep and as large as a full-sized swimming pool. The dirt was piled all around, and he had to fling it higher and higher each time just to get it out of the hole. But after a half-dozen shovelfuls he was done. His body was torn. He tried climbing out, but his hands were blistered and he couldn't grip anything solid. There wasn't enough strength left to even pull himself out.

He crawled his way to the shaded side of the hole and sat with his back against the dirt wall. He saw what he'd done as if seeing it for the first time. This hole. It consumed him now. It was all around him, and he knew it would only grow. He felt like crying. But even that required more energy than he had left.

Daddy would kill you if he saw what you done here, he thought.

But daddy was already dead. His body buried at the cemetery in Hope, a little town twenty minutes east of this hole. And here

Eli was. Digging a hole on his father's plot. His father might have made a sermon out of this. There was very little his father said outside of the pulpit. And even outside, he spoke as though he had a point to make.

"We can't save our own selves, son." He had said this with a bedtime story smile. As if Eli was supposed to find joy in the statement. He listened and watched his father die.

"Sometimes, things go unfinished. Because it's not up to us to finish them." His father's eyes looked up, watching for God. Those words would be his last sermon. An hour later, he died. A man of faith—even through the affair, abandoned by his own wife—always faith.

And yet those words had echoed such faithlessness in his son's mind. Where was there to go but down if you could neither save yourself nor finish business before dying?

And this is what all those years of faith had produced: a trailer, three acres of land and a divorce. His mother had pushed for the split when Eli was twelve, when he still held dreams of becoming his father, becoming a preacher. She said faith and God had turned Eli's father too rigid. Eli's father said her loss of faith had turned her loose, like the chaff in the wind, swept off her feet by some stranger blowing through town.

Eli had pieced together the story of the affair only in bits through the years. His mother had wanted to travel the world. She was brash and unsatisfied. Meanwhile God had kept his father anchored here in Oklahoma. The affair was brief, but it was enough to take away his mother. Father spoke very little of it, and Eli could never understand how a woman might leave her twelve-year-old son behind like that.

The last thing she said to her husband before leaving for good was, "You will leave your boy nothing but demons." She said this as though she meant to protect Eli from his father's God-fearing superstitions.

After she left, Father mourned, "Even God's children must suffer, son."

In the end, Eli inherited everything his father's faith had gained. The old man, who had devoted his entire life to Almighty God, received this scrap of land in return. Eli had desires for college, for another life, but how could he abandon everything his father's faith had produced?

When his father died, less than a year ago, Eli went to the church to gather his belongings and discovered his father's journals. An entire bookshelf filled with notebooks, dating back years, pages filled with drafted sermons and reflections on biblical passages. He read hours worth of eloquent essays about man's need for Christ and God's glory. He read his father in a way he appeared only in front of the pulpit. In a way he rarely appeared in everyday life. Emotional. Charged. Passionate.

Eli went back ten years in the journals.

The pages following his mother leaving were filled with scribbles and hurried drawings. Occasionally a few comprehensible lines made it onto the pages. Phrases like, "The snake came into the garden and took away my fruit. I never had a chance to eat or taste 'the full serving of life." The scribbling became worse with each page. Drawings crept into the corners. Deformed human figures devouring their own limbs. Two dogs fighting over a puddle of vomit. There were so many pages of violence. Violence that never came through in his father's tone of voice or touch.

The worst images were the children prying out of the darkness with knife carvings across their features. Those were the most terrifying. It made Eli wonder if the violence inside his father was getting to be too much. He wondered if his father had ever wanted to enact those carvings on Eli's twelve-year-old face: the only thing left in the old man's life. God had taken everything else. Why not destroy the only thing left?

He took the journals home and paged through them for days. That's when the demon children began chasing Eli through his dreams.

And only now he'd found a way to stop them. Or at least escape them. Through digging. Digging to save himself. And his heart told him his father was wrong. If you couldn't save yourself, then who could? Who else had the right to do so?

Surely not some god impaled to a wooden plank. Not a god who was so afraid of death that sweat had poured out of him as blood. Only Eli could. From his dreams. From his demons. From this life.

He lay there inside the hole, eyelids flickering from fatigue. Today was Saturday. He had the next day off, so he went to sleep, worrying only the children would be there once he closed his eyes.

They weren't.

He woke every few hours, checked his watch, looked up around the edges of the wall to make sure he was still alone, and nodded back to sleep. When Sunday finally came, after several odd patches of sleep, he was still in the hole. He hadn't gone to church since his father's last sermon, and today would not be the day he started again.

Dear God. Too damn sore.

He wasn't sure if that was meant to be a prayer, an apology or some absent-minded thought.

He remained sitting for several minutes, and his mind drifted to the man and the three straws. He thought for a while why someone might need those three straws. The mystery amused him, however trivial it might have been.

I'll ask him next time I see him.

Just then, he had a moment of fear that maybe that man wasn't a regular. That maybe he was never going to come back to that diner again.

He'll be back. He knows Rosie.

This thought calmed him, and he was able to sleep again.

He eventually made it to his bed and slept through most of Sunday, his day of rest, and thankfully, those children never came. Maybe he had beaten them. Maybe he had found the cure. Work yourself to near death, and you're safe. It almost sounded reasonable. In fact, it was the most reasonable thing he could think of.

Monday night, Eli returned to work. As he had hoped, the man came in, ordering eggs over easy with toast and downing several cups of black coffee. When the man asked for the check, Eli returned with three straws in his hand.

"Would you mind, sir, telling me what these are for?"

The man looked up at him from the stool, bright eyed, and smiled.

"I'm building something," he said, the charm all there, wrapped up in those words. "But that's all I'll say about that tonight. Good night, young man." And he took off.

Eli tried for a while to think what a man could build with straws. Nothing reasonable came to mind. Some kind of sculpture, maybe. Like an animal. A small ship, perhaps. Three straws at a time.

When Rosie came to him with an order, he grabbed her wrist to get her attention. She jumped.

"My dear heaven, honey, why'd you grab me like that?"

"Just wanted to ask something."

Steam lifted up to their faces from the grill. She said nothing, expecting him to say something and then finally, "Well?"

"The man with the straws…"

"Who?"

"The guy I just served. Do you know him?"

She looked at him with amusement in her eyes. She cocked her hip and drew in closer, a sign Eli had come to learn of a woman who senses the opportunity for gossip.

"You mean Charles? The old charmer?" she asked.

"Him, yes. Does he always ask for straws?"

"Oh yeah. Three, every time."

"What does he do with them?"

"Oh I've never been able to get him to tell me that. I stopped asking after a while, and I usually don't serve him anyway. I just go up and talk to him 'cuz he's a sweet man and knows a lot about the world."

"He told me he's building something with them."

"He told you that?"

Eli nodded.

"Like what?"

"Wouldn't say."

"What could he build with straws?"

"I don't know. What would you build with straws if you could?" he asked.

She thought about it for a while. Her eyes spaced out for a

short moment and then returned to him.

"I would build a giant butterfly," she said. "Or maybe a playhouse for my lil' ones to run around in."

"Yeah, I guess," he said.

She seemed offended by this.

"Okay, so what would you build?"

"I don't have a clue."

"There then." There was sass in her tone. "My butterfly ain't so dumb after all."

"Can you imagine doing it only three straws at a time?"

At that, she responded with silence. And he knew what she felt in that moment, because he felt it too. It wasn't sadness. Not quite. But it was very close. It was more like anxiety, but a slow one, without all the rush and the panic. A quiet, slow sense of anxiety. Like counting a jar of sand grains, knowing you will lose count and start over again and again before ever reaching the bottom.

Three straws at a time.

Whatever it was Charles was building, he would never finish it at that pace. The man was old. The thought of him never finishing felt… heavy. He felt it in his chest.

"Honey?" Rosie said. The word called him out of his thoughts.

"Yes?"

"Your eggs are burning."

"Oh," he said.

But neither moved. They both stood there for a minute longer.

That morning after work, Eli lay in his bed thinking of drinking straws, and all the things you could build with them. His sense of imagination wasn't good. So instead, he kept picturing piles and piles of white straws with pink stripes and bendable necks. They kept multiplying in his mind, which was okay. Even that was better than the children. But then, there it was. That's all it took. Just the word brought their faces back, and their teeth were sharp, exposed behind their chewed, cut-up lips.

He burst out of his bed. He hurried out to his backyard, where the hole was now as big as a basement. It could have devoured his small little trailer, it was so big.

He didn't have it in him to keep digging. The strength wasn't there. But he had to. It was the only thing that would stop him from imagining the faces. So he dug. Slowly. Pacing himself.

"Could I stop at three?" he asked. He didn't know who he was asking, but the question was valid. Could he shovel three scoops at a time and stop?

He tried. Stabbed, scooped and flung the clump of dirt over his shoulder. Stabbed, scooped and flung. Stabbed, scooped, flung.

Eli stood there, his hands clutching the shovel's handle. He tried to calm his breathing, his nerves, but now he felt as though the piles of dirt might fall over him and bury him there.

I can't stop. I can't do it.

So he went on until the pain was too much, which was better than anxiety, and the hole grew deeper. Which was fine, because this would eventually kill him. He would never finish the hole. He would die before he would see the bottom.

What the hell are you digging anyway? What is your purpose? What will you do with all this dirt?

He knew those questions. They were all false. Even if he did come up with a purpose to his digging, he would always know it for the lie it was. He was digging because he was digging. He was digging because he wanted the faces to stop. There wasn't a larger scope, a deeper meaning to this work. There was no redemption at the end of this act. He would just have to keep going. This wasn't an obsession. It was consumption. He wondered how long before he tore a muscle.

I hope not long.

Why he prayed for this harm, he had no clue. But he welcomed whatever physical pain came of this. He invited it. Begged it to come.

Only the rising of the sun came, and he finally reached the point of exhaustion that would bring him through sleep: in one end and out the other, without any trail of cut-up children's faces in between.

For several days, Charles didn't come to the diner. Eli feared that maybe the man had died after all, his project unfinished. Who would find it first? Would the police searching his house pause to observe his masterwork in the making, or would they rush through, pick up the body and send him to the nearest morgue?

Then Charles did come in one night. At the end of the man's meal, Eli brought the check and a whole box full of straws.

"What's this?" the man asked.

"You've been gone."

"What is this?" He sounded alarmed.

"Your straws."

"I need only three."

"But you've been gone. You missed four days."

The man chuckled at this. It was obviously a nice gesture, that the young man showed both concern and a willingness to help.

"This diner is not the only place where I get my straws, you know?"

"Why don't you just buy them? They're not expensive."

"Well then, if your establishment regrets handing out straws for free to their customers, I can go somewhere else. I always pay for my meal, and I don't cause a fuss."

"No, listen, that's not what I'm saying. Here's a whole box of them. You can have them. You can have them all. Take them." He wanted to push the box into the man's chest.

Truckers and other customers stirred at this—took a look at the counter where the two men argued over straw—and then returned to their midnight breakfasts.

"It's not about that," Charles said.

"What's it about?"

"It's about building something."

"Okay. Then here. Build. Build with these."

"I have to pace myself or—" he caught himself, stopped, breathed through his nostrils and finally pressed a thumb to his lips as if to prevent himself from saying more.

"Or what?"

"Don't you have some orders to make?"

"No."

"Then refill my cup, would you?"

Eli looked down. The black liquid came up to the brim of the mug.

"It's cold," Charles said, with a sort of forced kindness.

"Fine then."

Eli went back into the kitchen, dumped the coffee, came back out and refilled the cup. He set the coffee down on the counter and exhaled deeply. He lowered himself with his elbows on the countertop, fists under his chin. Eyes level with the other man.

"You're pacing yourself, aren't you?" he asked.

"I am." Charles managed a bright smile at this, but it was dishonest.

"Why?"

"I have my reasons."

"How? How can you do it? How can you stop at three every day?"

"I just know I have to. When you get to be my age, you learn a little about self control. You become friends with patience. When you're young, like you, there is none of that. Everything is here. Everything has to be now. Even here, miles away from big city living. It's like you think you can solve everything just by…" He couldn't find the words to finish.

"Digging," Eli said.

"Digging?"

"That's what I'm doing. I dig. I have to down a bottle of painkillers just to pour you a damn coffee. And there's no rest for me. There ain't no pacing."

Saying all of this—it felt a lot like a confession.

"What are you digging for, young man?" Charles asked.

"What is it you're building, old man?"

Charles didn't say anything. He just stared at his coffee while stirring it with a spoon, even though there was no sugar or anything inside to stir.

"It's a sculpture." the old man said without looking up. "But I can't say more."

"I'm digging a hole. But I can't say more, either," Eli said, finding spite in his own tone.

"It's nothing," Charles said.

"It's gotta be something. Else you wouldn't be building it."

Charles didn't respond. He placed exact change on the table for the bill, picked three straws out of the box and walked out.

For another month, Charles came in every night. His original glow was back. His charm. His wit with the waitresses. "You old flirt," they called him. By then, Eli had finally managed a schedule of digging that would probably kill him before the year's end. It's what he wanted. By then he had managed to see a doctor and receive a stronger prescription for the pain. Took three a day even though he was supposed to take only two. Originally the labor had helped put muscle onto his frame, but now he was beginning to wear out his own body. His skin became pale from all the pain and all the medicine. On the nights that Charles came in, they didn't talk. The old man went on flirting and Eli continued to fill his coffee.

That was it for a while, until finally one night, on Good Friday, Eli saw an old man at the counter with his head low and his clothes wrinkled.

"Can I get something started for you, sir?" Eli asked.

When the man lifted his face, it took Eli a long moment to recognize him. He looked at least eighty. The lines underneath his eyes as deep as slits in the earth. His shirt's collar looked as though someone had clenched it in a fist.

"Charles?" he asked.

They stared into one another's eyes.

"Are you alright?"

The old man didn't say anything. A shiver shook him, but then he composed himself. There was a young teenage couple in the far corner of the diner, and three men in black business coats chatting in one booth. Rosie took orders and refilled drinks. None of them paid any attention to them.

Eli didn't know what to do. He felt a panic in his chest seeing this man who had been so upbeat and charming become so sullen. He had an urge to hide him, as though he was afraid of anyone seeing him like this.

"Do you need to talk?" Eli asked.

"I don't know what I need. Want to grab me a coffee?"

Eli did and brought it back.

Charles grabbed three packets of sugar, ripped them open, and let the grains fall into the liquid. Then he grabbed a small handful of creamers, peeled the lids and poured them in. This was the first time Eli had seen him put anything in his coffee.

"I like it sweet today," he said looking up, and smiled. All of the lines around his eyes wrinkled when he did.

"Yeah. No problem."

"Are you still digging, Eli?"

Eli didn't answer. He simply stared at the man. His body was so worn he looked like a boy made of straw.

"I've had dreams," Eli said, as if trying to explain something unspoken.

Charles smacked his lips, took a long sip of his coffee and brought the mug back down without a sound. Eli kept trying to find some form of smile on that face. It was there somewhere. The man's eyes were aged, but they were still sharp.

"We all have dreams, Eli."

"No. Mine are terrible."

"No more terrible than any others." Did he look like he wanted to cry? He blinked, and the moisture in his eyes was gone.

"We can't save ourselves, you know?" Charles said.

"My father said that."

"I think your father was right."

"But we can try," Eli said.

"No. That's a lie. We can't try."

"What about the straws?" Eli asked. And with that question, a small realization came to him. Charles had been pushing something away with the straws, too. Perhaps not dreams, but something of his own.

"It's finished."

Finished, Eli thought.

Eli had hoped he might hear that word some day come out of the old man's lips. Finished. But he had expected it to sound glorious and full of accomplishment. Instead, it pained him. Even through all the painkillers. The pain of that word found a way to touch him.

"Can't you add onto it? Can't you add more straws?"

"I could, but it wouldn't be any less finished if I kept going."

"So you're done? You're just going to abandon it?"

"You don't add any more words at the end of a story when it's over. It ends when it ends. Painful or not. Adding more straws would just add to the pain."

"You don't know pain," Eli said. He wanted to show this man his prescription bottle with the infinite refills he planned on acquiring. However many refills it took him to finish digging the hole. However many it took to kill him. That was pain. He could barely get out of bed some days because of that pain.

"I really thought I would die before I would see it finished," Charles said. There was longing in his voice now, like a man speaking of a road trip across country. "I really thought I would escape..." before finishing the sentence, Charles brought both hands to his eyes and rubbed them with his fingertips, as if to force back an image.

He feigned a yawn.

"Boy, I'm tired," he said.

"You can still escape. We both can."

Charles raised a hand and touched Eli on the shoulder. There was tenderness in that gesture, but there was a shock in that touch. A tiny jolt. The young man stood there, staring at the old. And he knew this man would die soon. Maybe even tonight. And Eli would be left to his digging. He didn't know what else to say to the man. He didn't know what else to give him. He wanted to say, I'm sorry. He wanted to say, I tried. I tried to help you and help myself.

They stared at one another until Eli couldn't bear looking at him anymore. He was so damn old. Eli wanted to squeeze the sorrow out of the man. He wanted to grab him and shake him and tell him no. Tell him he hadn't tried hard enough.

He opened his mouth to say something. Stopped and closed it again.

Eli turned away. He went back to the kitchen, and grabbed an opened box of straws.

He stood over the garbage can with a pair of scissors in one hand. Snip. He cut one of the straws in half. Then in half again. Then once more. He breathed and stared at the little piece of tube left in his hand. He cut it again, feeling the plastic squeeze between the blades. Charles wouldn't need them anymore. How much hope had he placed in these?

He cut a second straw. Then a third. Smaller and smaller until he found himself holding a tiny ring between his fingers. He put down the scissors and held up the circle of straw to the light. He looked through it as if through a window. As if through a hole.

In one end and out the other. On the other side of the hole, on the other side of the kitchen, he saw the back door. He brought the hole down. A couple of orders hung along the track above the grill. He would go home early tonight, he decided. He would finish those orders, throw away the box of straws and go home. He pictured himself ripping his father's journal and letting the pages flurry and fall into the hole.

Then. Maybe. Perhaps. He might have enough strength left to dump the dirt back in.

A Voice
with Reason

Trevor was about to step onto the road, his mind consumed by the book in his hands, when suddenly, something told him to stop. His foot, already lifted and about to take that next step, paused and retreated back to the curb. A city bus went past him in a monstrous rush, passing inches from his face.

The vacuum created by the passing bus sucked him in; his narrow frame stiffened at the rush of air. Then a second gust swept him sideways, and he tensed his pencil-thin legs to hold his ground, jeans and shirt fluttering in the wind. His neatly parted hair was left disheveled.

"Well, that was close," he said to no one. His eyes never left the book in his hands.

The thing that had spoken to him hadn't been a voice exactly. It wasn't a conscious thought that took place in a world of grammar or used words to frame its message. It had been more like a subliminal flash that sparked in his mind. It was nothing more to him than the usual divine intuition—what others thought of as instinct. Trevor licked his thumb and turned the page.

He waited another minute for most of the traffic to pass and then stepped onto the road without looking in either direction. A shimmering Cadillac swerved around him, the driver honking and flipping him the bird. Trevor lifted one hand and offered a quick wave, never taking his eyes from the book.

Once across the road, he hooked a right and weaved through the thickening crown of pedestrians. A few of them brushed up against him, but mostly he was able to keep out of their way. He walked another three blocks before finally reaching the bank's entrance. His hand reached for the handle—

"Not this bank," a voice whispered to him calmly.

Trevor's hand stopped, and he looked up from his book for the first time. He looked around but saw no one there.

His hand stretched out again, but the voice came back once more.

"No. Not this one," the voice said patiently.

Trevor realized then that the voice was coming from inside his head, and oddly it reminded him of what had warned him earlier about the bus. Except now... he was hearing actual words: clear, audible words. Those warnings had always come to him as flashes before. As snippets, flicks, tweaks... and always, he had paid attention to them. This was different though.

He stood there a moment longer, one hand half outstretched for the bank's entrance, while the other held the book limply by his side. Strangers walked past, and some looked at Trevor as though he were a misplaced statue.

Trevor chuckled, shook his head, and decided to walk in

anyways. Divine intuition was one thing, but voices? No, voices were not something you listened to.

As soon as he stepped inside, he realized that he should have listened, though. It was Friday, after all. It was the last of the month. It was payday.

The line leading to the tellers stretched all the way back to the front counter where a young woman greeted Trevor with a forced smile.

"Can I help you?" she asked him, her torso turned to another customer.

"Uh…" he stammered.

Just walk out, hang a left, and walk five more blocks to the next bank.

The voice made his ears tense up.

"Is there another bank around here?" Trevor asked the woman at the counter.

"Sure there is. Make a left out here and walk… six blocks maybe? You'll see it off to your right on the next street over."

"Thanks," he said.

"I doubt you'll have better luck there, though. They might be busier than we are."

Hearing this, Trevor considered staying. He didn't want to walk all the way there and find the bank packed with people again.

Go to that bank, the voice said, but sounded more gentle than commanding.

Trevor opened his mouth to argue with the voice but thought twice about it. There were people here. He didn't want to look crazy in front of them, even though that's exactly what he was starting to feel like.

Instead of arguing, he shrugged, said thank you one last time, and walked out. He made a left and walked the distance to the next bank, finding it just as the voice had said. Five blocks, not six. This bank didn't face the downtown traffic, which seemed promising, and it stood surrounded by its own parking lot. Not many cars in the lot, either. He took this as a good sign.

Three men in business suits stood in front of the door.

Trevor walked up, still reading his book, until he bumped into one of the men.

"Excuse me," Trevor said embarrassed.

The man did not move. Neither of the three did. They just looked at him.

"Just trying to go in, that's all. Didn't mean to bump into you."

They stood there. They looked at each other, then back at the kid.

"Gentlemen," it was a woman's voice. She looked like she might be a bank teller or a clerk. "Gentlemen. Excuse me. You can't block the entrance like this. If you're not coming inside, you're going to have to leave."

The men left without a word.

Trevor managed a smile now, but his hopes dropped the second he stepped inside. This bank was maybe twice the size of the last one, with twice as many tellers, but unfortunately, even the line was twice the previous one. Trevor simply groaned, able to do nothing else.

He burrowed his mind back into the book. The story he was reading was turning dark. No use in going back to the other bank now, so he stepped into the end of the line. Noises all around him came in waves, but he shut them out, muffling them all outside his mind. Ten or fifteen minutes passed when a commotion stirred around him, but something told him to keep reading his book, so he ignored it. Then a voice spoke to him, this too muffled, but he thought, Dear Lord, please not again with the voices. Please. I'm too young to go insane right now. I've just—

Something tapped on his book, and his prayer stopped abruptly.

"Are you freaking deaf?" someone screamed, and it sounded nothing like the voice that had told him to come here. This voice was curled with anger and clogged with cigarette tar. That voice let out a whole stream of swear words.

Finally, Trevor's eyes looked up. They looked up only to find the barrel of a gun pointed at his nose. He gulped, but his throat scathed without saliva.

"Everyone stay down, all right?" another voice said far off to his right, this one more cordial than the first. "Just stay down, be calm, and don't move, please."

"We're robbing the place, Priest, not asking them to fill out a survey," said the man holding a gun to Trevor's face. The men wore a black ski mask, a camouflaged jacket, and brown leather gloves. The one with the gun to Trevor's face was built like an ex high school wrestler who had let himself go over the years. Trevor didn't dare take a look at the other man. "Just point the damn gun at them, and they won't have a need to move, alright? And no need for you yapping your mouth."

Then he turned back to Trevor. "You wanna get down like the rest of 'em, or am I going to have to shoot you down?"

Great, Trevor thought. I listen to a voice, and now I'm getting robbed. Just… just fantastic, that's all.

"Okay, are you listening to me? I have a gun. Do you see this? A gun, for Christ's sake. How many times am I going to tell you to get down?"

"Please don't blaspheme," Trevor said, and immediately

clenched his jaws. I didn't just say that to him did I?

"Oh so you're playing deaf, but you're no mute at least."

All Trevor wanted now was to get down. All he wanted was to lie flat on the ground, squeeze his eyes shut, bite his tongue, and just wait for the robbers to flee with the money so that he could have himself a heart attack. A heart attack at the age of twenty. That, truly, would be splendid.

Except he couldn't do it. He couldn't get down on the ground because all he wanted was to run. To run like crazy or even faster, praying that maybe he'd make it out alive. And he realized then that if all he wanted was to get down, and all he wanted was to run, he was stuck there in the middle of both and being able to do neither.

And even though he couldn't move, his limbs began to tremble, and that was the worst of it all because now his fear was visible. He felt the shake in his ass cheeks, shivering all the way down to his toes like a house on stilts that was about to crumble. Yet he still couldn't bring himself to the floor. He cussed to himself, and that's how he knew he'd lost it completely because that was the first time he'd cussed in months.

"What do you want me to do, Lar—" the one with the bubbly voice began.

"You know what to call me and what not to call me, Priest."

"I'm sorry. Pope. You're right. What do you wa—"

"Get the damn money. What do you think?" From one far corner of the bank a woman began crying, pleading and begging not to be killed. Others whimpered. Trevor saw none of them. His face was unmoving. He might as well have been alone in here with that barrel pointed at his face.

Pope turned back to Trevor. "Now I'm going to give you one last chance. You either get down, or you'll stay down forever."

Tell him to shoot, the voice spoke calmly inside Trevor's head. Tell him to go right ahead.

What are you crazy? Trevor argued back in his thoughts.

Have you faith?

"Faith? Faith! What does faith have to do with any of this?" now Trevor was screaming. Pope's eyes narrowed into slits, confused. His lips tightened, and his head tilted sideways just a notch.

Sweat covered Trevor's face in descending patches.

Faith has all to do with this.

"I can't believe you brought me in here!" Trevor said screaming, "I just can't believe I even listened to you in the first place! I have to be crazy. That has to be it."

"What the hell are you talking about?" Pope screamed back at him, all of his patience running out. As he screamed, he shook both fists as if he were strangling kittens. "Can't you see I'm going to shoot you? Why won't you listen to me?"

Pope cussed three, four times. Each time with more furious disbelief. Like punching a wall.

In the name of the Lord, proclaim him to shoot you.

Suddenly, Trevor thought he understood, which made him feel even crazier. Which made him feel so displaced, so spun and so twisted. Which made him feel... like laughing. He looked at his book, looked back up, and laughed. The story he'd been reading in the book wasn't religious. It wasn't about God or angels speaking. But it was about voices, and now here he was, listening to one.

He decided to trust it.

"God love you, squeeze that trigger," he said between gasps of hysterical laughter.

Pope blew into a snarl. His fingers squeezed. Trevor didn't even close his eyes. The gun didn't fire. Instead, it blew up inches from his face, metal shards shooting out. Every piece missed him completely.

"What the heck happened?" Priest said, running back to his partner and finding him dropped to the floor.

Pope looked at his hand. His index finger was gone, and his middle and pinky were barely hanging on. Priest gasped, a sound that stood at the edge of a scream. Pope could barely manage a series of choked up breaths. Then, somehow, he screamed a shout of torment and pain so loud that the people on the ground shuffled around.

"All of you stay the hell down!" Pope yelled at them all, his voice shrilly and filled with panic.

Then Priest raised his own gun to Trevor's face, but his hand wasn't as steady as Pope's had been. The barrel quivered.

The voice spoke again in Trevor's mind, filling him with confidence and soothing his veins with its words. He listened to it carefully, gaining a surprising calm now. His bones had stopped trembling, the laughter had even ceased, and he repeated out loud what was said to him.

"You're not going to shoot me."

"I will. I'll shoot you," Priest shouted, but he didn't sound convinced of himself.

"Do it," Pope snarled from the ground, clutching his mangled hand to his chest.

"No. You're not," said Trevor ignoring Pope, "You're not because none of this was your idea."

"How would you know? How would you know anything?"

"I know for the same reason I know that your mother's name was Susan."

At this, Priest dropped the bag of money. A few clumps of

wrapped bills fell out, and Pope snatched the bag with his good hand.

"Shoot him, Priest. Just shoot him!" Pope said, looking up at him intently. He let out a scream.

"And for the same reason I know that she's in heaven right now."

Priest's lips tightened and his eyes began to quiver wetly. "There's no need for you to talk about my mother, all right? She has nothing to do with this. I make my own choices. I need this money."

"She's crying right now, John. She's in heaven, and she's crying right now because of you."

Priest shivered. His hands slumped to his sides, and the gun dropped from his hand, clunking to the ground like a stone. Pope withdrew from it, afraid of even touching it.

Rolls of tears draped from Priest's eyes, wetting the rims of his black ski -mask holes. "You see this, Ma?" he said, "I'm crying too now."

For a long moment neither of them said anything, but only stood there staring into one another.

"You want to get out of here, don't you?" Trevor asked. Priest nodded slowly. "None of these people will say you were ever here. Isn't that right?" There was a low murmur among the crowd, agreeing.

"I suggest you get out of here too, Larry," Trevor said to Pope. Everyone remained still for a long stretch. In those moments, Priest and Pope considered their limited options. Finally, Priest tore off his ski mask, revealing his face to Trevor. The gesture was like a handshake.

Before turning to leave, Trevor crouched down in front of Pope, outstretching his book to him. For a moment Pope only looked at him, holding his breath, tasting the air, but then he actually took the book from Trevor's hands. The bag of money lay next to him, forgotten and unimportant.

"You can have it," Trevor told him. He smiled. It was a young smile that seemed to say, I had no clue any of this would happen, but I'm glad it did, and despite the pain in his hand, Pope actually chuckled at this.

People around them began to stand up, first one, and then the others followed little by little. Pope could do nothing about it. He couldn't even tell them to get back down. He couldn't bring himself to touch the remaining gun.

As Trevor stood back on his feet, the joints in his skinny bones popped. Pope watched him silently, questioning how in the hell this man—this boy really—could have possibly stopped him in his plans. Together with Priest—with John—Trevor walked toward the door, a conversation already forming between the two of them.

Pope had nothing left except the book. It was just an anthology collection of short fiction. Inside was a bookmark holding the place to a short story. "A Tin Can Mind," read the title. That didn't make any sense. He had been hoping for something greater. Something that might shed light on what the hell had happened here. He left there before the police could arrive. He left the book behind.

Blessed Are the War People

Helicopters landed and flew off again, each time blowing out gusts of air from the spinning propellers. Myron walked into the wooden shack, his uniform already sweaty from the heat and his shoulders sore from the weight of the ballistic vest. He still had the old version that strapped in the front with Velcro, rather than the newer one that swung over his head and distributed its weight evenly. Myron was a skinny guy, his head too small for even the smallest-sized Kevlar helmet and the vest didn't hug his hips the way it was designed to, but instead, pulled at his shoulders with all of its weight.

"Got a flight?" the man behind the counter asked. The counter was almost too high, coming all the way up to Myron's chest.

"That's why I'm here," Myron said, smiled and gave the man his ID.

Life was too easy, Myron thought. Sometimes he had to remind himself he was at war. *You're at war.* As if the two-hundred-and-ten rounds clipped to his vest weren't a reminder enough. He'd locked and loaded several dozen times since coming to Iraq and never fired a shot. Every time he returned inside the wire, cleared his weapon, it was always the same round that jumped out of his M16's ejection port. It was always the same round he bent down and picked off the ground and slipped back into the same magazine. That was as tough as this war got for him: he still carried a rifle the size of a musket while other soldiers had the shorter and lighter M4 or even an M9 pistol. Plus, as a photojournalist, Myron carried a Nikon with a massive telephoto lens hanging from his neck.

Other than that, life was easy in Iraq.

Getting ready for "war" each time he left the wire was harder than the war, itself.

The man behind the computer had a fat belly and his jelly-like neck seemed to roll from the collar when it moved. He was a civilian.

The man checked Myron's flight information.

"It'll take a minute," he said.

"I got time." He smiled again.

At the other end of the counter, another civilian employee talked on her cell phone, nearly shouting.

"Girl, you have no *idea* how blessed I was this weekend."

Myron's focus shifted to the sound of her voice. She was blonde, fairly attractive and very animated. Even in her chair she seemed unable to sit still. Crossing and uncrossing one leg. Waving one arm in emphasis, as if the person on the other end could benefit from the gesture. Leaning in, leaning back. A silver cross swung from her neck as she moved.

"It was such a *blessing* from God."

Myron listened, caught in curiosity. He enjoyed hearing people talk about God. It lightened his mood to hear people praise Him in everyday occurrences. It didn't matter where Myron was, at the chow hall, at the barbershop, at the Green Beans. It just didn't happen enough, he thought. He heard people boast about sex in public more often than he ever heard them praise God for His grace. So Myron kept an ear tuned to the blonde woman as she talked, hoping the conversation might lift his spirit before he left the wire for another mission.

"So I was at the PX looking for a bigger TV for my room, and all they had were the regular twenty-inch with bad color, not even the flat-screen. So I'm looking and looking, and after about twenty minutes I'm about to give up when I run into a girlfriend of mine. I say hello, you know, and she says hi and she asks what I'm doing. So I tell her. And wouldn't you know it, she's about to go back home in a week and she just *happens* to have a flat-screen she's trying to get rid of. I was like, *wow*. What a *blessing*. 'Didn't even want anything for it. It was just amazing. Here I was about to give up, and send God a little prayer, you know, ask him for a little help, and even before I can ask, there was my answer. I just felt so *blessed*."

Myron stood there, wanting to stare the woman down, but instead looked away and didn't say anything. *You gotta be kidding me*, he thought.

"I'm not even kidding!" the woman said. "And that's not all. Then I'm looking for cables for the TV because I got that new progressive-scan DVD player, you know, the HD kind, and the cable alone is over eighty dollars, and a man overhears me talking to my girlfriend and says he has a spare of the *exact* cable I'm looking for and tells me I can have it. Just like that. I mean, I am *so blessed*. Really praise God for that."

Myron had the urge to talk to the woman, though he had no clue what he would say. He couldn't explain his emotions then. Couldn't pinpoint it as simple anger, though at the very core, that's what it was. Right there. Anger. Lodged in his chest. He made a half-step toward the woman, but then the other attendant called him back.

"You're good to go, Sergeant. Enjoy your flight," and handed his ID back to him.

It was another hour before his bird landed. As he walked to the helicopter he stuffed his earplugs into his ears and the whopping of the rotors became muffled like the sound of hands in gloves patting sand. He hopped in the Black Hawk and made it a point not to grab the hurricane seat, but instead took the seat closest to the door on the opposite side. He fumbled with his seatbelt and almost blew a fit when he couldn't find the one strap. Then he realized he was sitting on it, yanked it out and finally managed to buckle all four clips. No matter how many times he flew, putting on the seatbelt was always a pain in the neck.

These were his biggest worries: staying away from the hurricane seat and fumbling with his seatbelt.

The helicopter lifted off. He loved the feeling. It was like ungluing yourself from gravity. The helicopters always flew in twos, and Myron snapped half-a-dozen photos of the other chopper through the frame of the open doorway. The sun was so bright it washed away the landscape in the pictures.

He watched below as houses glided past. Apartment complexes all seemed packed in small nucleuses of urban living. Their roofs were covered with dust. Everything sepia. Everything boxed in and drifting and then, like a break in a map, sand. Sand everywhere for miles and miles with nothing living. Then clusters of date palms. A lone, mud hut in the middle of nowhere and a fence that made it only partly around its property. Whenever they flew over a herd of goats, the animals seemed to scamper and then recollect only fifty yards from their original spot. This happened several times, each with a different herd.

This country looked so barren from above, and yet Myron had walked its streets. He'd snapped hundreds of photos of children shouting, "*Mista, Mista. Pen, Mista.*" Children wanting pens, wanting candy, wanting anything just as long as it was a U.S. soldier giving it to them. A few of the very young boys reminded him of his own son, Joshua. Deep olive skin and shiny eyes that held in the sun.

He'd seen markets and villages return to life, smiles on the faces of men and women he'd been told were incapable of decency or laughter. This was his first deployment, and on the job he interviewed soldiers who were already on their third tour. It was his job to record this war through the lens of a camera. Some days he had a hard time believing this place had ever been as bad as the news at home had depicted it. They had called it a civil war. They had called it a lost cause. And maybe it had been both of those things at some point, or worse.

You're at war, he reminded himself, though the word felt vastly exaggerated now as he hovered over the quietness of sand.

He closed his eyes and napped and didn't open them again until the turbulence from the helicopter woke him. At first, he jumped as if bracing for a crash landing, but then he remembered this is how it was—how the Black Hawks vibrated, violently almost, just before landing.

Myron hopped off the bird. He was in Babil Province now on a base just a few miles outside the Babylon ruins, though nothing he saw gave him the inkling of the rise of civilization, nor of God's creation. He was surrounded by twenty-foot T-walls just like every other base. The sky flattened above him with the sun burning as hot as ever. It was a wonder that life could survive under this sun. His boots crunched across the gravel. His steps slipped and sunk into the multitude of rocks.

A young second lieutenant greeted him as Myron stepped off the landing zone. Myron saluted. The lieutenant returned the salute and then shook Myron's hand.

"I'm Lieutenant Evans," he said.

"Good to meet you, sir. I'm Sergeant Downing."

They had to shout to hear one another, but then the choppers took off and Myron pulled out his earplugs and peeled off his helmet. His hair was damp with sweat.

"You're the journalist from Division, right?" Evans asked.

"That's right, sir." Myron pointed to his Tenth Mountain patch.

"Good to have you."

Myron realized right then how young the lieutenant looked. He was maybe twenty-two and had a face untouched by hardship. Yet, the lieutenant's uniform told another story. It showed he was not a soldier with many amenities. His uniform was stained with sand that had glued to sweat, and at best it had been washed in a bucket of water for the past eight months. Myron doubted they had laundry service out here. The post was no bigger than a patrol base or a joint security station.

"Hey, when you're out with my guys, do you mind if we get a copy of your pictures?"

"Not a problem, sir. I'll make you a CD."

Sharing his photos with soldiers was usually his best bribe for getting outside the wire. Most of the convoys didn't want him around if they thought he might get in the way, so he bought a little love by giving out pictures. Some infantry soldiers didn't want him around at all for even breathing the word "journalist." It didn't matter that Myron wore the same uniform as them. But for the most part, he'd been well received, and the lieutenant's welcome reassured him it would go okay this time. It wasn't like he was going out on a hot operation. Most of the missions he joined were to distribute medical supplies or award grants to local business owners, not dish out bullets and hunt down terrorists.

If it weren't for the ballistic vests, loaded weapons and up-armored vehicles, Myron would have sworn he had deployed with the Peace Corps, not the U.S. Army.

Evans showed Myron around the base. There wasn't much. The chow hall was tiny but homey. They didn't have a PX, but a fat Iraqi man owned a Haji-Mart on post with electronics and tobacco among other useless things people bought.

"We just got bunks to replace the old cots but we don't have linen." Evans pointed at a tent behind a wall of concrete barriers and sandbags.

"AC?" Myron asked.

Evans laughed. "Naw. Sorry."

"Well, at least you guys got Porta-Johns. I was down in Amarah last week, and all they had was a drain in the ground and a fold-out chair with a hole cut into it as a john."

"Yeah. I've seen worse."

"I could write a book about soldiers' resourcefulness."

"Where you stationed at?" the lieutenant asked.

"Victory," Myron said.

"Nice. I hear life ain't bad up there."

"Reminds me of a little vacation resort," Myron said jokingly, though it wasn't far from the truth.

"You guys got a pool up there, don't you?"

Evans was smiling when he asked this, much like a child might smile when asking his parents about the wonders of the North Pole. Yet, something about this place made Myron withdraw from answering. Telling this lieutenant they had a pool at Camp Victory was like serving a bowl of canned soup to a homeless man, then telling him about the turkey dinner waiting for you at home on Thanksgiving.

"They shut it down for maintenance," Myron told him.

"That's a shame," Evans said, and gave the sergeant a hesitant glance. "Any case, if you wanna crash for a couple hours you can go ahead and get settled in at the tent. I'll come grab you when we're ready to roll."

"Thank you, sir."

Myron's eyes had to adjust to the hazy darkness as he stepped into the tent. The wooden floor creaked and he felt the stuffy air cloud over him as he stepped further into the midst of bunks. He found an open bed and dropped his gear. As he sat on the mattress, the bed dipped so low he thought the hinges from the frame might snap. He unzipped his blouse and hung it on the bed post. It was soaked in sweat.

He looked around and watched as soldiers either napped on their sunken bunks or buried their faces into small DVD players and game consoles with tiny screens. Then he saw a soldier who caught his attention. Myron stood and walked over to him. He was just a kid, maybe seventeen or eighteen, a PFC with a bushy caterpillar of a unibrow. The private was wearing ear buds, listening to music, but his eyes were fixed on the pages of a small Bible.

"Are you a believer?" Myron asked.

The boy looked up, half-startled, half confused. He stared at Myron as though he were in trouble and popped the buds out of his ears. The music was loud enough that Myron could hear a tinny sound coming out from them.

"I didn't mean to interrupt you," he said.

The boy watched him as if he didn't understand.

"I was just wondering if you were a believer," Myron said.

The kid looked at him longer, then nodded, but only as if it were instilled into him to do so, to agree on command. Myron suddenly felt embarrassed, even though it was the private who seemed confused. He felt as though involved in some kind of misunderstanding.

"Whatcha' reading?" Myron asked. He smiled. Perhaps the kid had thought Myron meant to menace him, or at the very least razz him for reading the book.

"What?"

Myron wasn't sure if the private had trouble hearing because of the music he listened to or if maybe it had been IEDs and 50-caliber rounds. He dismissed the thought.

"I was just wondering what you were reading."

"The Bible, sir."

Myron remembered he wasn't wearing his blouse, giving no indication of his rank to the boy. Maybe that played part in the boy's confusion.

"I see that," Myron said, smiled again. The boy's puzzled expression didn't leave his face. "Which book are you reading?"

"Revelation, sir."

"Well, that's good."

"Yes, sir."

"It's good you keep up with the Word."

The two stared at each other.

"I'm Sergeant Downing by the way." He gave his hand for the kid to shake.

"PFC Lewis."

"Good to meet you."

"Yes, Sarn't."

It bothered Myron when soldiers chewed up the word, "sergeant" but he didn't say anything. The kid was unnerved enough as it was.

"Okay. I guess I'll see you around."

"God bless you, Sarn't."

Myron stammered, opened his lips to respond but didn't know what to say, surprised perhaps by the private's sudden direct—and yet meek—words. He gave a smile and turned away, wondering how he'd managed to say nothing meaningful at all throughout the exchange. He walked back to his bunk feeling silly and puzzled by what just happened. He tried to get his mind off it.

He sat there for a while before deciding to open up his own Bible.

He wasn't sure at first what he was looking for, so he scanned the back pages through the Bible's index. There, the word he wanted caught his attention. He thumbed the pages quickly, flipping back, eager to jump to the passage.

The chapter and verse brought him to Jesus' Sermon on the Mount.

He read, "Blessed are the poor in spirit, for theirs is the kingdom of heaven. Blessed are those who mourn, for they shall be comforted. Blessed are the meek, for they shall inherit the earth. Blessed are those who hunger and thirst for righteousness, for they shall be satisfied. Blessed are the merciful, for they shall receive mercy. Blessed are the pure in heart, for they shall see God. Blessed are the peacemakers, for they shall be called sons of God. Blessed are those who are persecuted for righteousness' sake, for theirs is the kingdom of heaven. Blessed are you when others revile you and persecute you and utter all kinds of evil against you falsely on my account. Rejoice and be glad, for your reward is great in heaven, for so they persecuted the prophets who were sent before you."

The passage reminded Myron of the woman at the counter from earlier in the day. He wished now he hadn't felt so angry then, but instead had simply opened up this passage to her. He didn't know how to quite sort out his feelings. The passage he read was like a discovery, coming at the perfect time in the context of the day's earlier events, and yet... he also felt it had come too late. Myron wished now, more than ever, he had paused to talk to the woman. There was a kind of desperation in that thought, as if he'd missed out on an opportunity. He felt cheated—by the passage for not having come sooner, and by himself, because there really was no one else to blame.

Myron tossed the Bible into his assault pack, suddenly disappointed. But he couldn't keep his eyes off of it, so he snatched it up again and decided to put it in his cargo pocket.

A few hours later, Lieutenant Evans came by to grab him. Myron picked up his gear and followed him out to the convoy staging area. Myron didn't see any MRAPs around, just Humvees, which meant it was going to be a crammed ride with no leg room at all.

The convoy commander, a gruff sergeant first class with a big chin and small eyes, called out names, reviewed the mission, driving speed, order of vehicles, tactical procedures, radio call signs then asked, "Any questions?" And of course there were no questions because this was a daily routine for them.

"Oh," he then said, as if absent-minded, "We also got PAO coming with us," and pointed at Myron with a thumb. "He's doing a story on SoI, so none of y'all act up, alright?"

The gaggle of Soldiers looked at Myron. His camera was a giveaway. A couple of them groaned. He could picture himself in their eyes: a skinny soldier with a camera lens almost as big as his rifle and a Kevlar helmet that made him look like Darth Vader.

"Birdsong," the convoy commander called, to which a big-eyed staff sergeant looked up, slowly.

"Yeah?" Birdsong asked. He was leading back on the hood of a Humvee, smoking a cigarette pinched between his thumb and forefinger like a joint. The smoke clouded his face.

"PAO's riding with you," the convoy commander said.

Birdsong swore under his breath. "Man, I ain't got no room," he said.

"Make room."

Birdsong glared at Myron. His eyes narrowed.

"Let's roll," Lieutenant Evans said, and everyone got moving.

Myron knew his place. Shut up and get in the vehicle and don't talk unless someone talks to you first. He opened the back door to the Humvee and saw a cooler in his seat. There was gear and junk all over the place.

"Is it cool if I move this?" he asked, pointing at the cooler.

"Do whatever, man," Birdsong said. He was still smoking the cigarette as he strapped on his helmet and sunk in the front passenger seat. "Just hop in."

Myron pushed some stuff aside and cleared his seat. He pulled the door shut, which was heavier than hell. Claustrophobia crippled him for a long moment as he was reminded there was no room to move. He took up his entire seat and tried to find space for his weapon between his legs.

"Hey," Birdsong shouted back at Myron. "Put on your headset."

Myron hated the headsets. Those things were so awkward to wear as they looped around the back of his head and strapped over the top of his helmet. It made him feel completely immobilized because turning his head made the frame dig into his skull. Also, he knew that once these things were over his ears, there was no escaping the conversation inside the Humvee—it would go straight to his head. And he knew well how soldiers talked.

As he switched on the set, he caught their conversation in mid-sentence.

"… you know I'm working it, man, why you have to be on my case?"

Myron thought it was the driver talking by the way he was bobbing his head.

"Oh, you workin' it, is that it?" Birdsong said. "Has she even noticed you yet?"

"Man it's just a matter of time. Let me do my thing."

"Oh, I know what *that* means then."

"What's it mean?"

"You ain't even close."

"I *am* close," the driver said defensively.

"Pryce," Birdsong said, as if trying to reason with him. "When *I* say I'm close it means my fingers are already wet."

"Oh shut up, dude, that's nasty man—"

"Let me see your fingers," Birdsong said.

Birdsong reached over to grab for the driver's hand. Pryce pulled away, the vehicle swerved left and right as Pryce yanked the wheel and readjusted.

"Will you guys quit messin' around down there?" It was the gunner. "This damn road's bumpy enough at it is."

They bantered with one another for a few more minutes, keeping up the sex jokes and finding ways to use the F-word as a noun, a verb, an adjective and an adverb, all in a matter of a few phrases. Plus they punched in some cuss words that Myron had never heard used in such ways before.

Myron groaned. He would do anything to not have to listen to this. He tried to tune it out and watch the road signs pass them by, but it was impossible to ignore them. Everything they said pressed into his ears. He thought of switching off the headset but was afraid he might miss something important if anything should happen. Instead, he tried to divert their conversation.

"How long have you guys been deployed?" he asked.

"Too damn long, Sarn't," Pryce said.

"How long is too long?"

"What is it? Going on twelve? Yeah, I think twelve."

"You like what you do?"

No infantry ever answered, "yes" to this question in all the times

Myron had asked it. Yet, at the same time, every grunt he'd met was somehow proud of his job. Proud of the hardships. And if any politician or Hollywood star should say something bad about soldiers or their fighting force, any one of them would be quick to defend what he did. And they did so genuinely. Myron noticed that perhaps not many soldiers liked what they did, yet they had a love for their work all the same.

"It's all right," Pryce answered. "I mean, it's not bad, or anything. Just long hours, lots of convoys. Same ol' crap every day, you know how it is."

Myron asked them more questions. Somehow, they found ways of sneaking in a cuss word into every answer. He wondered if they were capable of forming a full sentence without it. It was like their head might explode if they didn't swear every time their lips opened.

"Have you guys been hit in a while?" Myron asked.

"Naw. Not really," Pryce said. "Roads have been pretty quiet around here lately."

No cussing that time.

There. That wasn't so hard, was it? Myron thought.

"I was expecting a little excitement to be honest," the gunner chipped in from above. "Hell, man. It's been getting boring. I ain't killed no one in *months*."

"Shut up," Pryce said. "When was the last time you even killed anyone?"

"Last deployment."

"Freakin' right. You make it sound like you're some kind of Rambo or some hotshot just a few months ago."

"Dude, I'm just saying, man. I was just expecting to shoot some bad dudes this time around, that's all. Ain't had a chance to get nobody yet."

"Well, that's a good thing if you ask me," Myron said.

"Yeah, I mean… Whatever. I *guess* so."

"This is what we wanted. This is what winning's about," Myron said. "Not the number of people you kill, but the number of people you help feed."

"Don't be getting all peace-loving hippy freak on me now, all right PAO?" Birdsong cut in. "This your first deployment?"

"It is."

Up ahead, Myron saw a little village. He could see people standing by the side of the streets. Some waved. To his right, he saw a little farmhouse with the land in front tilled, ready for sowing seeds. A tiny, little boy without shoes or socks ran after them. He ran to greet the soldiers. His parents stood by, watching, smiling. He wasn't going to make it in time before the convoy passed him by.

"Then you don't know," Birdsong said. He let out a cuss word directed at Myron. "You don't know squat. This is my third, and only reason it's quiet now is because we had to kill a bunch of terrorists. A bunch of bad freakin' dudes who blew us up in bunches just a year ago."

"Well thank God it's not like that anymore at least," Myron said.

"Yeah, *thank you,* God. Really. Thanks, buddy."

Myron opened his mouth to say something, but he shut it again feeling the rage pressing at his jaw. He wasn't going to speak in anger.

"Though it is nice being out with the people," Pryce said. "You know. Without worrying about none of 'em trying to shoot you."

"Shut up, Pryce," Birdsong said.

"What? It's true. It *is* nice. How many times we been to Sheikh Hadi's house? Like a dozen and he always makes us Chai."

"Man, that one feast last week was good, too," the gunner said. "Remember how you had to eat the eyeball, Pry? Man, that day was a trip."

So they talked about the Iraqi feast for a while and Pryce being forced to eat the eyeball straight from a goat's head, and how gummy it had been. When asked, Pryce said it tasted just like what you'd expect an eyeball to taste, and they all laughed. This was all right for Myron, because talking about eating eyeballs was better than shameless talk of sex. So they bantered for a while, cheering and laughing. Their cussing still made its way into the conversation, but there was little to do about that. Myron still felt the anger linger in him over Birdsong's earlier taunts, but he tried to push it aside. *Let it go*, he thought, and he tried.

Then the chatter quieted down, as it often did during long rides. Myron was relieved. It was growing warmer in the car. He felt sleepy again and closed his eyes, trying to take another nap.

He woke again perhaps twenty minutes later with laughter in his ears. The chatter had resumed again.

"Good God," the gunner said.

"Yeah, that's what yo' girlfriend calls me when I'm with her," Birdsong said. "*Aw Gawd! Aw Gawd!*"

Both the gunner and driver laughed at the high-pitched mimics Birdsong made.

More swearing and banter between the three of them.

"Shut up, man. You know nothing about my girlfriend, and if anything she'd be screaming for you to get your small pecker away from her."

"Hills, you damn well know the good Lord blessed me with a big one. I'm His number one man. He take *care* of me. Just like I take care of your girlfriend. It's what God put me on this earth for."

"Alright, hey," Myron said into the little microphone. All this talk was hurting his head and now he was getting sick of it. "Can we please…" He stammered, didn't quite know how to spit out the words.

"Please what, Cameraman?"

"Can we stop?"

"Stop what? Stop talking about my—?"

"*Yes.* Please."

"What's the matter? Can't handle it?"

"Can we just cut out the language? That's all."

There was a moment of tinny silence. It made Myron's ears feel hot. The silence before the storm.

"Hell no we can't cut the damn language. This ain't your vehicle, Cameraman. We talk how we damn well please."

He let out a whole ream of expletives for good measure. Just to make his point.

"Come on, listen—I'm not getting aggressive with you. I'm asking nicely."

"*Nicely?* Listen to you! You think we're in the business of *nicely* here? Does my nametag say Staff Sergeant Nicely? You got virgin ears or something? Or do I just offend you?"

"My ears aren't any more virgin than yours," Myron said, by which he simply meant he was no more innocent than anyone else. He was trying to humble himself, trying not to come off as holier than anyone else in the vehicle. It was an admission, not a comeback. But that was the problem with humility. Nobody understood "humble" anymore, and in this case—like many others—humility came off as a presumptive cockiness, not as a gesture for making amends.

"Whass'that suppose to mean?"

"Nothing. Listen… Nevermind."

"Yeah, damn right nevermind," Birdsong taunted. "It better be nevermind. I don't want to hear jack from you."

"I don't have to put up with this." Myron said, more exasperated than defiant.

"You don't have to ride in this vehicle is what you don't *have* to do.

But you in. So yeah, you *do* have to put up with this."

"Alright, you know what, you're right."

"Damn *right*, I'm right."

"Pryce, stop the vehicle," Myron said.

"What?" Pryce said.

"Stop the vehicle, I said. You heard Birdsong, I don't have to be in here."

"Don't listen to him, Pry. He ain't the TC. I'm the TC. Keep driving."

"Stop the truck."

"Drive," Birdsong insisted, then to Myron, "Cameraman, quit being such a girl."

Myron yanked on the battle locks and pushed the door open, which swung out slowly because of its massive weight. The Humvee was rolling no faster than twenty miles an hour, but with this six-hundred-pound door now open, that speed felt close to deadly. A sudden stop might cause the door to swing open and bounce back shut again, slamming its quarter-ton frame and crush Myron if he tried to jump out.

Pryce slowed the vehicle. Everyone was screaming at Myron to close the damn door. Then, slowly, the Humvee came to a halt and Myron stepped out.

Birdsong dismounted, the whole time shouting.

"You're a freaking child, man. A *damn* baby. Can't take a little bit of language? Well, *screw you* then. You don't belong in my convoy anyway. Pro'lly don't even know how to fire your own weapon, your fingers are so glued to that camera."

"You're supposed to be a professional, sergeant," Myron said. "Isn't that what the creed calls us?"

Of course that was the trump card. Calling out an NCO on his lack of professionalism was like questioning his manhood.

"What do you know about professionalism?" Birdsong asked, and in a swoop he was upon him, one hand grabbing hold of Myron's vest, the other hand holding back a fist.

"By the standards you've shown me today, I think you and I have different interpretations of the word."

"Oh, you a talker. But you a fighter?" Birdsong's head bobbed from left to right at the two options.

Myron saw the fury in the man's eyes as Birdsong clutched his vest. His eyes meant violence. In that moment, he wondered how they had gotten here. How had they gotten to this very instant, out in the open in the middle of an Iraqi market, Birdsong daring him to exchange blows while all Myron had wanted was a bit of decency? Here they were, though, and there was no turning back. What to do, then? Fight? No, fighting was never Myron's thing. He might get angry, he might even shout in that rage, but fighting was a last resort. Not because he was a peacemaker, as the Sermon on the Mount required, but because he was smaller than most guys he came up against.

Dear Jesus, what do I do now, he asked.

His eyes looked away. Away from Birdsong's savage eyes, which were like two bottle caps holding back fury. Looking away helped Myron distance himself, and he realized just then that a whole street full of Iraqi villagers was watching them. Birdsong didn't seem to notice at all, stuck in his own tunnel of violence, and Myron suddenly felt embarrassed for the both of them.

He saw a small gaggle of children clinging onto one another next to a market stand. Afraid and watching. A row of red cuts of lamb meat hung by hooks. Fluorescent, colorful fruit draped around the columns of another stand. He wanted to take a picture of all this, but he didn't dare touch his camera. He didn't dare make a move.

An old woman with tired, watchful eyes took a step away into the shade, clutching onto her black dress. A man with scraps of tattered clothing clutched a pipe, grooves of age in his face, the tobacco smoke rising as if it were moving through water.

Almighty God, please bless these people lost in the ruins of war, he prayed silently.

"They're watching us," Myron said.

"Let 'em watch," Birdsong responded, though he didn't seem to have heard what Myron said.

There didn't seem many options now. Fight this angry man or return to the vehicle. Myron didn't want to do either.

Myron shrugged. By his side, his fingers touched something hard in his pocket. It was the Bible. This is all he had now to defend himself.

"I forgive you Birdsong," was all Myron managed to say.

The words cooled him. They washed away his own anger. He even felt a chill pass through him despite the heat. Despite the sweat. Despite the burning sun beating on them.

"Whad'you say?"

"I forgive you," he repeated, the words more tender still.

"I don't need your forgiveness, you sorry ass. If you don't wanna fight, you don't wanna fight. Just don't give that forgiveness bullcrap."

Birdsong clutched Myron's vest tighter, pushed him off and then released as if disgusted by him. At this, the Velcro strap from Myron's vest stripped open.

"Get back in the truck. This is war, and I outrank you. You want fuss, we'll take it up the chain."

"This is war," Myron said, repeating Birdsong's words as if in a trance. His eyes returned to those of the angry soldier before him.

They stood in the silence.

"*This?*" Myron asked, his vest draping from his shoulders like an open curtain. He made a gesture to the crowd, to the market, to the color of it all. "*This* is war?"

"Get in the truck. I'm ordering you."

Myron's rifle was hooked to his vest by a carabiner. He thumbed the clip with one hand and let the weapon drop. Some of the villagers jumped, startled by the rifle smacking the ground.

"What are you doing? Pick that up. Pick up your weapon."

Myron stood there, as still as a statue. Then he raised one hand, unsnapped his helmet. He tilted his head to the side and the Kevlar came flopping off, hit the ground and rolled a couple feet before finally bobbing on its shell like an upside-down turtle.

"What the hell are you doing? Put it back on. Where do you think you are!" There was so much panic in Birdsong's voice it was impossible to ignore it. Children and elderly looked at each other. No one dared to step close or try to grab any of the items on the ground.

"Where are we?" Myron asked, his words tainted with defiance now.

"What?" Birdsong asked, confused.

"I said, where are we?"

"We're in Iraq, man. We're in Iraq."

"Yes, but where are we?"

"What the hell you talking about? I just told you!"

Myron grabbed his vest with both hands and swung it off his shoulders. It too flopped to the ground. Only his camera remained dangling from his neck. His only shield was the book in his pocket.

Birdsong's face dipped. Anger gone. A face of bewilderment remained.

Myron lifted his camera to eye level and snapped a picture of that face. Birdsong's anger resumed at this, but he didn't move.

"We're at war, you're right," Myron said. "Except it's not the one you think. The enemy's in the mirror, when we claim to be the hero."

"What the hell are you talking about? You don't make no damn sense."

"We want to save this country yet we can't even save ourselves. We want to offer them peace and hope, but we won't dare to do so in the name of Christ."

Myron knew he was exposed and felt it. An IED could explode and send shrapnel shooting out and plant itself into his skull. A sniper somewhere could sink two rounds in his chest, right into his heart and make it pop like a pimple. Those things would kill him the way only men could kill one another. It didn't take much to take a life, yet it took a drastic act to save one. To save a man. To share your blessings with him.

"I forgive you," Myron said again, his face sullen, his words as deliberate as bullets.

"Screw you!"

"God bless you."

To this there was no response.

What was there to say to a soldier who had stripped himself of his vest, his helmet and his weapon, fearing only God, a God who smashed towers and scattered languages.

"Okay, man. It's cool. Let's just get back in the truck and be on our way."

Now the gunner from the vehicle behind them was yelling something, his voice too distant to tell exactly what he was saying.

"Listen, I'm sorry. Let's just go, okay, let's just go."

There was desperation in Birdsong's voice.

Myron didn't respond to his pleas.

Instead he asked again, "Do you know where we are? Do you know what this is?"

"I don't know man. I don't know whatchu want to hear. You're going to get us all busted. Come on, man. Please."

"I just want you to see. Look around."

"Man, my first sergeant is going to tear me a new one if you don't get back in the vehicle, okay? I can't have this."

"Let him tear it then. But first you need to look."

Birdsong's eyes twitched. He looked around finally, though his eyes jumped so fast from spot to spot he barely could take in the scene or absorb it.

"What do you want me to look at?"

"If you don't see it, I can't make you see it."

Then the gunner started shouting down at them from the turret.

"Sergeant, you guys might want to get back in the vehicle. LT is calling up on the radio asking what the hell's going on."

"Tell him everything's fine," Myron said, never taking his eyes away from Birdsong. "Tell him Cameraman is just taking some pictures. Lovin' life."

Birdsong watched the people who were still watching them. Some of the children had gone back to playing, bored with the two soldiers' interaction. Yet, more and more people had gathered around to witness this weird exchange between the Americans, pointing in confusion at the one without his vest or weapon, pointing then to the ground where it all lay.

"Do you see it?" Myron asked.

"What do you want me to see?" Birdsong said. He looked like he was holding tears back in his eyes, as though he was trying to see, really trying, but simply couldn't. "I don't see what you see. Tell me what I'm looking at."

"Then I can't make you."

Myron bent and slowly picked up each piece of his gear.

"Wait—" Birdsong pleaded. "Com'on, show me."

But Myron didn't wait; he didn't even say a word. He simply put everything back on that he had torn off. When he was finished, Birdsong was still staring at the crowd, confused. A little lost, maybe. Myron snapped another photo of him. He would give it to him later as a gift. But for now he stepped back into the vehicle, closed the heavy door and waited for Birdsong to return to the truck. When he finally did, they drove off again, and nobody spoke again of sex or flesh.

They drove in silence to their destination. The gunner and driver were left confused over what had happened outside. Birdsong was left a little stunned, but the drive cooled his anger.

Myron felt that tension he had felt earlier, when he should have taken the time to talk to the woman about God's true blessings. Also, when he failed to express his passion for the faith with the soldier reading the Bible.

Once the convoy arrived, the troops worked with village elders on an upcoming farming project. Myron took photos to cover the event and wrote down notes and quotes for the story.

That tension remained with him: That lack of courage.

When would he find the courage to express his love for Christ and share the Gospel with these soldiers? On the drive home, perhaps. He might give it a try. Inside that cramped Humvee, he would try to find the courage and the words to talk about God's blessings and of His grace.

Amidst Traffic

Lyonya defined her life by the tattooed words scribbled on her skin. They ran like trails of broken thoughts. Idioms lost, clashing against one another like cars mangled across a stretch of highway. Those tattoos. They were a habit among her many.

In all her scribbling, those tattoos etched out messages, dates, thoughts, ideas… reminding her of things she couldn't keep track of in her head. They had all been remarkably brilliant in the speck of time in which they were fabricated, all short-term memories printed into permanency. But fading.

Her first mark was gradually dissolving into a smeary, blue stain, becoming blotchier and blotchier by the year.

"*Believe!*" it read, now with the blemished ink finding depth in her skin. Fading. Becoming like the rest. Defining her with words she once defined. There were hundreds of lines and phrases, running all the way up her arms and shoulders, some on her thighs and calves, some hidden beneath her foot, self-tattooed as if the act of writing could help her remember more than the ink itself.

But she couldn't remember.

There was only the illusion of remembering.

Lyonya stared at that first word etched onto her wrist. *Believe!* Believe in what? It wasn't something magical or promising. Believe in believing, is all she could think of. Like a knotted rope meant to be untied so it could be knotted again.

Believe!

The word itself was becoming submerged by all the other scribbles that surrounded it. Too often it sunk beneath reams of bracelets, which kept it hidden through most of the day. Now she had so many of those bracelets she had lost track of how many there were. Each of those stood for a week, a month or a year she had found remarkable at the time. Every one of them stood for a memory, each one holding a folded symbol.

They were all she had left: those symbols. They were moments lost in her tattoos and bracelets and necklaces that draped down to her chest. Yet, she felt the necessity of those symbols. She felt the necessity of her written words.

Just like now.

It was time for another tattoo. She needed to write this one down. Now. Before she forgot. Because forgetting was her biggest fear.

Make it permanent before it fades, she told herself, and this thought brought her a moment of calm.

She sat at her frail kitchen table with rust gnawing up the wobbling, metal legs. Among the piles of papers and trash, she found her homemade tattoo gun. She used a guitar string for the needle, which made the humming of the little motor feel musical when she wrote.

She had become quick with the ink.

On her forearm she found a spot of untainted skin that squeezed between *I hate people* and *Like a glorified majesty on the 21st*. She had to slide the reams of jangling bracelets up her arm to find the vacant spot. Her writing hand became steady when she tattooed. She brought the pointed guitar string to her blank, pale skin. The metal needle pierced and drummed. An emotion took charge of her, and all she felt now was the need to place it down into permanency. If she didn't, she might forget tomorrow. She might forget an hour from now. The letters formed like petroleum scratches.

Make Zephan

Before she could complete the phrase, her cat, Adara, meowed from inside her purse, breaking Lyonya away from her ink.

"What is it?" she asked delicately. She switched off the motor and put the needle down.

"Hungry?"

They made contact with their eyes, a glare she found brilliant in her cat. She stood from her creaking chair and went to the cupboard. Among the glasses, some clean, others not so much, she pulled down the bag of cat food. She grabbed a handful of dried cat food and dropped it in Adara's bowl. A few bits spilled and rolled onto the floor along with the crumbs already settled there. Adara crawled out of his throne—her purse—and moved to his bowl. The dried bits crunched between his teeth. Lyonya crouched low, watching him in adoration.

He made gentle purring noises, confessing his love for her.

"I love you too," she said.

With a sense of unfitting calm, she brought both hands to her chest, pressing them against her own solar plexus—the central gate to her soul, she believed. She moved her fingers up to her neck, where dozens of necklaces draped over one another. There were hundreds of beads, mostly wooden, bound in hemp. Her fingers reached for one of the necklaces. It was the only one made of pearls.

Pearls in the banana sun.

This was written somewhere on her left thigh. She had found the necklace in the trash at a market place downtown. Someone had thrown it away because the clasp was broken, tossed right on top of a pile of garbage, tucked inside a banana peel. A treasure amidst trash. Anyone looking at Lyonya with her newfound pearls didn't seem to care. Her awkwardness of digging through trash fazed no one. It had seemed fitting somehow. Around her, the market stands had displayed flowers and fruits against the backdrop of gray buildings that shot upward into the city sky.

She had grasped the pearls into her fists and held them against her chest. Nobody would miss them. They were just more proof to support the truth of displacement. The truth of belonging by not belonging at all. The truth that things—objects, emotions, thoughts, fears—were found only if they were first lost. It was among the chaos of loss and displacement that finding anything was possible. There was no other way for discovery. She made this her truth.

The door to the apartment slammed; an angry mood vibrated through the walls. Lyonya rose, peered out from the kitchen, and asked, "Did you get it?"

There was no hesitancy in her voice. She had been waiting for him.

Drake stood at the door with their little boy in his arms.

Sometimes it was hard to believe he was five. He was so small. So sheepish and quiet. Some days, they hardly noticed Zephan playing by himself in the room.

Drake's hair swooped low, down to his neck, curving around the front like thick blades of grass. He carried a gaze in his eyes that a poet might admire, locked in a dream-state within every watchful saccade. He peered back at Lyonya, jaw clenched.

He set the boy down.

"Did you get it?" she repeated.

He shook his head, eyes unblinking. There was something lodged in his stare. Lyonya couldn't tell exactly what it was. Sadness? Guilt? Yearning?

"What do you mean, *no*?"

"I just couldn't, okay?" he answered in a groan.

She took this for annoyance, when it could have been fatigue or sorrow. They miscalculated one another's tones. They misunderstood one another's signals often. It was easy to do by now. It was easy to pretend you found what you expected instead of what was actually there. Expecting the worst usually meant you would receive just that.

Lyonya made a gesture to her boy.

"Come Zephan. Come to mums."

The boy looked up at his mother with sheepish eyes. His hand tightened around his father's.

"Go on and play with your trucks," Drake told him. "Go on."

Zephan scampered toward the trucks in the corner of the living room. His little shoes made no sound. He sat in the corner, facing the wall, barely touching his toys.

"Why'd you bring him with you?" she asked, now looking back at Drake.

He remained silent, staring back, eyes flinching—an accusation held in their own language. She scratched her arm between the reams of her bracelets.

Make Zephan

Those words standing. Itching. Make Zephan what? Already she couldn't remember. Already the thought had dispersed. She turned her face back to her boy, trying to regain that dwindled emotion. A rose bloomed somewhere inside her for a long moment. A quiver strummed her spine like a cord. A guitar string pierced through her solar plexus. Spreading. *Make Zephan,* she thought, and felt she could regain her claim on that emotion. A boy of five years. Her boy. Once born of her womb, fed of her milk, now distant from anything she had to offer.

The boy had always preferred his father. The way he cried any time he left the house. The way he refused to eat unless it was his father feeding him. The way he played trucks with his father but wouldn't when she tried. The way he hid behind his father's leg when he was trying to run from her.

Make Zephan

"Another one? You got another one, didn't you?" Drake asked.

With two steps he reached her and grabbed her wrist, which felt like a malnourished branch in his grasp. His hands were large, big enough that he once used those hands to hold her shoulders close to him for comfort. Big enough to hold her heart and protect her from harm.

But this was then, now lost in the presence of their tempered habits. She with her tattoos. He with his unfinished poems. Both of them with their snorting coke. An addiction they both loved and devoured as greedily as it devoured them. A love for the same violent powder. The same hard, quivering high.

"You can't go on like this," he said with an expression she read as either remorse or disgust. But it could have easily been pained compassion.

"Don't *can't* me. Not *me*."

There was a lyrical beauty to those words, even though she thrust them with contempt.

Holding her wrist, he traced the traffic of words trailing up her arms with his eyes. She could see him reading, searching, rephrasing. He pushed up her bracelets then, and saw the new branding immediately. He knew her markings better than his own poetry, just as she knew his poems better than her own ink.

"Make Zephan," he read. "Make Zephan what?"

The question stunned her. Was he curious? Interrogating? Accusing?

"I dunno," she said. "I knew a moment ago. I swear. I *knew* this time. I *knew*."

"Lyonya. Maybe it's too much. Maybe you oughta stop."

This hurt, of course. Even through his gentle tone, it hurt.

It had been his hands that taught and guided her fingers through her first tattoo. It had been *his* poetry that convinced her to believe, offering a context for keeping the symbols fixed. It had been *him* who said her tattoos would serve as her own poetry. *We can form poems,* he had promised. *Together. The two of us.* Now he was telling her to stop, which was the same as telling her she should quit searching for something to believe in.

"And you? What about *your* poetry? Why don't *you* stop?"

"Damn it Lyonya, it's not the same," he said, striking each word from his lips.

And there it was. There was his quickness. There was his temperament rising with little prodding. There was his selfishness for wanting to keep his own poetry while telling her she should leave hers behind. Just like when she was pregnant, when he told her she should stop snorting coke while he could go on. Somehow snorting was bad for the baby only if *she* was the one doing it.

"It's different," he repeated, calmer now, but his anger had left its stain.

Different, she thought, and saw the word for the lie it was, because in truth, it was all the same. They were both dependent on the need for symbols. They had the same need for snorting a drug that mended the world so they could break it apart. Break it apart with their own words. She, on her body; he, on his journal's pages. Both of them with ink as permanent as their mediums allowed.

"*This* was different," she said to him, pointing at her latest tattoo, and she recognized her words for both the lie and the truth they presented. Yes, this tattoo meant something more this time, but how could it be so different if already she couldn't remember what that *more* was?

She sighed.

He twitched.

There was love in those gestures. There had always been love between them, right from the first moment when they met eyes at the marketplace downtown. He had complimented her pearls, and she had admitted to their discovery. Both of them gazed at the other with watchful eyes, dazed in adoration for a long poetic moment.

Sure. Love was there.

But the problem was that Lyonya understood love as something contextual. She understood it as something that needed to be rediscovered each and every day. Something lost among the chaos of life. Lost, so it could be found again and again. Drake understood love as an interpretive force. Something that needed to be understood and explained with new terms, fresh words and stunning metaphors. These were two different kinds of love. One was discovered, the other explored.

Over the years, they had fooled themselves into believing they both wanted the same love. They both gave it the same name, calling it *poetry* as a synonym for something so big it could be found or explained only in pieces. Except in the end, for two people to believe in two different breeds of love was like splitting one God into separate beings. Even their love for cocaine split them in half, often turning Drake to violence and Lyonya to self-loathing.

Drake twitched again.

And that was all it took to give him away. There was actually nothing like poetry in that twitch. It was a twitch she knew how to read. It meant only one thing.

He had some.

"You lied to me," she said.

Her face changed with those words. She could feel the ripple of her lips, brow and eyelids tightening.

"What? No. I don't have any."

"You *lied* to me," she repeated.

"You're crazy. You're freaking crazy. I don't have any."

"Give it to me. Where is it?"

"Get off me. I said get off me."

He swore at her, but her arms and tattoo-battered wrists wailed at him, hitting him. Her one hand scooped into his jacket pockets, digging into one, finding nothing, searching another, while her other arm kept swinging and striking his body with frantic anger. Drake finally pushed her off, hard. Her spine struck the wall.

"*Fine,*" he shouted at her. "Is this what you want? *Is it?*"

He held his arm outstretched, dangling a small baggie before her.

"*Give me,*" she said, and lunged toward him, but he pushed her off again.

The boy cried and wailed from the corner, but neither of them paid him any attention.

"*It's not yours,*" Drake shouted at her. His voice devoured oxygen.

There was drama in that voice. Drama he was always trying to stress. His hand shook the bag with each word, fingers clenching tighter. He had always been one for the dramatic.

Lyonya felt her heart drumming, shaking every vein and artery that clung onto its beating. Her breathing quivered with yearning. Her eyes stared at the brilliant white powder dangling before her face. She wanted. She *wanted.* It was just one simple truth, confirmed by everything else inside her. It was a want that smeared every other desire. It smeared even the desire to quiet and soothe her boy's crying, making it distant, pushing it far and away.

Her lips puckered with yearn. Drake enjoyed seeing that look on her face. It was like a child's lust for chocolate. It was a look he liked to deprive.

He licked his lips. A gesture that mocked Lyonya's wanting.

"This," he said, giving the baggie a quick, angry shake.

"Listen, Drake…"

She was pleading, but that was okay. Pleading might work. Anything. She'd do anything for just a little. A tiny, little bit. She wanted. She just *wanted.*

"*Shut up,*" he said.

"I just… It's simple—"

"*Shut up,* I said."

Adara wrapped himself around her leg as if to protect her. She barely felt his fur. The moment stood silent and then… Wails of tears again. Louder somehow. Closer. But not close enough because in an instant Drake thumbed open the baggie and put it against one nostril.

Before Drake could inhale, Lyonya swatted the baggie from his hand. The white dust flew through the air and dispersed. It fell to the ground. A slow, white mist.

For a while, neither of them could hear anything but the sound of cocaine falling. The powder became lost in the thick strands of the carpet. They would not be able to recover it. Then the sound of their child's crying consumed them both. They looked at one another, ashamed, and then looked at their son, ashamed more still.

Lyonya was the first to pick him up and hold him. Drake touched the boy's shoulder, touched the boy's chin. They both apologized to one another and to the boy in silence while Adara weaved in and out of their feet like a rhythmic dance. After a long time of shushing and kissing him, the boy's crying exhausted him and they both put him to sleep in a makeshift bed Drake had built with scrap wood.

They made love because this was the only way they knew how to speak their apologies. "I'm sorry. I'm sorry," they said, over and over again. And while Drake hovered over her body, Lyonya watched the small pearl tattooed just above the tuft of his pubic hair. He had the pearl tattooed there on their first anniversary as a gift to her. It was the only tattoo he had ever allowed anyone to needle to his body.

He fell asleep after making love, like always, and she stared at his singular tattoo.

It was just like poetry, that tattoo, where the fewer the words, the more impact it was intended to have. Drake said poetry had to have an echo longer than an epic novel, be more powerful than a short story, more secure than an anecdote, more intrusive than a dirty joke.

Lyonya envied that pearl because it would always achieve more than all her lost scribbling. It was so easy to find. It was so easy to remember what it stood for, lost in the most perfect place. It was private.

She stared at the ceiling for a long, long time. She wondered what might have happened if she hadn't slapped the baggie from Drake's nose. Lyonya pictured her husband snorting up all that coke, his eyes bulging with pleasure. His eyes growing so big they might burst like small bubbles of jelly. His knees popped instead, joints shifting like slabs of unevenly stacked bricks. She pictured him falling to the ground and overdosing on the one substance they both so violently loved.

The sound of honking came from the streets outside. Lyonya slid out of bed and walked to the window. She stood there naked, clothed only by all of her scribbling. The words ran up her legs from her ankles, rose over her buttocks, wrapped around her waist, curled around her breasts, spread out to her shoulders and fell down her arms to her wrists.

She opened the window and felt the rain pelt her face and shoulders. Below, the street was packed with cars moving slower than creek water. Amidst the traffic of vehicles, a man in a dark suit walked between the cars. Lyonya could not see the man's face. He had black hair. She imagined it was filled with searching. She pictured herself with that man, holding their child, walking away. How could she make her boy love her? How could she make him the central focus of her life and purpose?

The drugs needed to stop.

Car drivers honked and some shouted at the man to move out of the way. The man moved through the traffic, between the bumper-to-bumper cars, up stream. Lyonya followed the man with her eyes until he became lost in the distance and she couldn't see him anymore.

Lyonya looked down at her newest tattoo.

Make Zephan.

She thought, in that moment, that she might finish that sentence.

A Tin Can
Mind

Some nights I'd step out from work, step into the cool of rolling darkness, and I'd hear voices. Cars passed by on Banksville Road. The median between the crossing lanes stood there to prevent disaster. The voices I heard were mechanical. They sounded like the revving of dirt bikes and movie car chases. But really, they were more like one voice coming from everywhere. I couldn't tell if it streamed down from the north, the south, or from the dumpster behind me. It was the kind of voice you might hear announcing at the racetrack, fuzzy with megaphone mechanics.

And it echoed… right through my tin can mind, opening it up like homeless food and spilled beans. Bouncing off everything.

I could never understand that voice. I didn't know what it said. I didn't know if it was speaking to me directly or if it was shouting at a cultivated audience waiting to watch some spectacle. Some disaster. Some victory. Some clash of wins and losses. Maybe it was just the rush of traffic passing by that whirled into something that sounded vocal. Or maybe the cars sweeping by just dragged the air behind them, carrying lives and voices along.

Melodies and furies.

Maybe there was a show somewhere down the road and the overhead speakers were turned too high. But every Friday night, it seemed, I heard that mechanical whirl. When throwing away trash or getting ready to hop into my car and take off, the voice spoke to me.

It was all just a wind of buzzing vowels and consonants. I couldn't understand a word. It might not even have been English.

One night, I walked back into the pizza shop and asked Nick if he's ever heard that voice.

"What's it sound like?"

"Like someone shouting through a megaphone."

"Maybe it's the refrigerator upstairs."

I've never heard refrigerators talk. Hum, maybe, but not talk. And out of every place where that voice could be coming from, I didn't think it came from upstairs.

I turn my head left and right, looking up and down Banksville Road, turning my ears to find its source.

There's a power tool shop across the street. There's a Johnson's Florist. To either side of the restaurant we have a beer distributor and a Jackson Hewitt Tax Service.

Everything is dimly lit by overshadowing lights. No race tracks anywhere in sight.

The pizza shop where I work used to be a coal mine. The tunnels inside were airshafts that burrowed into the hillside. In 1886 a fire broke out, cremating the mules used to carry the coal, but everyone else survived. I can't even say the place is haunted.

'Unless the voices belong to the mules.

Yet, this isn't the first time I've ever heard voices. I hear them all the time. When sitting in thick traffic with a green light beaming ahead and no cars moving, I hear at least two of them at once. One telling me to ram every car in sight, scraping bumpers, running down grannies, tearing up asphalt, whatever the hell it takes. And the other telling me to remain calm. *Relax. Enjoy the music. You've only heard this song a couple hundred times. One more won't kill'ya. Happy thoughts. Smile.*

But those are internal voices of debate and reason. The little devil and angel battling one another from opposite shoulders. They're the little insanities of my mind that keep me sane.

Every one of us has heard these voices.

They give us reason. Sometimes, they give us hope and reassurance. Other times, not so much.

One time I heard a voice telling me all will be okay and the troubles of the world were only temporary, and I believed it.

Another time I heard a voice telling me I was a loser and would never find a good woman who would stick by my side, and I believed that, too.

A voice telling me I was a damn good writer and my name would be known some day, and this pizza job was just temporary, and I believed it.

Another convincing me that I might as well swerve my car off the road, crash myself into the cliff below because no good can come of life.

I almost believed that one.

Inside my head I have more voices than I have vocabulary. The darkest voice I've ever felt—the most hushing by far, the most chilling—belonged to Bobby Black, my alter ego. It would be too simple to call him the evil side of me.

He was the sly and collected one.

Does everyone have this voice inside them? And if so, how did it get there? Where do our inner voices come from?

Bobby Black first whispered into my ear one summer day when I had the house to myself and a BB gun to my side. Rifle in hand. No one home to tell me what I could and couldn't do. I was fifteen and determined to kill something. My friend, Dante and I had practiced shooting that gun for weeks. Setting up stacks of beer bottles at one end of the driveway and taking aim from the other. The crash of that glass splintering brought vigor to my heart every time.

Yet now, Dante wasn't with me. Only me and Bobby Black. Instead of a small, rounded BB, I slid a .177 inch pellet down the barrel of the rifle. The kind of pellet that breaks the skin. The kind of pellet you can load only one at a time and sold in boxes with warnings signs printed in extra bold font.

The round slid down that rifle's barrel like a scream in the darkness. I stood by the side of my house and waited for birds to rest on the telephone wire across the road. In less than a minute, a pigeon perched on the wire like a fat businessman on a throne. I took aim and Bobby Black walked me through every step.

Aim it up right, Jack. Cross the sights with the bird. Steady. Don't shake now, relax. Easy. So easy. Just pump some air, that's all, and let 'er rip.

My first shot missed, nipping the wire. The pigeon just waddled over a few steps to the left, unfazed.

Bobby Black laughed inside my ear.

'Kay now. Try again.

My second shot blasted through the pigeon's head. It tried

to fly off for a second but instead remembered it was dead and plummeted down on the concrete like a spinning airplane made of bricks. I ran toward my kill with a laughter that filled my chest but wouldn't leave through my lips. I was in disbelief. How the hell did I hit it?

As I stood over the kill, my neighbor ran out of her house, screaming at me.

"What if someone went around and shot your dog?" she said.

I tried not to picture that, tried to see that killing a dog and killing a filthy pigeon were two separate things. But for a moment I did see Brownie there, dead, small and twisted where the bird had been just a second ago.

"I'm sorry," I said looking up at her. Her hands were on her hips and her face held disgust. Bobby Black was gone. He would have told her to screw off and to leave me alone. But instead I was left with seeing myself the way this lady saw me. Some little neighborhood scumbag wearing baggy jeans and a wrinkled wife beater.

If Bobby Black is inside each of us, what do we have to counterbalance him?

What voice can we hope to redeem us for killing pigeons out of sheer fun?

That wasn't the last time I heard Bobby Black inside my head. He became my pseudonym for the stories I wrote that felt too dark to put my own name on them. He kept me calm throughout Army Basic Training and eased me into firing my first real weapon.

Bobby Black...

That voice...

Just like shooting a BB gun, he said. I felt the cool of the world rushing through my lungs when he spoke. The kick of the M16 felt like a brotherly fist to my shoulder. That weapon was just an extension of my arm. Bobby Black was just an extension of my mind.

But voices weren't the only things that ever boiled inside my tin can mind. With my trial and error rendezvous with Mary Jane, images and colors have pinched at my nerve endings like aromatic fruit flavors rushing at my face through my nostrils. Everything coming in at once through a single gateway. LSD once. Mushrooms a couple times.

I've seen the Tasmanian Devil with wings in the sky. I've seen pumpkin faces as stairway steps and holes in the ground that shot straight into hell. An eel tried to bite off my face once. A swarm of ants crawling at my feet, making me laugh because the ground looked like liquid waves moving along. The gears of the world twisting, and my sister's nose on the floor like a misshapen Picasso piece.

Yet those were all drug-induced visual pop-ups. Voices are something else. And this voice especially, this one in the midst of night, coming over to me in this Banksville Road parking lot... It wasn't just a feeling inside my chest. Not just a tumbling of indecisive consciousness. It was true *sound*. Pressure waves and vibrating eardrums. My tympanic membranes were *moving*.

I had to find that voice.

The next day I asked my boss, Gary, if he had ever heard it.

"What, like an announcer? Yeah, there's a football stadium just over there." He pointed across Banksville to the shallow hill sloping on the other side of the road. That whole day I couldn't get my mind off that voice. I had to find it. I stretched dough, and thought of that voice. I baked pizza crusts, and thought of that voice. I roasted wings until they sizzled brown, and thought of that voice. I was determined to go out and find that stadium.

Gary had pointed in a general direction when he told me where it was—like pointing out into the sea and saying, "Land is ahead."

It was up to me to find it.

After my shift, I stood outside under the reaching night and waited to see if that voice would come out again. It didn't, so I hopped in the car and skidded out of the parking lot, tearing into Banksville traffic. I shifted lanes like a bad twitch. The noise of the radio disturbed me. I turned it off. I needed complete silence.

I missed turns and took random roads, convinced that all things would point to the stadium. In the back alleys of suburban streets, I chased for my voice. I made two lefts, and suddenly… there it was. The stadium's sight opened up like an egg cracking upwards in front of my eyes.

After parking my car, I stepped out in a hoodie and heavy feet. My steps walked the street. It was just a stadium. An outstretched chain-link fence surrounded the field. All was quiet for a moment, but then things were happening I didn't understand.

A black car with a droning muffler passed me from behind, stopped, the passenger door opened, someone was getting out— no, getting back in—they threw something out. The car backed up, drove ahead, stopped, backed up again, laughter muffled inside, then took off. The banners surrounding the field read, "Golden Eagle Pride," followed by "Castle Shannon Dormont Green Tree." A school united? A person in the distance walked past without making a sound. More cars purring past in the distance. Then a whistle somewhere—like the *whizzz* of spinning firecrackers. That whistle, too, sounded like a voice. Everything did. Everything was.

I began to understand, but I let the moment surround me.

All was scattered amidst the night. All of it outside and beyond the fence.

Then a shape approached. A man. A figure. Call it whatever you want, but really it was none of those. Bobby Black approached me like a shadow. Walking up the road at the speed of sound traveling underwater. And he looked at me. And he smiled.

His eyes were two dented holes punched into the face of night.

Come with me, he said, and nodded at the stadium.

There was so much brightness beyond the fence. The field, the bleachers, the goal posts. They radiated in that after burn that burns when taking peeks at the sun. But Bobby Black had no trouble staring.

Come discover it with me, he said. *Find your voice.*

And you know the feeling those words created. The feeling of being seduced by a persuasive, slender woman with little clothing, whose toes barely touch the ground.

Swept.

I wanted.

The words. The sound. The stadium.

All of it.

I stood there while Bobby Black walked to the fence, pushed his fingers through the links, and gripped.

Come, he said. *Listen.*

"It's too bright."

Do you remember the time you saw music transform into colors?

"I remember."

You said it was too bright back then, too. Remember the time you qualified expert at the firing range?

"I do."

I was the one with you those times.

"I buried the pigeon, you know."

I know.

"You weren't with me then. You weren't there when I put the bird in a plastic bag and dug a hole in the back yard and buried him there."

It was a good shot, Jack.

"It was."

Come listen to the stadium. He tilted his neck back and breathed as if listening himself.

"The voice is gone. It was just a game announcer."

How do you know it wasn't me?

I didn't have an answer for him right then. The only thing I could do was walk. Walk away. I never touched the fence that night. I never gripped the links or tried to listen, nor did I hop over to find that voice. There was maybe regret. I could have hopped over the fence and sat down in the middle of the field. I could have stood at the center of things. But it was just a simple high school football field. Turf grass. Polished, aluminum benches. Lights sparkling down over pristine restrooms. All of it clean. All of it a bit too shiny for a game of attrition and muddy shoes to have played the night before. It was all shiny objects caught by the eye, nothing about it that circled the ear. Composed and orderly.

In the middle of nowhere.

Return

I came down the hill and watched the football wobble like an egg to her feet. She stopped and bent down to pick it up. Her jogging shorts pulled as she did so. When she straightened, she pinched the shorts back down and turned to see where the ball had come from.

"Hey that's mine."

I don't know why I said that. Why I said it that way. Like she was going to take it from me.

She walked closer. Her legs were long and muscular. Her tank top was cut high and cut a across her flat tummy.

"How do I know it's yours?" She hugged the ball tighter in one arm, and made a gesture to me with her free hand. Her dark hair, in a bun, bobbled as she said this.

"Are you joking?" I didn't mean to smile as I said this. But I did. I smiled. I know how it looked, like I was flirting back, and I tried to cover it up quickly.

"I'm Hailey," she said and came a step closer. She had taken my smile as an invitation. "I'm new to the city."

A herd of bicyclists rushed past us, pulling the wind behind them. She smelled of cocoa butter. A familiar smell. Beyond the bicycle trail, a couple—a mother and father—took turns pushing a little boy on a swing. They laughed as they did, and it wasn't forced. The boy was much older than Joshua, maybe four or five.

"Listen, the guys on the hill overthrew me and the ball landed at your feet. Can I have it back?"

I knew what she was doing. I didn't want to play the game. I hated that I even had to ask for my ball back. It was mine after all. She didn't have a right to take it. Didn't have the right to question my ownership.

"Prove to me it belongs to you and it's yours."

"Well, it's *already* mine." That smile crept out again. My eyebrow cocked up.

She looked at me in a way that made me wish I was wearing my wedding band. So I could flash it casually, and this game between us would end. I pictured the silver ring with the three crosses etched into the metal, sitting in my car among the loose change. I don't even know why I still held onto it.

"Look," I said, and I tried to sound reasonable. "Right here," I reached across her body to touch the ball on a spot. My arm brushed against her. Her skin was soft. "That's the Tenth Mountain patch. I got the ball as a retention gift."

"Retention?" The word puzzled her.

"Re-enlistment. Army lingo."

"Were you in the war?"

I laughed. I couldn't help it. *The war.* The way she said it. The way she made it sound. Like the word held a spell over her. The boy on the swing was giggling now. His father tickled him and smothered his face with kisses. Was Joshua two years old now? Already? I couldn't remember. It seemed important.

"I was in Iraq."

"Oh. Well..." she stammered, searched for the words. She touched my arm. "I guess thank you. Thanks for your service."

I never knew how to respond to those thank-yous. I deployed as an Army journalist. Never fired a bullet in combat. What was I to be thanked for?

I looked at the ball. She held it like it was her own. Like I was never part of it. Like she might just turn around after her thank you and her charmed smile and walk away with it.

"Can I have my ball back?"

Why did I even have to ask for it? I thought of taking it from her. I thought of stripping it away from her grasp. I felt the tension in my face.

Was I being childish?

I was.

Calm down, I thought. *She hasn't done anything to you. Not her.*

"Are you guys playing catch up there?" She nodded toward the hill where I'd come from.

"Just me and some friends."

"Mind if I come play with you guys? I just finished my run, and I don't have much else to do."

Behind her, the father lifted the boy off the swing. Lifted him high for a moment. Then the boy kicked his feet in the air as his mom and dad held him up between them, an arm in each of their grasp.

"Lady. I just want my ball back, okay?" I didn't smile this time.

She looked at me like I'd slapped a child.

"That was rude," she said.

She pushed the ball into my gut without a word. I gasped because I didn't expect it. It took my breath for a moment. She waited for me to take the ball. She waited there with the ball pressed against my belly. And I took it. And she walked away.

I stood there a moment. I felt the anger lingering in my face. I breathed.

The family of three squeezed into a two-door coupe. They drove away together. Happy.

I turned and made my way back up the hill. Feeling as though something was taken from me once again.

Clouds in the Water

"I'm going to marry you some day."

"Ew, don't say that."

She giggled in his ear as they swung upside-down with their legs hooked onto the sturdy branch. It barely shook as they rocked, hovering low over the pond's water, holding firm like an arm reaching for the other shore. On the other side of the pond the grass turned wild and the West Virginia hills tumbled and rolled into one another. The rain was long gone from the night before, and the sky was a deep summer blue that came around only once every thousand breaths.

Samuel could see himself in the water. His gray eyes and pale face. He barely felt his youth when he looked into that face. The water was calm and as reflective as glass. His neck felt sore but he didn't want to come off the branch yet. He loved feeling his blood rushing up to his brain. It made him feel fuzzy and warm.

He rarely felt this.

Jenny swung beside him and grabbed for his hand. On her pinky she wore a small ring Samuel had made out of tinfoil and paperclips. The foil formed a small rose, fragile to the slightest bend. She wore it on her pinky because wearing it on any other finger would have been corny. As Samuel squeezed her hand back, he made sure not to crumple the rose.

Both in the pond and in the sky, the sun shone through the clouds, pushing through into beams of light.

"Look," Jenny said, pointing to the clouds in the water. "They're beautiful."

"They're just clouds."

"You're wrong. It's more than that. It's like floating."

It was true. For a moment, neither of them could escape the feeling, hovering between two skies: one above, the other below.

Samuel stretched for the water, extending one arm as close to it as possible. He could almost skim the pond's surface with his fingertips.

"Don't," she said.

"What, I won't fall."

"Not that. Don't touch it."

"Why not?" he said.

"I don't want the water to ripple."

He plunged his hand into the pond, stretching his entire body as far as he could, and splashed some of the water at her. Ripples shook through the clouds. The illusion was ruined.

"You jerk!" Jenny said, shoving him with one arm. He laughed the way only boys could when they teased girls. She shoved him again for laughing, but he laughed only harder. The branch bobbed a little now. Samuel scooted closer to her and tried to grab hold of her in his arms. His skin was clammy—the color of a boy allergic to everything. Pallid and splotchy.

The color of afternoon rain, Jenny tried to tell him once, but he told her that rain didn't have color.

Exactly, she had said.

This was his sickness, visible to everyone. The doctors said it was like eczema, but worse. Who knew simple allergies could make a child look so vulnerable. He slept with socks over his hands because too often he'd wake up in the middle of the night bleeding from scratching himself.

He looked down into the water, which was becoming calm again from the ripples. His neck was crooked, and it ached constantly. He didn't like to see himself and that crooked neck of his. He splashed the water again.

"Quit that," she said. "Oh, you always ruin everything."

"Oh yeah?" he said, smiling because he knew his mission of torturing her—a mission every boy has in life when it came to girls—was almost complete.

He reached over and grabbed Jenny with one arm, and ruffled her blond hair with his other hand.

"You're getting me all wet!"

She squealed in a pitch that could've shattered the pond's surface, but he didn't stop. His boyish laugher never even paused. He was a month older than her and that gave him the right to pester her. He loved to—

The wood gave a crack.

They froze.

"See what you did?" he whispered, trying to keep still.

"What *I* did?"

"Shh! Not so loud. Your voice is going to snap the branch."

"No it won't," she said through pursed lips and a squeezed frown.

They waited. Listened for the wood. Braced for it to snap. All they heard was the sound of the clouds moving and the water rippling out to the shores.

"See?" she said.

He gave her a big shove, and she almost slipped off the branch. She was about to shove him back when—

She froze.

Jenny pulled her arms tightly back to herself, closing her fingers into tiny fists under her chin.

"What?" he said.

"Bee," she said, a whimper.

"Oh please."

Samuel turned his neck, as sore as ever now, and looked for the bee. It buzzed in front of his gaze for a long moment, came closer, and rested on his chin. He strained his eyes to look at it. He could feel its fuzzy body crawling along his jaw line. It tickled him, and he almost burst out laughing again.

"See? No harm," he said as the bee crawled around his face. He tried to follow it with his eyes, but bee was just a blur out of focus.

"Get it away."

"Relax."

"It's going to sting you."

"It won't sting me."

"You're allergic."

"I'm allergic to everything."

"You'll get hives."

"Will you relax?"

"Flick it off or something. Ew."

The bee lifted off Samuel's cheek and came toward Jenny. She squirmed, trying to lift herself up with her legs, but they were sore from hanging so long.

"Ew-ew-ew—get away from me."

"If you yell, it'll sting you."

"Do something."

"It'll go away."

"It's not going away. I'm gonna scream."

"Don't scream."

The bee flew away, but then it swooped back around and charged toward Jenny again. She squealed—that same, high-pitched squeal that could have torn through the clouds. She tried to swat at the bee, but as she swung with one elbow her legs twisted and she slipped from the branch. She fell, plunging into the water. Her voice cut off into a gargle.

Samuel couldn't contain his laughter. It choked him up and tensed his chest like a ball of knotted twine, bringing him to a coughing fit. His legs buckled from the coughing, and he too fell in the water holding his chest. He saw the clouds as he dropped. Saw them everywhere.

He floated in the water. The pond was deeper than its size suggested. Samuel clung onto his tightening chest with one arm as he lunged and swam through the water with the other. His hand pulling and pushing. His feet kicking. He needed air.

Air!

On the shore, Jenny was already waiting for him. His coughing fit turned to laughter again. He was laughing so hard he couldn't even convince her that his chest was in pain. As he crawled to the shore, she lunged for him, but he rolled to his feet and ran towards the barn.

His lungs tightened like fists. It was hard to breathe. He needed his inhaler. He wheezed and wheezed as he scurried to the chopping block where he'd left it. With every step, another wheeze. Jenny followed behind, mad at him for laughing at her. How dare he tease and torture a girl like that, and then just run away. She could *run* for a girl.

"You crooked-neck jerk! You pale-skinned freakazoid!" she screamed at him.

Samuel stumbled over his feet before reaching the chopping block. He lay on the ground, wheezing and coughing in bursts. Jenny was about to give him a good kick in the tush when—

"Where's your inhaler?" she said frantic. In an instant, she was no longer mad at him. She looked around for the inhaler.

He motioned with one hand. She ran toward the block, remembering, grabbed it and brought it back to him. They were both drenched and sticking to the lush grass. He took a puff, waited, took another, gulped. Each rasp of breath sounded like a leaky suction in his lungs. Jenny kneeled beside him, curving and hovering over him. She ran her palm over his hair, over and over and over. Smoothening it out. As if the gesture were meant to calm her as much as soothe him.

With another burst of coughs he was laughing again. Crackled, but laughter all the same.

"It's not funny," she said.

"Sure it is," he said, his voice still wheezing.

"You could have died, so no, it's *not* funny."

He just smiled and looked up from the ground, still breathing heavily, looking at the world upside-down.

"So you wanna marry me now or later?" he said.

"Shut up you jerk."

She jabbed him in the chest with the palm of her hand.

"Oof," he said, and started coughing again.

"I'm sorry, I'm sorry."

They lay there for a minute.

He saw the barn. The door was left ajar from this morning. He remembered someone had stolen all the bales of hay overnight.

Samuel's father had called the sheriff and then took off to find out whose skulls he needed to crack.

Just then, Samuel remembered the hive.

"I want to show you something," he said to Jenny, his voice calming down. In fact, it held a mesmerized quality to it.

"What is it?"

"Come with me."

He got to his feet slowly and walked to the barn. Jenny kept beside him. Neither of them said a word. Sawdust was scattered in front of the barn's entrance, damp from last night's rain. Muddy footsteps stretched back and forth from the barn to the dirt road sloping behind a small trail of brushes. Samuel turned his neck to the house. Nobody was home. He pulled open the door to the barn, a door as big as heaven's gate, when Jenny's fingers clamped down on his arm, hoping he'd stop.

They stood, looking into one another's eyes for a moment. He saw the clouds in those eyes just then, caught by the illusion. He could tell she saw the same in his own.

Inside, the barn was as empty as it had been that morning. The interior was unpainted. Bare wood. Quiet. The smell of the stolen hay lingered in the air. The ceiling was high, and the walls seemed wide enough to box in a house. There must have been fifty or sixty bales in here, now all gone. Samuel had never been in the barn when empty. It had never looked so huge before.

"Someone stole it all last night," he explained to Jenny as he pointed to the hay scattered on the ground.

"Who did?"

"I don't know. But they took it all. Daddy was as angry as a bull when he saw this."

Samuel felt sorry for whoever stole the bales. Their bones would be hurting if his father ever found them.

Only one thing remained in the barn.

Jenny looked up in the loft. She saw something strange up there.

"What is that?" She asked.

"That's what I wanted to show you."

With the barn empty, Samuel had discovered the sculpture.

Samuel could hear the buzzing zipping around in the far corner of the hangar. At the sound, Jenny rushed back for the door. Samuel reached for her and hooked one arm around her slim frame.

"It's okay," he said. "They're just flying."

"Is there a beehive up there?" Jenny asked, her voice trembling.

"Better," he whispered, his voice honey.

She tugged at his arms.

"Let's go," she said whimpering, but he didn't ease his grasp.

"Do you love me?" he asked. It sounded silly to him asking that question at thirteen, but he knew it wouldn't sound silly to her. Her body eased, melting in his grasp. She whispered yes to him—a hush. What did *they* know of love?

"Then do you trust me?"

"I hate bees."

"They're not bees. Do you trust me?" He said the two as one sentence.

She pressed her lips. Not responding.

"Do you trust me?" he asked again.

"Fine. Yes. I trust you."

"You won't be afraid anymore, okay? You'll see they can't hurt you. I'll show you. I'll be with you, and we'll bring a stop to fear together."

"What if they sting me? What if they sting *you?* You're allergic and you'll die. I can't. I can't. Let's just—let's leave. I don't want them near me."

"Com'on," he said in an easy hush, leading her by the hand. She hesitated only a moment before following him. The stillness of the barn felt sullen over her thoughts. Only the buzzing of wasps held the authority of sound.

"What are we doing?" she tried to say, but couldn't tell if he had heard her, or if she had even spoken at all. The buzzing was wavering now. Droning. Vibrating inside both their minds.

She followed Samuel and climbed the ladder to the upper loft. The wooden ladder groaned as the steps adjusted to their weight.

Once at the top, they had a better view of the thing he wanted to show her.

"What is that?"

"My grandpa Charlie made it before he died. This was years ago. I was really little, but I still remember this thing. He lived in Oklahoma. My dad said grandpa was going insane in his last days. So he made this thing. After he died, it was shipped to us. My dad didn't know what to do with it. I thought he threw it out. I didn't know he kept it here."

Jenny was mesmerized by the sculpture. It was hard to describe the shape. It was multi-layered and it twisted around itself. It was like a hive of a sort or a cocoon, but with hard lines to define its edges. It was as big as a person.

She came closer to inspect it, and saw it was made of thousands of plastic drinking straws. It was beautiful, and a shame that it was left hidden up here, only to be overgrown with cobwebs.

She moved around the sculpture to study it from another angle, and there, in its center, she saw a hive lodged inside its heart. The nest was as big as her head. Bigger. It was a spool of grey matter.

She gave a yelp, and then covered her mouth.

One of the wasps came out, and she almost stumbled backward and off the ledge of the loft. Samuel caught her. Then another came out and circled around them. She squirmed.

"Let's go," she said in a shaky whisper, her body tense. "I'm not scared anymore, okay? Let's go."

"Stop it. They'll know you're afraid."

"I hate bugs. I hate *wasps.*"

He just stared, saying nothing.

"You're allergic," she said, as if she needed to be the one reminding him. She said it as if the thought would bring him back to his senses. Because this was stupid, and only a stupid boy would make her do this. He was allergic, and he was the one who was supposed to be scared, not her.

"Don't you know you're allergic," she said again, this time accusing him of treason. Accusing him of carelessness and of youth.

He gave her a smile as if to say, *Should my allergies stop me every time? Should we find a million excuses to be afraid? Should I quit living my life now? At thirteen?*

She tried to brush off that look of his from her mind but couldn't. It was filled with so much assurance. It was a look of righteous youth. It was a look of love that unfolded beyond boy-girl relations. It was love for life—untouched by allergies.

All the same, she tugged on his drenched shirt to encourage him they should leave. More of the wasps came to see who the intruders were. Jenny clung to him tightly. She grasped his drenched shirt, wrinkling it in her fists. Within a breath of time, dozens and dozens of wasps spun and wrapped around them like little buzzing strings. Jenny whimpered. Samuel's eyes widened, his lips barely touching. It was like breathing inside a vortex.

"Don't leave me," she said to him.

"What?"

The buzzing was all he could hear. A white noise. Every passing second, more wasps circled around them. Jenny started to cry. Tears spilled from her eyes. They leaked down to her cheeks. *Don't leave me*, she kept saying. *Don't leave me.* She repeated the words like a mantra. The air around them whirled. There were so many wasps now that the vortex seemed to become a cloth of knitted threads spinning around them. One noise. White noise. A sound like waterfalls coming upon them with the crashing of waves. Their wet clothes glued them together. Samuel and Jenny. The circling wasps forced the two of them closer. Closer. Into one being.

"Make them stop!" Jenny screamed. "Make them stop, *please!*"

Her squealing voice shattered through the sheet of wasps. They scattered for a moment, and she thought of fleeing right then. They were giving her enough room to slip away. But she thought twice of it. She couldn't leave Samuel behind, alone and fragile to their stings. So she clutched tighter onto him, biting down on her lips so she wouldn't scream. She tried to absorb Samuel's wet body into hers.

"Open your eyes," he whispered, lips against her ear. Somehow the sound of his words made it through the maddening buzz of flying insects.

She opened her eyes slowly and looked into his own. They were shiny and bright. Like ponds. The wasps kept circling around their bodies, making Samuel and Jenny feel as if being swept away. Alone with the wasps. It was beautiful. She remembered the tin foil rose on her pinky. The thought of that ring made her want to protect him. She wrapped her arms around his frail, skinny body, his white, glowing skin. There was this sense of shielding him that rose in her chest. It made her body vibrate. It excited her.

"It's like floating," he said.

And it was. Not just an illusion, but a presence. It was like hanging above the stilling pond, surrounded by displacing clouds, moving with the circling winds. Spinning wasps, and floating.

"Like floating," she repeated.

Clouds in the water, she thought. And that was their youth, step in step with the illusion of hanging. Protected and untouchable. Holding on to one another as if to one self. This was theirs. For now. Hung within the revolving voices of time. It was theirs.

"Clouds in the water," they both said, and they believed it.

Lost in
the Night

The sound of his own cell phone ringing alarmed him. Somebody was having sex upstairs. There was something violent about it. Unpleasant. It was almost animal like. He couldn't remember where he was. The phone rang again, and he felt himself trying to focus. The glow of the moonlight shone through the window. He was down on the carpeted floor. The sounds from upstairs went on.

Finally, he picked up the phone, feeling as if he had taken too long to answer. "Hello?" he said. He tried to shake the confusion from his voice and asked the word again.

"Kevin?" It was a girl's voice. Familiar. Scared. Crying.

"Grace?" he finally said. The wait felt like trying to breathe under water.

She was in tears and incomprehensible from the other end, trying to talk but coming through with only bawls. The sound of her cries shook him awake. It brought his senses to alarm. It was like rising above the surface of the water and taking that first real breath in hours. Air. Upstairs the sex continued. Kevin was over Mark's apartment, he remembered now, and he'd fallen asleep on the floor.

"Grace, what's the matter, baby?"

"They…" the word came out in tumbles, as if tripping down a flight of stairs, still mixed up with her own crying. After a while, in broken-up vowels and consonants, she managed to say, "They ripped my shirt."

Kevin felt angry now. Protective.

"Who?" He demanded. "Who ripped your shirt?"

"I don't know," she seemed to be gaining some composure now, slowly.

"What do you mean you don't know?"

"I don't know, okay? Some guys. Two guys."

"Are you hurt?"

She seemed to think for a second. "I'm okay."

"Where are you? Where did this happen?"

She was in Oakland, Pitt's campus, down on Craig Street. It was just a few blocks away from his friend Mark's apartment. She managed to tell him how two guys had tried to grab her as she was walking back to her car. Kevin now wished he hadn't drunk half a bottle of Vladimir. His mind felt like it was pushing through fumes.

"Can you meet me at Mark's?" he asked, he didn't feel stable enough to move on his own.

"The car broke down."

"What? Why?" He realized the tone of blame in his voice and tried again, "What happened?"

"I don't know. I didn't *do* anything." She was on the verge of tears again. He could hear it in her voice.

"Shhh, it's okay. Grace. Everything's okay. I'm right here."

Kevin was looking around for his shoes. He tried to think of everything he had brought when coming over tonight. He always emptied his pockets and took off his dog tags before going to sleep because their jingling bothered him. Now he was fumbling through the darkness to find everything. Wallet. Keys. Cell phone. Where was his cell phone? Where'd the hell he put it? His hand. He was talking on it. *Damnit Kevin, wake up!*

"Can't you come here?" Grace said, pleading... Scared. "I'm in my car."

"Just meet me at Mark's. I'm calling the police."

"No. Don't."

"Why *not?*" Again, his voice.

It was hard to concentrate, especially with the noise going on above him.

"Please. Just don't. I'll meet you there, okay?" Her voice was childlike, that of a little girl who was afraid of making her father angry.

"All right. I'll wait for you outside."

As he hung up, the rush and pain of guilt knocked against his chest. He shouldn't let her walk at night after what just happened to her. She'd been attacked, she said. He didn't know anything else, and now he was afraid that something worse might happen to her while walking across Pitt's campus. He ran down the stairs of the apartment building. The outside air touched his face with a night breeze. Summer air. This helped him to think a little. The moon wasn't out after all. He realized he'd been fooled. What he thought had been moon-glow shining through the window was just a pile of city lights.

In the distance he could see the Cathedral of Learning poking into the sky from above the surrounding buildings. It glowed in a hazy, orange light, jutted against the blackness. From high above somewhere he could hear drunken speech. College kids partying on rooftops. The sound of a glass bottle shattering and people yelling. The smell of liquor rose like blooming petals and thorns. His own smell.

The apartment buildings stood skewed around him. The street was lined with them. Abandoned couches and mattresses and trash bags half-ripped open dotted the street. Things that could easily be set on fire. Drunken shouting and noises scattered through the street. His veins felt warm with blood, but he found it hard to breathe and slow his pulse.

The minutes passed. He crossed his arms in his chest, even though it wasn't cold outside. Where was she? Why was she taking so long to get here? He tried to calm his rambling. *She was attacked,* he told himself. The phrase softened him.

My baby. My Grace. How could somebody try to hurt her?

That made him angry again, this time at whoever could do such a thing. He felt a vigilante kind of violence in himself. He wished he had a gun or a bat right now.

Something. Anything that could inflict a lot of pain. Insurmountable pain. Immense amounts of pain. Disastrous pain. In his head, Kevin tried to grab hold of the biggest words he could think of. The bigger the word, the more pain it would mean for whoever had hurt Grace. To him, the bigger the word, the better he was able to think.

He pictured himself bashing the head of two faceless strangers. Blank faces.

Anybody's faces. As soon as Grace got there, they would go hunting the streets together, he thought. They would inflict punishment. They would return their hate with interest.

His hand was flipping his phone open and shut. Flipped open with a flick of his wrist, and closed again like a switchblade. The minutes passed like a dull blade carving into wood. Kevin checked the time to see how much had passed, but then realized he had no clue when Grace had first called him.

An hour ago? he asked himself. To him, that sounded reasonable. Too long ago.He flipped the phone open again and dialed 911. It was all a reflex.Before the operator could finish her sentence, Kevin blurted out, "My girlfriend's been attacked."

"Please remain calm, sir. Is your girlfriend all right?"

"*No,*" he shouted, "I mean, I don't know. She's on her way over here. She's walking in Oakland. I don't want anything bad happening to her. She told me two guys tried to grab her. I don't know anything else, but if I find out who they are…"

The words boiled on his lips. He forced himself not to finish the sentence. He let the words hang. It was clear what he would do.

"Okay, I'll dispatch someone to come right over. Please remain calm."

"I'm calm."

"Can you tell me where you are?"Kevin thought hard before remembering the street name. He looked to the face of the building and gave her the apartment number as well. He heard himself speak the words as if he were repeating somebody else's voice telling him what to say.

"We'll send somebody out—"

"Just hurry," Kevin said, and shut the phone. He'd been pacing the whole time and just now realized it. He was aware of his actions only after the matter. Two or three steps removed from himself. Reacting instead of acting. He didn't like this.

He waited.

Voices argued in the distance. Shouts peaked and dove in volumes. Laughter. Whooping and taunting. Somebody was picking a fight.

None of it made the time go faster.

He sat there on the steps, hunched over his own body. Flipping open and shut his phone because he could do nothing else. *Helpless.* He repeated the word in his head. *Helpless.* Who? Who was helpless? Was it Grace or himself? It didn't matter.

Helpless.

Then, her figure appeared from the far end of the street. She walked the stretch of the sidewalk holding herself—arms wrapped around her own body. She didn't run to him. Kevin stood and watched her walk slowly to him. With one hand he gripped onto the steps' railing. His other hand held a fist. Grace walked all the way up to him, never taking a quick step until reaching him, when she flopped against his chest, hugging him and crying. A moment passed before Kevin returned the hug.

"Hug me," she said.

"I am."

"Hold me."

His arms closed tighter on her shivering body.

"Let's go inside. Let's get you out of the cold," he said. The words felt right even though it wasn't cold out.

Inside the building, they walked through the tight hallway. The walls squeezed over their silence. He led the way through the corridors because they were too narrow for them to walk side by side.

Upstairs, inside his friend's apartment, Kevin held Grace's hands in his own. The one side of her wavy hair was twisted and knotted, as if tugged by a fist. Mascara ran down to her chin like black scratches. Her jaw quivered and her eyes were brilliant with tears. Her baby-T with Grumpy the Dwarf on the front was ripped from the collar down to her chest. She wore a second shirt underneath, which calmed Kevin's rage a little. To have seen her exposed would have made him snap.

"You're shaking."

She nodded in awkward head bobs, pressing her lips tightly.

"Who did this to you?"

Her lips pressed tighter still, her eyes looking into his. She didn't know. He lifted the flap of her ripped shirt to her neck, as if trying to patch it up, but when he let go with his hand it just flopped loose again.

"Did you see their faces?"

"I don't know."

"Well *did* you, or didn't you?"

"I don't know, okay?"

"Fine, can you tell me what happened at least?"

She composed herself. Breathing. She told him, slowly, how she had dropped off her brother with some friends in a parking lot downtown. She ended up in Oakland because of the construction. Her car broke down, leaving her stranded. When she walked to the nearest gas station looking for help, there was no one there.

"Then two guys were asking me for directions, and before—"

"What were you doing driving your brother downtown? He's got his own car."

"He asked me as a favor. He's my brother." She could hear the defensive tone in her voice.

"What the hell did he have to do downtown?"

"He was meeting some friends. Said they were going out."

"Oh, Tubby's got friends now."

"Listen this isn't about Simon," she said, keeping an even yet defiant tone. She didn't like it when he made fun of his brother's weight. "It's about me, okay? Simon's got nothing to do with what happened."

"Then what *did* happen?"

She hesitated. She took a few steps back and leaned against the wall. The room sounded hollow for a while. Kevin took a step closer to her, but she crossed her arms, holding herself, and brought her face low, resting her chin on her shoulder. For a short sober moment, Kevin saw how beautiful she was. Even in her hurt. Maybe because of her hurt. He traced the lines of her face with his eyes.

"I was trying to tell you…" she said. Her voice was soft now.

"Go on. Tell me."

"Two guys. I didn't see their faces. They asked me how to get to Bouquet Street, and before I could tell them, one of them grabbed me."

"How'd you get away?"

"I pushed him off me. He got angry. The other one was just sorta' standing there. He didn't seem to know what was going on, but I slammed the door into his knee. I locked myself in, and the one guy kept shouting, 'You're no fun. You're no fun' and I just—" she began sobbing again.

Kevin tried to hush her into his arms. He hushed like a soft, calming wind into her ear, telling her it was okay, she was okay.

The grunting from upstairs resumed.

"What is that?"

Kevin gave her a look as if to say, *Take a guess.* They both fell quiet for a long moment.

Grace looked ill.

"I want to kill them," he said, only half aware he'd spoken.

"It's okay. They're gone."

"I'll be okay once I kill them."

"Don't talk like that, Kevin."

He fantasized the idea for a moment. Running the streets with his girlfriend in search of the two guys who hurt her. Like a vigilante mission. They would search the streets.

They would find the guilty together. The idea felt almost exotic in his head. But he dropped the thought. It was fantasy.

"You have to talk to the police, babe."

"No I can't. I can't."

"Yes."

"Kevin, I just can't do it."

"What if they attack someone else tonight? Some other girl?"

"I know, I just…" her voice sounded breathless.

"Babe. Yes. You're going to talk to the police."

"You don't understand," she said, pleading with him. "You don't know how—"

"Quit being so damn selfish, for a moment. If we don't do anything, think of who else they might hurt. Some other innocent girl."

The anger returned in his voice. He thought he had handled it so well. He thought he had managed it into a tight ball, keeping it enclosed and away from his words. But it had exploded back in his throat, tainting every word he shouted at Grace. The grunting upstairs sounded ravenous. His voice matched their tone.

"What about *me?*" Grace asked, half angry, half crying, all tears. "*I'm* the innocent girl. They attacked *me*."

"I know, honey. That's why you need to talk to the police." Calm again. He wondered how it was possible for his mood to switch so quickly, from composed to shouting, from yelling to hushing, all of it in leaps and sputters of emotions with little transition in between.

"No. You *don't* know. You have no idea what it feels like to be judged by their eyes when *you're* the victim. Okay? I won't talk to them."

"Has it..." Kevin caught himself. *Has this happened before?* he wanted to ask. But he didn't want an answer. He dreaded the thought—the possibility—that this may have happened to Grace before. The idea of her body violated in the past without him being there to protect her. In his mind, he tried not to picture a huddle of cops blaming her for someone else's lust.

She stood there, staring in his eyes, nodding a tiny nod.

"Well, I already called them. We might as well talk to them." He fought the tears.

"You what?" she said, words falling off her lips like stones crumbling into dirt. "I asked you not to."

Kevin caught hold of her arm, gripping his fingers around her clammy flesh. The touch of her skin made him draw back, flinching his hands away from her. Her skin was cold and untouchable. She stepped backwards, away from him, stumbling over her own feet. The fear on her face—It overwhelmed everything else.

Kevin made a move towards her, slowly, hoping to appear trustworthy. But instead of stepping closer to him, Grace rushed out of the apartment and stormed down the hallway steps. He ran after her, shouting for her to stop, calling for her name, feet pounding down on the stairway steps. The hallway walls shrunk around him, his brain felt woozy and full of blood—lightheaded and drunk once more.

He finally caught her as they both burst through the building's front door, grabbing her with one arm, and clutching onto the railing to snag himself in place. She tried to push him off, but he held her there, feeling all right and sorry for the both of them. Grace tried to fight him, but he wrapped her tighter, apologizing and crying alongside her. Apologizing, mostly, for the disgusting nature of the men around him. Apologizing for—

Red and blue lights flashed like flames burning up oxygen in the air. Grace pushed him off as a last effort to get away. He let go of her, half-numb, and she tripped over her feet, tumbling and screaming down the short stretch of steps, hitting the concrete walkway below. Kevin ran down to her, but stopped midway the stretch of steps at the shouting of police telling him not to move.

A police officer stood by his driver's side door. His bald head reflected the dim street lights.

"Stay where you are. Don't you move!"

A second officer, from the passenger seat, called something into his radio.

"We have a possible two-forty here. A ten-sixty-six just pushed a young female down their apartment steps." A crackle of radio. Someone answered back, streamlining words back at the officer.

"I didn't do anything," Kevin was saying, holding his palms open, fixed in the air. "I didn't do anything."

He said it over and over, unable to stop himself from repeating the phrase. Grace was crying, curled and bruised on the ground. Kevin's eyes jumped back and forth from her to the bald officer, who came closer to him. Kevin breathed in quivers, and before he could finish his next breath, the officer was upon him, slamming him back against the door.

"I didn't do anything. I didn't push her. She fell, I swear." The cop twisted Kevin's body, pushed his chest against the door, and grabbed hold of his hair.

"Stay still," the officer said. He pulled and slammed Kevin's head against the hard wood. "That'll teach you to hurt girls."

"Grace, please tell them! Tell them I wasn't the one who hurt you. Tell them I didn't do anything."

She kept on crying, sitting up now, planting her face into her own hands. The other officer approached her, trying to soothe and calm her tears.

"You don't understand," Kevin tried to object, but the bald officer pulled Kevin's hands behind his back and handcuffed them.

"We'll get this sorted out," the officer told him. "You better pray that girl's not hurt bad."

Kevin kept shouting and roaring and screaming for Grace to fix everything. To set the details straight. He tried to yank himself from the officer's grasp but couldn't. The rage mounted inside him like a flame catching fire to straw drenched in liquor, setting aflame the connecting nerve-endings in his temples. He screamed and screamed, feeling cheated and blamed, ashamed and righteous, vengeful and violent. The officer forced him into the back of the police car, but that didn't stop him from screaming. He hit the window with his shoulder. He hit the glass for being accused. He hit the glass for feeling cheated. He hit it for want of vengeance. Tears streamed from his eyes, begging to be recognized for his innocence. Spit flew from his lips as he screamed, speckling the glass.

He hit the window for that, too.

The officers ignored him.

For a while longer, he kept hitting the door. If not with his shoulders, then with his feet and knees. It wasn't until Kevin lost his voice from screaming that Grace found the courage to talk. It would be another hour before they sorted through the details. By then, Kevin no longer had any urge to talk. He had stopped hitting the window a while ago. His body had drained itself. The bald-headed officer opened the cruiser's door, letting Kevin out, making no eye contact.

"Turn," the officer told him.

Kevin did, and the man un-cuffed his wrists, which were sliced with pain.

"Go on upstairs," the officer said. "We'll give Ms. Shuster a ride home."

Kevin searched inside himself for some emotion. He glanced at his feet. He glared at the moonless sky. He didn't care if another girl got hurt tonight. Grace brushed past him and lowered herself into the cruiser's back seat.

"Kevin," she said, eyes watery, fixed on him.

He said nothing. He didn't turn towards her.

"Kevin."

He listened for drunken hooting in the distance. He listened for the grunts of sex coming from his friend's apartment. He heard nothing, yet felt sick imagining those sounds anyway. Something had been lost, and he tried to imagine what. He tried to imagine the loss as if it had a face to fill.

"Kevin?"

"We'll find it in the morning," was all he could say, his throat sour and bundled tight. He walked back into the stone-faced building, trying to picture what it was they'd lost. He tried to imagine where they might look to find it.

Midnight

How did this happen? One moment you think you're in control, with your old man's Beretta in hand, telling everyone inside the Circle K to get down on the ground—and they do, of course they do—and the next moment... Damn. The next moment's gone. It's all blanked out, and now I'm outside pointing the same Beretta to Black Man's head over here, with beams of white light bleaching into my face, and the cops shouting that everything's going to be okay.

Right.

Everything's going to be hunky-dory.

Who in the hell ever invented the happy ending?

The Black Man I have the gun pointed to, he's not really black. In fact, his skin is as pale as worn wooden shingles, bleached white by the sun. And now, with these lights beaming unto us, his skin— it glows. It's like little, shiny particles are dancing all around him.

Or like droplets of fine mist bouncing off his body and reflecting the light in all directions. I call him the Black Man because of his clothes. Because of his hair.

Man, you'd never think that hair could be so dark. So thick. He keeps his neck tilted because the barrel presses against his big mulch of black hair, and it's like the gun could be lost in it. I'm afraid of pressing the gun any further, not because the metal might dig into his skull, but because his hair could swallow the gun and my whole hand with it.

The man wears a black tux, matched with a silk tie and deep black, oxford shoes. His shirt is the only thing whiter than his skin. When I first entered the gas station, I asked myself what a man like this could be doing here, on the side of the highway in the middle of the night. Was he running from his own wedding? From his own funeral?

He had opened the cooler doors, reaching for a jug of milk, and a fresh breeze of air licked my face. I pulled my gun out then, and the shouting began. At first I didn't think Black Man would get down. He opened his jug of milk, took a long swallow, and just stared into the barrel of my Beretta. But then, slowly, he sat on the floor while everyone else seemed to be hugging it.

The clerk was an old Mexican man without any facial hair. On the ground in front of the counter, some teenage kid clutched a Red Bull in his right hand. He wore a T-shirt too tight for his chest. Some older woman cried, and as she sobbed on the ground, I could only see the back of her head, filled with silver hair. I screamed at the clerk to get back up, to open the register, while fixing my gun at his big, brown nose. The whole time, I kept looking back at Black Man, who would twist his milk open, take a long drink, and twist the cap closed tightly again. Then every time I looked at him, he would do the same again, somehow always thirsty for more.

His eyes grabbed me each time.

I couldn't see the color of his eyes from where I was standing, but his black pupils seemed big enough to swallow the night's sky. Remembering that detail makes as much sense to me as watching kids dress up for Halloween. Or as much sense as religion. How can you judge the size of a man's pupils, but can't tell the color of his eyes?

The old woman was crying, forming half-sentences about fuses for a car and not wanting to die. The kid's Red Bull rolled away, hitting the base of the sunglasses stand, and he formed himself into a ball, hands over his head, taking quick peeks at me like a series of bad twitches. This is the point where my memory stops, and somehow reforms with me outside of the store, holding Black Man with one arm around his chest and my gun sunken into his hair.

I don't even remember if I shot anyone. Or if any of the register's money made it to my pockets. I just know that I entered the store minutes before ten, and now the big, digital clock above the Shell station across the highway reads eleven-fifty-three. Two hours passed through my frame of mind like a shot in the dark. Untraceable.

And somehow, beyond and above the shouts of the cops, all I hear is one voice. Black Man says, "Chill."

He pronounces the word fully, slowly, with a sort of authority somehow pocketed inside his voice. And just then a chill *does* penetrate through my neck, because his voice is so cool. So indifferent. Then the cops' shouts continue, and my muscles regain their wooden stiffness. A prickly heat flares over my skin, and I can feel droplets of sweat covering my face.

"What's your name, pal?" Black Man asks. Except it sounds nothing like a question normally asked by a stranger. It sounds more like an inquiry posed by someone wanting to be friends.

"I'm Benjamin Franklin. What the hell do you care?"

"Come on. Give me a break, here. You could at least tell me your name."

"I don't have to tell you anything," I tell him, twisting the barrel harder into his temple. He tenses hard into my grasp as pain digs into him, and that makes me realize how real this is. It makes me realize that the man I'm holding hostage is of flesh and bone, and not just a random stranger in a black suit. This is a life I'm in control of. A life that will end if I pull the trigger. The reality of this fact tumbles inside my stomach, and I grow warm all over. The heat that was just on the surface of my skin sinks deep into me.

"My name's Adren," the man says next to my face.

"Shut up. Don't tell me your name."

But now the name is already in my head. Adren. He's flesh and bone, and has a name. Now he's not even a stranger. Once you know a man's name, he's no longer just a person out there that doesn't matter. He becomes part of your life. You could piss next to some guy in a public restroom and be okay with it, but if he tells you his name then it becomes awkward. Pissing next to each other becomes meaningful, somehow, and that's just wrong. Now me and this guy, Adren, we're pissing buddies.

"I imagine you didn't expect this to happen," Adren says. He chuckles, and his laughter is a bouncing ball rolling down a hill. Gleeful and worriless. He laughs as if I'm the one who's supposed to be surprised, here.

"Yeah, like you knew you'd have a gun to your head tonight."

"Not like you're going to shoot me," he says, coolly as always.

"Oh, you're so sure, huh?"

A man in an unbuttoned suit and a loosened tie steps forward from the blue and red flashes of police cars. He speaks into a megaphone. His voice is crackly through the thing, but I can make out most of what he says.

"Son, please remove the gun from your hostage's head. It's making everyone here real nervous." The guy talks to me as if we're old college buddies. Great. Next he'll tell me his name, too.

"Please lower your gun, son," he says again. His hair is white, and that to him makes me his son. "I'm agent McAfee. You can call me Bruce."

"Screw you!" I scream, flashing my gun up in the air. My voice is shrilly, exploding from my throat and scrambling into shards of glass. As I scream, the cops tense up. Some back away. "The next person to tell me his name, I'm going to kill him, damn it!"

"Smooth," Adren tells me. "Real smooth. Way to gain their trust there, my friend."

"I'm not his son, I'm not your *friend*, and don't tell me what to do, okay?" I say through my teeth, clenching them against his ear. I press the barrel back into his temple, and somehow more of the gun disappears into the hair than before.

"You don't want to get shot, do you?" Adren asks me, as if he were the one holding the gun, but could care less either way if a bullet landed inside my head or not.

"That's why I have you as my shield, *Adren.*"

"Much good that'll do you pretty soon. They're already setting up firing positions."

I look around. To my far left, the exit ramp coming off the highway has been blocked off. Men with flashlights stand there next to rows of orange cones and road blockades. To my right, a Taco Bell joint stands lit but deserted. Farther down, cars and people watch from a distance at the Economy Inn motel. Suddenly, a helicopter blares overhead, and I look up quickly to see that it's a news chopper.

"Where?" I ask Adren.

"Tell me your name, and I'll tell you."

"No, you tell me where the snipers are, or I'll shoot you."

"You won't shoot me." And he laughs. How the hell can you laugh at a moment like this?

"What makes you think that? Huh? Huh?" I jab him twice with the end of the gun, and his laughter stops, but I can see his profile, and his lips hold a smirk. I back away two steps towards the Circle K entrance, keeping Adren close to me. I twitch around, searching with my eyes, looking for snipers. I see none.

"You won't shoot me because you have no choice to do so. If you kill me, you're left exposed."

"Tell me where the snipers are."

"Tell me your name," he says indifferently.

"Damn man! Where are the snipers?"

I look back at the digital clock across the highway. Eleven-fifty-seven. Only four minutes passed since I last looked. Adren breathes in and out deeply. He sighs on the exhale, as if waiting patiently for something. His back relaxes against my chest.

"You don't know," I say, testing.

He says nothing.

"You don't know where they are."

Nothing still.

"There's no *snipers*," I say, but I look around still, focusing on the roof of the Economy Inn where I catch a blurred silhouette. It's too small and too far away to tell what it is. SWAT rifleman?

Chimney? Satellite dish? In any case, if I can't tell what the hell it is, then how could Adren?

Yet the sound of his voice… It's like that of a man requesting nothing but trust. But for whose benefit?

"I'm in control here, okay?" I tell Adren.

"Of course you are."

"Tell me where!" I snarl into his ear, pressing my cheek against the barrel of my own gun. My finger is a fragment of a pound of pressure away from firing off a round.

Blast, and the game is over. Either that, or just begun. Hell. I don't even know what my options are.

"Okay, fine," I say. "Daren. My name's Daren."

"Spelled with one or two 'R's?" he asks.

"What the hell is this? Am I applying for a bank loan? Just tell me where the snipers are."

"It makes a difference, you know."

"What difference does it make?" I yell this, while whipping him around from left to right and back, looking for any man with a gun and a good shot to kill me. Now Bruce, the cop, talks into his megaphone again, but I don't hear a thing he says. All of his words are mechanical blurs.

"It makes all the difference in the world," Adren says, not even phased. "Because Daren with a single 'R' means 'Born into the night.' While Darren with a double 'R' means 'He who upholds the good' or even 'Dearly loved.' My guess is that yours is the first. Am I right?"

And I can't help but laugh. It just bursts out from my lips, taking me by surprise. "And I don't seem 'dearly loved' to you?"

"Your name fits you. It fits your situation."

"*My* situation?"

"Look around you, Daren. Take it in and feel it out."

My eyes jump once again. Flashing lights. Nervous cops. Meshes of shouts. None of these are anything new. I close my eyes, and breathe in deeply. Adren's body feels calm against my chest. His coat is warm and dry, like lint out of the drier. The nerve endings to my skin flare like foot stomps. I'm shaking.

My ears twitch.

Below every other level of noise, the wind whines in a soft blow of air. Everything feels meaningless. With my eyes closed I still can't remember the part of my memory that's been blotched over by a black spot of ink.

"Tell me something, Adren," I say with a quiver in my voice.

"Anything."

"What did I do in there?"

The man shrugs in my grasp, exhaling deeply. I wait for him to inhale the breath back into his lungs, but he doesn't. I wait longer, holding my own breath, but I give in before he does. I inhale through my throat, and the noise it makes is that of a croaking old man giving in. Somehow, I feel oily inside. My veins and arteries chug crud in both directions. Finally Adren breathes in through his nostrils. He opens his mouth to answer.

"You—"

I stop him before the word fully leaves his lips. I don't want to know. I don't even want to go back inside the gas station, safer or not, for in fear of knowing.

"Nevermind," I say, feeling that blackness moving slower inside me. "Tell me this instead. What are my options?"

"Not many." He pauses. "And you won't like the one best for you."

"I'm not surrendering."

"You have 'til midnight to make a decision," Adren says, and my heart twists tightly inside my chest, like a small, suffocating creature. It's not the word, "midnight," itself that punctures me, but the idea that I'm limited by time. As if until now I believed that I had an infinite amount of time to think, to wonder, and to analyze the options around me. But that makes no sense. Soon the cops will have run out of patience, if not already. Soon Bruce, my old pal, will give the command to blast my head into cranium splinters. The clock across the street reads eleven-fifty-nine.

"Why midnight?" I ask in a panic.

"Because midnight marks a new beginning. Midnight is your limbo, Daren. You're stuck forever in it if you don't make the right choice."

Then Bruce's voice seems to come in close from far away. All I catch from what he says is, "… are you listening to me, son?"

He stares, and I stare back. Before, the cops and lights were coming from just one general direction. Now, as I look back to reality, they've formed an arch around me, guns pointing and somehow creeping closer.

"After midnight," Adren says, "It'll be a new day. You can start by becoming a new man tonight."

"Born into the night," I say mesmerized by his earlier words, only half aware of it.

Bruce talks into a radio, and a high-pitched squeal shoots from the megaphone because he's holding both items up to his mouth. He drops the megaphone and continues talking into the radio, looking toward the motel.

Bruce nods.

For the first time this night, Adren tenses in my arms. I feel like the child who clutches back for the father who isn't there.

Midnight strikes on the clock across the highway. Midnight strikes everywhere, and a standstill surrounds my frozen world.

Adren breaks through the frozen time and presses back against my chest. We fall backwards, and a whizzing sound darts through the air, inches before my face. *A bullet.* It cuts right through Adren's nose—in one side and out the other. His face bursts open with blood. The sound of his nose cartilage crackling resembles that of wet leaves ripping. A sound of childhood memories.

The bullet hits the ground, and a chunk of concrete pops upward. Adren just saved my life. We fall to the ground, me on my right shoulder, and him on top of me. My grip loosens from around his torso, and my gun tumbles out of my hand, flipping cartwheels towards one of the cops. The officer panics, tensing his arms and shaking from his knees up. My gun stops short and lands with the barrel pointing back into my eyes.

Every weapon within a mile radius is aimed at my head.

Adren crawls over to me, pushes up with one hand, and crouches before me. He wears an odd smile, and half of his face is covered in blood. He turns to the police, arms spread, covering me from the light. Covering me from death.

He tilts his head to the side and says to me, "Do you want to be born again today, or die tonight?" His voice is a fog, distorted by gashes of nasal sounds. He looks deeply into me, and this time his eyes are visible. His pupils have shrunk, each of them swallowed by a blue halo of energy. Blue. His eyes are blue. And even though every light is shining from behind him and his face should be a silhouette, the color of his eyes is as visible as a breath of air is vital. And it makes no sense.

"Live," I quiver. My voice is a harsh whisper. "Live. *Live!*"

Back at the cops, Adren tells them not to shoot. Bruce screams something into his radio. My skin trembles, and my every nerve twitches. Then the officers are on me, shouting at me not to move, and fisting their big hands against my body. One of them strikes me in the face. He shouts, "Why are you moving? I told you not to move!"

"I'm not!" I say.

Someone else's elbow cracks me in the back of my neck. They drag me away reading my rights, my hands cuffed behind me. Paramedics surround Adren and lead him to an ambulance. I want to shout his name, but he disappears into the crowd, and I'm pushed inside a police car.

On the clock across the highway, the time is still midnight. Still midnight. Still midnight. Movement catches my eye, and I look away to the gas station's entrance. A spray of blood streaks the glass of the Circle K window.

Oh my God, I killed them. Oh my dear God, I'm sorry. I'm so sorry—

But then three cops walk out from the store, each of them escorting someone beside them. The woman with silver hair coats her face with her hands, shaking and sobbing. The tight-shirted kid walks out with a blank stare. Every few steps, he twitches. The clerk holds his shoulder with one hand. Blood seeps through his fingers. He walks with heavy steps, his weight supported by the cop beside him.

The knots dissolve from around my heart.

My world moves on another minute.

Consumed

I opened my eyes to the sound of my phone ringing. A thin arm held onto my body, fingers pressing on my naked skin. Resting over my chest. Smooth. Lisa's. The ringing went on like a child's finger jabbing at my temples. I didn't want to know what time it was.

Lisa's cheek rested on my shoulder. Through her long blond hair, her lips pursed out and her one cheek was smooshed in. Her hair came over my neck and I brushed it aside. I shifted aside in bed, piles of blankets moving with me, and her hand fell to my stomach, pressing firmly to keep me close. I pushed her off and reached for the phone on the nightstand.

"Yeah?" I answered. My alarm read seven-twenty-five a.m. and I realized it was Sunday morning.

"Is that how you always answer your phone, Sergeant?" The voice was cheerful and somehow familiar.

"Who is this?"

"It's Sergeant Crawford. How are your Class As?"

I groaned.

"My uniform's fine," I said, and I knew already what this was about. Over the phone he told me he needed a volunteer for a military funeral. I owed him one, he said, for skipping drill last month. The whole time he talked, I scratched at my chin covered with stubble, and I thought of the dumb coincidence of it all. My dad died a year ago today, and Lisa and I were going to go see him at the cemetery. Now I was stuck going to see some other dead man. I decided not to tell Crawford about my father—it was easier not to explain the details sometimes. I just kept listening and scratching. The chapel, he said, was forty minutes north of Jackson. It wasn't even far enough to get reimbursed for gas.

Lisa sat up on the bed, stretching her back and rotating her shoulders. "Was that work?" she asked as I hang up.

"No. Army."

Her eyes sagged. Her face was smeared with makeup she had forgotten to wash off before coming to bed the night before. Her blotchy lipstick made her lips look swollen. She wore the same Paul Simon T-shirt and silk panties she had on at the bar with my mother. Thirty-year difference and they thought it was okay to go out to the bar together.

I asked her why as my girlfriend she felt a need to have margaritas with my mother.

"They're friends," she'd said. They liked to talk greens. Flowers and gardening she meant. Lisa was a flower shop girl. I told her the only greens my mother ever cared about were the kind with dead presidents on the front.

"I have to get ready," I told her. She held the makeup-smeared pillow in her lap.

"I thought we were gong to go visit your dad for his anniversary," she said.

"Don't call it an anniversary. You make it sound like we're celebrating."

"Sorry," she said. "Are we still going, though?"

"Later. I have to do this funeral first."

"Who died?"

"It's military. I didn't get the details."

"Did he have family?"

I turned away because I couldn't stand the look on her face. That look of sad mourning over someone neither of us even knew. And as I looked away, her questions stopped. It worked that way. When I broke eye contact she knew to stop. Like when I first got promoted to specialist a few years ago, and she wanted to know what I was becoming a specialist of. "You don't understand," I had told her. "It's a rank." But she had kept asking until, finally, I looked away. Only then she had quit. That was my unspoken cue.

"I'll help you get dressed," she said now in her little voice, proud of herself for being a good little helper. I pulled the bottom drawer to my dresser and found my black socks. Last pair. They were rolled up next to my three white undershirts that I never used. Behind me, I heard Lisa at my closet, sliding jackets and shirts, hooks scraping against the metal bar. *She better not screw up the order of my uniforms.*

"Will you not slide those hooks so loudly?" I told her.

She slid the hangers more quietly, until she found what she was looking for.

"Here," she said. She had my camouflaged uniform in her hands.

"Not that one," I told her. "I need my Class A uniform."

She gave me the blank look of a deer.

"The fancy one with all the medals pinned to the pockets," I said. She put the camo back and grabbed the right one. I thanked her and placed a kiss on her forehead. She smiled out of the corner of her lips.

"I'll call you later so we can go see Dad."

I stepped out the door, leaving her behind.

I arrived at the Good Shepherd Chapel and parked far enough to leave room for the family once they got there. The sky hung overhead, consumed by the vast blur of clouds stretched beyond the hills. The chapel's walkway was lined with dried flowers in pots blown over by the wind. A cold breeze fluttered my black overcoat, and my jaw stiffened as I waited for it to pass. Brown, poplar leaves scattered across the ground, grazing low and smacking against the trunks of trees and against the side of the gray chapel.

The entrance door opened, and a man in army greens stepped out. There was a white scuff on the tip of his black oxford shoes. *He ought to buff that out.* Then my eyes jumped up, and I caught the gold bar on the front of his beret.

Great. A butter bar.

"Morning Sir," I said, holding up a salute. He gave me an awkward laugh and waved a quick salute back at me.

"You don't have to do that," he said, holding out a white-gloved hand for me to shake. His mustache was too wide, reaching over the corner of his lips and touching his pudgy cheeks. *Army regulations*, I wanted to tell him, but then again he was the officer here.

"I'm Sergeant McKinley," I told him. "I'll be your flag folder."

"Glad you could make it. I'm Lieutenant Tamary. Call me Dave."

A moment of silence hung between us, and he gestured for us to go inside.

The chapel's interior was small. Tiny, almost. The center isle led to a floor opening in the front, just wide enough for the casket and some walking room. Three short benches stretched from each side of the isle.

To the right of the podium the Tennessee state flag draped from a pole display next to the American flag. On the back wall, a mural depicted a shepherd leading a flock of sheep up the peak of a steep hill, cutting off into a cliff at the far end. Leading them into suicide, I thought.

"I have an extra pair of gloves for you," Lieutenant Tamary said, handing them to me. They felt tight over my fingers. He told me the casket and family wouldn't arrive for another hour, giving us some time to practice. He took an already folded flag, and unzipped it out of its display carrying holster.

"I don't need practice folding, sir," I said, "I'm pretty good with that."

"You've done this before?"

"Folding or funeral, sir?"

"Either one," he said. He leaned against one of the benches, crossing his arms and feet in front of him, holding the triangular flag in one hand.

"Flag folding, I've done plenty of, sir. Funerals on the other hand—this is my first one."

"First ever, or just military?"

My dad came to mind again. Him in his death bed—his skin

pale from the tuberculosis eating him from the inside-out. His own wife wouldn't even be near him.

When she found out, I remember her voice, screaming at him. Screaming as if she wanted to shatter glass. "This is what we *get?* You spend time with those beggars, and *this* is what we get?"

She meant the soup kitchen. He didn't have an answer for that. Her life was defined by her Mercedes Benz and her tidy, little garden. In the end, she confined him to the guesthouse and hired a nurse to take care of him.

"Sergeant?" the lieutenant asked. My eyes snapped back up at his face. His brow twitched, waiting for some answer.

"Shouldn't we get started?" I said.

"You're all business, I see."

"Yes, sir."

"You got a girl?"

"Yes, sir. I do."

"I bet it drives her nuts."

"She's learned to deal with it," I told him, and I guess I must have had that dickhead look on my face I sometimes get because his smile turned flat, and he turned away. He talked me through our positions for once the funeral began. We started out in front of the small chapel where the hearse would pull up, and then he explained where we'd post back inside.

"When the priest is ready for us to go to the casket," Tamary said, talking to me from across the room and gesturing, "he will wave us over. If you can't see him from where you're standing, look to me and I'll nod. You take the foot of the casket. Taps plays, we salute, Taps finishes, we drop our salutes, I'll nod and we bend at the waist, taking the corners of the flag. We'll take a step back as we stand. We'll then "blossom" the flag, take two steps to your left.

And then you get to show off your folding skills."

Just then four men walked in, three of them holding rifles. All four were old, white haired from age and pink faces from the cold. They all wore military jackets and navy blue pants with creases in the front. They came over to us, shaking hands and making greetings. The man without a rifle introduced himself and his riflemen. They were all retired from the service years ago, and now this was their way of keeping busy.

"Once Taps starts to play," the old man said after all the introductions, "my men will fire three volleys. Afterwards, sergeant, when you're folding the flag, I'd like you to pause as you reach the blue so that I can tuck these in." He held three polished rifle cartridges in his hand and looked to me to see if I understood.

"Peaches," I told him, and he smiled.

We killed the minutes talking about funerals and the things that could go wrong. One of the old men said, "It's always embarrassing when the flag goes to the wrong person." They all grunted with some laughter at this.

Another one, the tallest of the four with a mustache that touches his chin, said, "Or when the rifles jam up. That one sucks."

They kept talking, but all I could do was think of my father. I wished I was at his grave right then.

I remembered the spittle of blood on his chin. I remembered the rasps of breath that sounded like they were leaking through his lungs. I remembered his eyes, losing more clarity every day. The disease kept digging at his lungs, already damaged from years of smoking cigarettes. "I hope this isn't the way you'll remember your father," he had told me. He made me promise I wouldn't remember him this way. He drowned in his own blood. After seeing him like that, I couldn't bring myself to go to his funeral.

When the hearse finally arrived, the lieutenant and I stood at the top of the pathway with the chapel behind us. A long stream of cars followed behind the hearse, little orange flags fluttering from every window. The hearse passed us, slowed down and then stopped. Men and women stepped out of their cars, some holding their kids by the hand. Others, holding themselves in the cold—all of their faces mourning. I wondered what really passed through their minds.

The lieutenant and I saluted as eight men pulled out the casket draped with the American flag. We held our salutes until they passed between us, and we waited until all the guests were inside before turning around to face the door.

Inside, the chapel was packed with people, most of them standing because of the lack of seats. Lieutenant Tamary excused himself in whispers as he moved through the crowd. We stood looking at each other from across the room. He couldn't keep himself still. *What are you doing, man? What are you so nervous for?*

A tall, bearded man stood up to the podium and started talking.

"At every funeral I've been to," he said, "there was never a person who could stand up here and succeed in saying words that could console me. When a man dies, no words can make you feel good inside, so I don't expect my words to do it for you. Though, I'll try." The man went on. The man in the casket could have been his son or a brother. He didn't say. His words sounded like they'd been recycled from a hundred previous speeches. He could have used it for the family pet if he wanted.

Finally, Lieutenant Tamary nodded to me, and we walked slowly to the coffin. He took the head of the casket by flag's field, and I posted at the feet. We faced one another. The lead rifleman read The Soldier's Creed from the podium. Tamary and I just stared at one another.

"Taps" started to play from outside. One of the three riflemen used an electronic bugle to play the slow-moving, tune that fell around us. The song of the dead. Lieutenant Tamary and I raised our hands slowly, saluting the song and the man in the coffin. Sniffles grew from the room, some quickly turning to cries and sobs. My eyes fixed on Tamary's. *Don't do it. Don't start crying on me, too.* His eyes wavered.

Then a child started screaming. His wails filled the chapel, and slowly a throb grew in my neck from nowhere. The first gunshot fired outside, and I flinched. *Damn. I flinched.* The boy's cries grew louder.

The throbbing in my throat took up a pulse, beating, beating, beating… My collar became tight. Tighter. My necktie strangled me. I breathed through my nose, but it was not enough. I wanted to swallow the pulse back down to my stomach, but I couldn't gulp, I couldn't move. I had to stand still. The pulse grew faster with each of the child's cries. It felt like a fist pumping into my throat.

The Lieutenant's eyes became glassy. His lower lip began twitching, and he struggled with himself to keep still. A second gunshot burst, suffocating even the small boy's cries. And I flinched again. *I did. I know I did. Damn it, I can't even keep still.*

Tamary gulped.

With the third gunshot I sensed the crowd stirring. They

moved into my periphery, and then I could make out a shape running toward us. It was the boy. He made it to the casket, crying, pressing his tiny palms against the coffin.

"Daddy!" he screamed. His hands gripped the flag, and he started to pull on it. Then, a woman wrapped her long arms around him. She was graceful, swooping him up, but the boy screamed only louder. I still hadn't dropped my salute, and the lieutenant didn't know how to react.

Keep still, I mouthed to him. *Don't do anything*. But he didn't even look at me. The boy clutched the flag in his hands. His mother told him to let go, trying to quiet him with a hand caressing his cheek, but he wouldn't, and as she pulled him away, the flag slipped from the casket.

It can't touch the ground.

I swatted my left hand on the flag to stop it from slipping, keeping my right hand as a salute, eyes fixed forward. The boy let go of his grip, and his mother took him away. From the crowd, every face, every pair of eyes was crying. Tears slipped from my own eyes. Their saltiness stung the corners of my lips. By now, "Taps" has stopped playing, who knows for how long, and I'd been holding my salute for nothing.

Tamary gripped his end of the flag. *Let's just do this*. He wiped his face on his coat sleeve, and I saw the tears blotching up the fabric. We performed the first two folds over the coffin, lengthwise, and then we took two steps to the side, leaving just a long rectangular strip in our hands, running from my hands to his. Most of the crowd was still crying, and a pulse surrounded my whole neck.

I folded. And with each fold, the room turned blank around me. The crowd vanished. Deafness coated my ears. This flag and my hands were all that existed. I folded and I stepped forward. Folded and stepped. I counted the folds, reached nine, and froze when the ninth fold reached the blue of the flag.

Panic.

What am I doing?

I couldn't remember what I was supposed to do next.

But the lead rifleman stepped forward, and I remembered. He stood beside me with three rounds in his hand.

"These—" his voice cracked. Silence rung. My ears popped. "These three rounds represent duty, honor and country. Captain Richard Banner sacrificed all in defense of this flag." He tucked the three golden shells into the fold of the flag, and nodded to me to finish off the last four folds. Lieutenant Tamary tucked in the remaining flap, and then paused to inspect the fold before receiving it. He looked to me, pressed his lips, and I handed the flag over.

I held a three-second salute, and Tamary nodded. I stepped away and marched to the door where the mother held the boy who had cried at the coffin. Tamary's practice flag was on the floor by her feet. Her face wept, cheek pressed against her son's head of hair. The boy looked at me with silent eyes. Silent blue eyes. The sky outside has never looked that blue in anyone's lifetime, and somehow that made his stare even worse. They carved canyons into me with their stare.

Looking at him now made me wish I had gone to my father's funeral. The courage to touch his coffin rested nowhere inside me. My mother wouldn't even touch his bed, yet she expected me to come touch a coffin. I couldn't bring myself to see my own father inside a casket. I pictured my father in his last days. When he coughed, droplets of blood would settle on his chin.

Deep red against his white skin.

"Smile," I told the boy, almost begging, and the word sounded so stupid coming out from my lips. His stare went on. I forced a smile myself, and he returned a shy one of his own.

"What's your name?" I asked the boy.

"Adren," he whispered to me.

I probably shouldn't have been doing this. Not while the ceremony was still going on.

Oh screw it.

"Hi Adren. I'm Alex." I placed my hand on the boy's shoulder, and right then wondered if that was the correct thing to do. "I want to give you something. Will you take it?"

He nodded, slowly. Lieutenant Tamary posted across from me, which meant he'd presented the flag to the bearded man already. I held up a finger to him—*just one second*. I crouched to pick up the flag by the woman's feet and unzipped it from its plastic casing. I glanced at Tamary to see if that was okay with him. He nudged his head at me, smiling, as if to say, *Go on.*

I didn't know the words I was supposed to use when presenting a flag, so I improvised. The boy's mother smiled while I presented it, but my eyes fixed on the boy's face alone.

"The Army wants you to have this, Adren. On behalf of our country, I want to present it to you. These colors all mean something. The red is for the sacrifices your father's made. The white is for the pain that will wash away. The blue is—it's for your very eyes, as big as the sky itself. This flag was meant for you."

Adren took the flag in his arms, hugging it tightly, and pressed his cheek to the cloth the same way his mother pressed hers to his black hair. I wonder what kind of mind roamed beneath that thick mulch of black hair—what thoughts and wishes he might hope for. The vast mind of a small boy. Just a boy.

Once the family members left, Tamary and I stood outside to enjoy the calm breeze. He sparked a cigarette and offered me one.

"No thanks, sir."

"Good job today. That was a great fold, Alex."

"Thanks, Dave—" I tried to catch myself at the last moment, but the word felt all right once out. I let it go. I looked at my white gloves. They'd turned pink at the edges from gripping the red stripes of the flag.

I looked down into the valley of my Dad's cemetery from up on a hill. Down below, Lisa sat by his grave with something in her lap. It might have been flowers, though it was hard to tell the color from this distance. She rocked from side to side, maybe humming or perhaps praying, but the air was thick and I couldn't hear a thing from that far away.

The trees around the cemetery stood still and the poplar leaves stopped blowing in the wind. The clouds became denser, but they'd grown white instead of grey. I thought of the child at the funeral, and a boyish energy grew in me. I ran. The hill was steep and my steps lunged forward. I felt my momentum growing, and soon I was running so fast that my tie whipped out of my coat and fluttered around my neck. Every other stride my oxford shoes slipped across the moist grass, but I kept my balance. The whole time I ran, I kept Lisa in my line of sight, but her blurry image jumped around like a shadow. When I finally reached her, she stood up, startled.

"You scared me," she said.

I didn't say anything. I was too winded and breathing too hard to talk. My hands were on my knees, and then I coughed into one of my gloves. One cough turned into a coughing fit, and then it was minutes before I could stop. When I looked at my hands, I saw blood and I panicked. My father's blood, coughed up by broken lungs.

Then my vision refocused, and I realized the glove was still only pink from the flag stains. I smiled, feeling silly.

"What?" Lisa said in her tiny voice, half smiling to match my own.

"Nothing."

"No what is it?"

"No, it's just—it's nothing. Really."

A sudden rustle of leaves drew my attention, and I turned to look. When I turned to Lisa again, her face was downcast and timid. The cue.

"There's nothing wrong, Honey. Nothing."

"Okay," she said.

"I didn't mean to look away."

"All right." She shrugged her shoulders but didn't look at me.

"Are those for my dad?" I asked, touching the bouquet of blue irises in her hands. They reminded me of the boy's blue eyes again. *The boy.* I want to tell her about the boy. Another cool rush of air passed, and I shivered as it went through me.

"Are you okay?" she asked. Her eyes were narrow.

"Peachy." I smiled.

"You don't have to be sarcastic."

"I'm *not*," I said, my tone sharper than I intended. She drew a step away. I tried to think of something to say to fix the awkwardness of the moment.

"How's my mother? Did she come by to visit him?"

She didn't say a word. Instead she looked at my shoes. I looked down and saw them splattered with mud. *I don't care.* I wrapped one arm around Lisa's torso and tried to hold her to me. Her body stiffened.

"Can I tell you about the boy?" I said.

"What boy?"

And I tried to tell her. I tried to tell her about the boy, standing there by my father's grave. But in my every effort, the right words wouldn't come. I couldn't describe his eyes despite how fiercely blue they were. I couldn't describe his cries even though they had cut into my emotions as they rose through the church. I couldn't describe his innocence. Even his name escaped me as I tried to think of his blue halo eyes and impossibly black hair.

"Maybe, tomorrow," I said after finally giving up because I knew all the words I told her weren't right. "Ask me tomorrow."

"Okay."

"Promise me you'll ask me tomorrow about the boy."

"All right," and I saw the worry in her eyes.

"*Promise* me," I said, maybe too forcefully.

"I promise," she said.

But she never did ask. So I never told her. And in all of my days, the sky never looked as blue as the eyes of that child.

Duct Tape People

The trouble was that there were three of them, and they weren't going to go away.

Jack Carlos let them in, knowing that if he hadn't they would have come inside one way or another. The third man closed the door behind him and then stood next to the other two, aligning shoulder to shoulder, and to shoulder again.

Blake, the fox terrier, barked at the three men.

"Hush, Blake," Jack said, and his voice croaked.

Jack cleared his throat, confusing the tears on his cheeks for droplets of sweat.

"Just a moment," he told the men, who stood there silently.

He let the dog outside, and then took a seat on his hand-carved, wooden chair.

He looked up at them from the antique chair, which looked more like a wooden throne. Only the man in the middle held his eyes open. The man on the left looked as if he was dozing off, while the one on the right looked to be in a deep state of meditation.

Who are you? Jack wanted to ask them. He wanted to scream it just to shatter their silence. *What do you want?* But somehow, he knew the answer to both. Not in details, no, but he *did* know it in part. He didn't know their names specifically, but he knew who they were all the same.

"David," the one on the left said, introducing himself.

As he spoke, his eyes opened—brown as a puppy's own loving stare. At the same time, the man in the middle had closed his eyes, and the one on the right had kept them as before, meditating. When the middle man's eyes closed, they didn't seem like they were reaching for nirvana nor peering into the doors of dreamland. When *his* eyes were closed, he simply looked dead.

"Victor," the man in the middle spoke, opening his eyes while David closed his.

There was something almost violent about Victor's voice, but Carlos tried to dismiss that.

Victor closed his eyes again, allowing the man to his right to introduce himself. "Adren," he said pleasantly. His irises were a placid blue, holding back gallons upon gallons of ocean. Then they closed once more, slowly, as if no hurry or rush had ever plagued them in their life. Adren's meditation resumed, and Jack Carlos looked to see Victor's mossy green eyes opened like sprung traps. He wasn't sure which he liked less, the man's eyes opened or closed.

All three of the men wore black, two-button suits that made them look like men of business, but not businessmen. Their shoes were glossy black, as reflective as used motor oil. Their pants were trim, each leg dashing forward with a striking, bold crease that could have cut through thin air and made it bleed. They wore silver cuffs. The one thing that made them stand apart was the color of their hair.

David's orange hair made him look like a fiery youth. Victor looked the oldest but wore spiky, blond hair. Adren's head was covered in thick, black hair that cascaded down to his jaw line.

"Do you know who we are, Jack?" Victor asked, stepping forward from between David and Adren.

"Yeah, I know who you are," Jack answered, "And I know you know who I am, but that doesn't put us on a first name basis. I'm Mr. Carlos to you."

"Then who are we?"

"You're the duct tape people. You cling like leeches to the catastrophes of the future, always searching for the next death-stricken disaster. But that's not exactly how David Booth would put it."

He spoke of the man—David Booth—as if he were a household commodity.

"How *would* he put it, then?"

"He calls you people the 'purveyors of apocalyptic visions of the future,'" Jack answered, eyes half-opened and uncaring, as if he were reciting something from an encyclopedia.

"Never heard him say such a thing."

Carlos looked at him with slit-thin eyes, wondering if Victor was trying to reel him in or if he was being honest.

"Probably hasn't said it yet. Or maybe what you think you know isn't worth a damn, Mr. Victor."

"Just Victor, Jack."

"I said to stop calling me that. You're no friend of mine."

"All the same. I don't trust men by the name of Jack, anyways."

"What's wrong with 'Jack'?" he demanded. He tried carefully

to keep his tone even with Victor's own. Tried hard not to show his bitterness and fear.

"Jack is a simple name, one spat out without even a trying care at originality. Your parents must not have given it much thought when you were born, for it is on your birth certificate, which leads me to a conclusion as simple as your own name."

"What are you trying to say?" Jack asked.

"Caring parents spend time with their children. Caring parents find purpose in a name. They give it meaning and expectations even before the child is born. Your name—Jack—has no meaning. Who knows how well a parent raises a child that he cares for not."

That last phrase reminded Jack of poetry. He felt mesmerized by the way Victor spoke, despite the passive aggressive condescension.

"*That* is why I don't trust you, Jack," Victor continued. "You, and other men of similarly simple names."

"Jack is just slang for John," he said, but sounded like a little girl flaunting a weak defense.

Victor's Adam's apple bobbed coolly in his throat, and Jack thought he was trying to keep himself from laughing. But that face knew no laughter. The skin stretching over it remained unmoving, without a flinch to disrupt its composure. Jack's eyes dropped, unable to compete with Victor's gaze, and fell to the height of the man's thumbs which were propped in their pockets. There, he noticed the odd, rounded bulge in Victor's left pocket.

Noticing Jack's eyes, Victor slipped his hand in his pocket and reached for the bulge, as if being reminded that he still had it. When he pulled the object out, it turned out to be a bundle of garlic, still wrapped in its papery skin. Victor's smooth fingertips rubbed and peeled the flakes of skin off the bundle, slowly exposing the interior cloves. The flakes of skin swooped down like fallen leaves.

With his careful, slow-moving fingers, Victor snapped one of the cloves from its bundle and ripped and twisted the skin off of that individual piece as well. He let the rest of the garlic roll back into his pocket, and more of those flakes zigzagged and spun their way slowly to the rug.

Jack thought he could hear them hiss and roar as they tumbled downward, but they made no more noise than falling snow.

Jack found himself nibbling at his lower lip in quick, gnawing bites. His foot rapped nervously on the floor.

"Could you pick that up?" he said.

"OCD about your rug?" Victor asked amused, but he knew well Jack wasn't obsessive-compulsive. They had been observing him for a long time now, almost six months, to know better than that.

"No," Jack answered, annoyed, "I'd just like my living room clean."

Victor didn't move to pick up the garlic skin. Instead he brought the naked, moist clove to his lips and bit into it as if it were an almond. His eyes remained solid, unblinking, staring holes into Jack's pupils.

Jack could smell the crunched garlic from where he sat. Victor's jaw worked the garlic between his teeth, as though he were eating something chewy and tasteful.

Jack looked away to distract himself from Victor's mouth. He watched the gas-fueled fireplace. The flames danced around two fake ceramic logs.

He wished the men would disappear.

Victor went on chewing for a second more, then he tongued his palate, swallowed, and clucked his lips the way a man would after stripping chicken meat off its bone.

Victor leaned in closer on Jack, wrapping his fingers around the chair's armrests for leverage. Jack drew away, unable to go anywhere but against the back of the chair, and his legs propped up a bit, as if trying to keep Victor away with his knees.

"Is *this* how the death of your parents smelled?" Victor spoke, breathing directly into Carlos' face. The stench of his breath was staggering, sharp enough to shoot a hole through Jack's throat—because all of the sudden he wasn't breathing the stench of garlic, he was *tasting* it. But it was more than just garlic that stained Victor's breath. Jack thought he could smell road kill in its aftermath.

Victor backed away, doing so just as slowly as he'd leaned in close on the writhing man, and stepped back between David and Adren, mimicking their stance only with his eyes open and theirs closed. He glared down at Jack with those mossy and gruesome eyes, and Jack felt himself withering beneath their glare. A heat choked his neck and then flushed his face in a wave of warm but uncomfortable tingles.

The shiver sprung Jack to his feet. The urge to swing a fist into Victor's jaw shook from his shoulders down to his knuckles. He pulled an arm back, unsure if he should swing.

Victor's eyes sank shut, drawing back to their deathly appearance, and Adren—the black-haired man on the right— opened his eyes with the same calm manner he held earlier.

"I wouldn't do that," said Adren, speaking as if giving life's advice to a young boy.

"Why the hell not?" But already his fist had lowered some. There was such a soothing calm to Adren's voice.

"Because his breath doesn't smell half as bad as the stench of your own decaying carcass would, Mr. Carlos."

Then Jack's wrist lowered completely, shoulders slumped.

"It wasn't right what he said," Jack muttered.

"He has that effect on most people." A long moment of silence stole over them.

Then, when Jack finally regained his composure, he said calmly, "My parents died when I was seven."

"Because of David Booth," Adren said, as if striking a match that would set a forest ablaze. The name sparked inside of Jack Carlos' mind, and his eyes widened.

"I never blamed him for what happened. Well, maybe at first I did, but not for long. It was easy to do in '79."

"Was that the year?" Adren's voice wasn't questioning yet, but leading.

"May 25th, yes," Jack answered. "You don't forget the date of your parents' death. You might not remember their birthday, but you never forget the day they died. We were living here in Chicago then, and they booked a business trip to California, so they left me at my uncle's for the week."

Wearily he realized that he wasn't talking to Adren. It wasn't Adren who the story was for because somehow he knew that these three men already knew all the details. Jack was telling the story to himself, or *for* himself, as he had always done when the topic came to subject. He went on.

"My parents worked for an insurance agency headquartered in Los Angeles. That trip was supposed to make both my parents a lot better off financially."

Jack stopped for a moment, eyes jittering in his sockets, thinking back to how much of those details he actually needed to remember to have the story sound right—to make it sound understandable.

"That flight, flight 191, never made it to Los Angeles. It didn't even make it outside Chicago. Before you knew it, the hydraulic fluid started to bleed, and one of the engines failed. The plane took a nose dive into a sink hole of a mobile-home park, killing two more, on top of the number of passengers."

Adren's eyes watched him coolly—not *coldly* as Victor's had, but calmly. His eyes tightened into slits.

"What?" Jack asked.

Adren didn't speak.

"What? What is it?" he demanded.

"How many times have you told that story growing up?"

Jack said nothing.

"Because you've actually grown to believe it. I see it in your eyes. It's been years since you've told it the way it sounded best, but you still believe it."

"What is it with you guys attacking me? First my name, now my *story?*"

"Your parents were never on that flight," Adren said without mood.

"They were killed in that plane crash."

"You're not lying about that, but you *are* about the rest. That plane crashed into your house—that hole of a trailer park—where your mother was probably cooking dinner and your father watching TV. You were at your uncle's when it happened, yes, but just for the day to help him paint the house. You were a good sport at seven, even though today you're still ashamed of what you were then."

"Who sent you? Did David Booth send you?" Jack shouted.

Victor and David didn't even flinch. Their eyes remained closed. The question had sounded ridiculous coming out.

"You *did* blame Booth, didn't you?" Adren said slowly, once again in that same leading manner, as if to help Jack search for himself. "You sent him hate mail for over a decade before you realized how much it hurt to shoot the messenger. And here you sat just minutes ago, quoting words that came from his very lips—calling us the Duct Tape People."

Jack needed to sit again. Slowly, very slowly, like an old man with a broken hip. He lowered himself back in his chair, looking up at Adren for a long moment before deciding to explain himself.

"I stopped the letters when *I* became the messenger," he admitted gravely. "But for ten years, yeah, I believed he had *caused* that plane to go down. Everyone all over the country knew he'd had dreams about it—for ten straight days he had those dreams. 'Vivid but fuzzy', he called them, like someone wanting to take the credit but not the blame. He said he never knew exactly which plane was supposed to crash before it finally did, but back then I still believed he *made* it happen all the same."

"He had warned the FAA about it," Adren said.

"I know, I know. And they didn't even believe him. They took a note and left it at that. Freaking jackasses. Three days after he told them about it, the plane crashed."

"You became fixated."

"With the crash. With Booth. With his dreams."

He exhaled. He let the confession linger between them before going on.

"And strangely I became obsessed with all sorts of apocalyptic visionaries. I became a duct tape man myself, just like you, hunting those who hunted down the future. Except soon, I found out it was the visions that hunted *them*, and not the other way around."

"When you were seventeen," Adren said. This was posed as neither a question nor a statement. The words were a piece of string for Jack to pull.

"That's right. That's when I stopped mailing my letters to Booth because I finally understood him. And I didn't like it. It disturbed me to know that it was now happening to me."

"What happened exactly?"

"In October of '89 I had a dream that kept coming back for a month straight. Except each time the images shifted, more images coming to focus. I thought, 'Damnit. That's not something a seventeen-year-old should be dreaming of.' I was barely into politics then."

Jack paused, breathing out heavily. Then he breathed in again, wondering if he had enough strength to go through with it. It was a long story, he realized. "I knew commies were the bad guys then—they had been since the sixties—but beyond that I was oblivious to the subject. The Reds didn't scare me any more than a kid in a Halloween mask did, and besides, the tension was already cooling off by the eighties.

"In my dreams I saw faces crying tears of joy, and then something being ripped and taken apart and crumbling. It was the Berlin Wall, but this didn't become obvious to me until the day before it finally happened.

"And in all, that wasn't so bad. I could take it. It wasn't any sort of horrifying series of dreams, and it *was* fascinating all the same. At the time it was enough to stop my hate mail to Booth because I could feel a connection with him. But then the dreams worsened.

"I saw Rodney King's beating—understood it even for what it was, and knew of the riots that would follow. I saw plane crashes, fires, murders, freak accidents. By the time I was twenty, I saw more deaths in my dreams than the world could ever have known about. Then days, weeks or sometimes months later I would hear of them again on the news, and every time I thought, 'Why didn't I stop them? Why didn't I do something?'

"And each time I thought of David Booth. I thought of him and all of the damn letters I sent him, damning him to hell for killing my parents. So many of those letters were anonymous, and none of them ever had a return address, but I knew he knew it was me all that time. So every time I thought I'd go to the police station announcing the next catastrophe, I was too afraid that the victims' families would blame me. It was practically illogical, but my own paranoia seemed to know no logic then.

"When I was twenty-four, I went on a job interview. The job came down to a decision between me and two other guys. It was for the assistant editor position at a horror magazine called, 'The Midnight Watch.' My credentials in literature and in the world of publishing weren't brilliant, but I must have done something right because I got an interview.

"I was way too young for that position, and everyone up that ladder knew it- including myself. The editor in chief who interviewed me was at least twice my age. But I knew how to tell a story, a dark story. I'd always managed to impress even myself with my writing. My tin can mind is full of them, somehow. That magazine had published five of my short stories before finally my connections with it became more personal, and so I found myself in their editor's office.

"When I met with Mr. Vlair—a fat, greasy man who couldn't have squeezed his way into a Geo Metro—he shook my hand, and I felt a jolt. The visions didn't happen when I touched him—it was only a jolt then. The visions started soon after when we were sitting face to face, talking shop."

Adren stood silently, looking down at Jack without making a

sound. He watched and listened. Jack went on.

"His whole office wavered a minute into it. It was like the air was expanding and then contracting, moving everything with it. Just then, subliminal snapshots cut into my vision like frames of film that didn't belong. You know? Like quick flashes, but there were so many of them that I couldn't help but see them. That night Mr. Vlair was going to rape a woman, and she'd die in the middle of it, choked to death. I ran out of that office horrified, not even five minutes into our interview, and didn't look back once."

"Did you tell the police?"

"That time I did, yeah. They heard my story, but didn't even listen to it. I sounded crazy to myself, so I don't think I could have sounded any better to them. They took a note just to appease me—to make me go away—the same way the FAA took a note when Booth went to them, and I knew they weren't going to do anything about it. So I went to the place where I saw it happen by myself, but when I got there I was too late.

"Mr. Vlair had left the woman dead behind along with a stream of sweat, like the fat snail that he was, slithering away. He had done it in the woman's bathroom of a small bar in the strip district. A place so *public.* So *risky.* He got off on that. And of course, just then two women walked in and saw what looked like the disaster I had foreseen. Except they thought *I* was the rapist. Before I could do anything, they ran out and seconds later four men ran in. One was the bartender, one the bouncer, and the other two were just drinkers tagging along.

"They grabbed me and beat the hell out of me. They beat me until I was puking guts. Then they held me down until a cop came and took me away. I was in jail three days before the DNA results came back negative on my part. I didn't go to anybody about my visions after that. I guess those ten years of hate mail had finally come back with 'Return to Sender' stamped across the front."

"And then on?"

Jack breathed out a sad laughter, one that should've been met with tears, but somehow he managed to hold those back. For now at least.

"From then on things turned worse before they got better. It wasn't just dreams that plagued me. The visions I had in Vlair's office sparked off a whole new breed of visions. In broad daylight or with friends I would start screaming, freaking out over things that nobody else could see. They thought I was crazy. And then I would think the same until what I saw actually happened, and that drove me even further into my own secluded insanity.

"In the past five years I've drawn away from others, and they drew away from me. It was fear. Fear grabbed hold of everything and fumed it with its own stench. To me, nothing seemed safe in the world anymore. The Oklahoma City bombing, the O.J. Simpson murder, Heaven's Gate mass suicide, the Columbine shooting..."

Jack found himself out of breath, chest heaving with its own hysteria, and realized how badly his hands were quivering now.

"And all this time I was trying to stay away from the Duct Tape People, so I said nothing. Nothing to anyone."

"But you wrote letters," Adren said mildly.

"I did. Sometimes. Those letters helped nothing, though. I never put a return address on the envelopes to clue in to who I was. But I guess there were ways, or else you wouldn't be standing here if there weren't."

Adren gave him a brief nod. His eyes never blinked.

How could they hold their eyes open like that for so long?

"And now?" Adren asked, reassuming his role of leading, both of them knowing that eventually they would reach the reason for their visit.

To his question, Jack gave only a confused look. *Now what?* he thought to himself, wondering what it was that Adren was asking. Jack looked around, sweeping his gaze across the room for clues or answers.

"The answer to what I'm asking doesn't hide in this room." But Jack barely heard him, and continued his search anyways.

David and Victor were still standing there, motionless, offering no more than impassive faces. Jack looked to his 900-watt Sony stereo system, the giant flat screen TV, propped on the wall like a blank canvas.

Looking at his living room now, he felt as if he had never even seen it before in his life. The materialism that plagued it—

"Quit stalling." Adren's voice was sharp now, full of reproach— something that moments ago hadn't seemed possible in all of his tenderness.

"And now?" he repeated the question. No patience this time. "Are you going to tell us what you know?"

Jack's face held a cold shiver, his head bobbing unsurely above his neck. His eyes were not focused on anything, and they seemed lost in their own train of thought. Adren said something, but Jack didn't hear it, and then—

"Haya Jack!" a new voice sparked, breaking up Jack's brief delirium. His face looked up and saw that it was David. The man held a smirk that resembled a ventriloquist dummy's grin. David's eyes were lucid, now twitched with quick jolts of energy.

Adren had fallen back into silence, eyes closed and thumbs back in pockets.

David took two zigzagging and jazzy steps forward and then

a quick hop, stomping down in front of Jack. His hands were deep in his pockets now, carrying a beat that slapped his thighs in fractured, parading intervals.

"You know who we are, Jack?" his voice sounded like it was hopping on hot coals.

Jack looked up at him with his face sagging in a grimace and thought, *Why are you asking me this again?*

Then David gave out an intrusive laugh, showing he was only kidding. "I know. You know us, and we know you. And you know we know, and we know you know... all of it going on until infinity and forever. Knowing is a complicated thing, Jack."

"Don't—"

"Don't call you Jack?" His face pinched, and then he laughed wildly, as if having said that turned out to be a lot funnier than he had expected. "I'll spare you the afterthought."

"What?" Jack said confused. He felt irritated and annoyed by this man. He would rather go back to smelling Victor's garlic breath than have to interact with this buffoon.

"Never mind."

"So what is this? What's going on now?"

"Nice place you've got going here, Mr. C."

"Yeah—thanks." Jack stammered, trying to think of what he could say to bring their conversation somewhere useful for at least a second.

David went on, "It's not cheap having such a nice home in the Chicago area. And you've got expensive taste. Especially those French doors. That indigo stain is fantastic, and the crystalline cut design... quite interesting. You had those installed just recently didn't you?"

"Yeah."

"Custom made?"

"How can you tell?"

"Because of the lining and cut of their frame. It's not symmetrical with the rest of the room. Very pretty, still. Must have cost you a fortune to have them installed."

"It was manageable."

"No, come on. Let's hear it. How much did it run you?"

"That's none of your business. Why is that even relevant?"

"Tell me, Mr. C. What's your state of employment?"

To Jack, this conversation felt sputtery and random, as if talking to a red-haired kid with ADD.

"I'm not employed right now."

"Oh is that so? Then how can a man without a job afford a sixty-some-inch plasma TV and a house with more bathrooms in it than a man can use in a year? Not to mention that you're only twenty-nine."

"Thirty soon enough."

"Things happened after your interview with 'The Midnight Watch' didn't they?"

"I already told this to him," he said, pointing at Adren. "I had dreams."

"Sure did. And it went beyond just your regular visions, too. It wasn't all gruesome stuff after all."

"Like I said," Jack admitted gravely like an old man forced to share an even older secret, "It got worse before it got better."

"And better it did."

Jack paused pensively before talking. "At first I thought they were dates, you know, of catastrophes bound to happen, but the digits I saw didn't fit the pattern of dates. I tried to decode them in every possible way I could think of, but I got nothing. I guess

I was fixated. I've had a lot of fixations in my life, and predicted catastrophes became one of them. I couldn't see beyond the possibility that these numbers told of deaths."

"But they weren't dates after all," David said.

"No, and the first time I realized this, I laughed so hard walking down the street that people must have thought I was a lunatic. *I* thought I was a lunatic. It all seemed so insanely good, like one of those work-at-home programs that guarantee you thousands a month to lick stamps and mail envelopes."

David held a grin that spread across his face. He cocked his eyebrows once.

"What I kept seeing..." Jack said, and laughed a staggered laugh, as if even now after all these years he still couldn't believe it, "Were stock market quotes, and winning lottery numbers, and all these other codes—most of which I couldn't decipher, but that didn't even matter. It became a fortuneteller's dream instead of a nightmare for once. One you'd think would never happen.

"A few times I thought I was making the winnings happen, not just foreseeing them. I felt like I was *making* the racehorse win the race with my mind. Like I was rigging the track."

"You never bet on horses."

"No. There were plenty of other things I bet on, and every time I wondered if I was controlling the events. I wondered so many times if my mind was *changing* the future instead of simply predicting it. Because, I mean, how could you tell the difference?

"Say you tell some kid that he'll get hurt if he keeps playing on the street. Then, the next day you follow a car with your eyes, right up to the very moment it runs the boy over. You saw it happen, watched it happen, and you almost convince yourself you made it happen. Now, is that a confirmed prediction or a metaphysically staged one? Did you *make* it happen, or did you simply *let* it?"

But the analogy wasn't quite right to describe how he felt about the lottery winnings. He knew that his visions didn't actually *change* the outcome of events. He knew he was simply in "receive" mode. However, did knowing something before it happen make you somehow responsible for it?

Jack's eyes rummaged through his past once again, this time holding a thinner smile on his lips. Then his lips pressed tighter, flattening like those of a child who doesn't want to take his medicine. His eyes flashed back, consumed by the glory of the remembered winnings, pretending that his mind had never left the subject. "This is what it's about, isn't it?"

David's face drew back as if evading a slap. "Money? You think we want the next big lottery hit? What's on our minds is more important than cash and prizes, Jack."

"Then it's the other thing," he said solemnly. The phrase stood on tiptoes between a question and statement.

David cocked his head sideways in a tilt. He nodded and lifted a brow while doing so. "We want to make sure that money and lotteries aren't the only things filling your brain lately."

"They haven't."

David's pulled his hands out of his pockets slowly, but kept his thumbs hooked on the outer seams. His eyes closed, and Victor's returned to life again.

"This one's the worst yet," Victor said, and his voice sounded like clumps of dirt shifting down an eroding hill.

"You can't even imagine." Jack's eyes fixed on the peels of garlic skin on the rug. But his mind saw something else. A vision that had plagued him for a month straight now.

"And you haven't told anyone."

"I don't know how. This is worse than Flight 191."

"We figured. You haven't seemed right since mid August, and just before we walked in, you were shrieking."

"Was I?"

"And crying."

Jack brought a hand to his sagged cheeks and felt the tears that had dried on them. The corners of his eyes felt crusty, and as he squinted, he felt the skin around his lids pulling.

"It's going to happen tomorrow," Jack said.

"You know the day?" Victor's voice sounded excited now, verging towards disbelief.

"I just told you, didn't I?"

"What's going to happen, Jack? You need to tell us."

Then suddenly all three had their eyes open, beaming down on him like searchlights.

A trembling sort of pressure shook Jack's chest, and he realized now why they had been taking turns opening their eyes.. He actually *felt* their stares pressing on his skin. Blended together, their stares radiated in temperatures. From hot to cold, they warmed his face to droplets of sweat and then chilled it down again.

Jack found himself unable to breathe, lungs collapsed and struggling for air. His throat creaked at each attempt to breathe, sounding like a cork twisting out of a wine bottle. He clasped his hands around the chair's handles, his knuckles screamed, turning as pale as Victor's hair.

"Tell us Mr. C,"

"Tell us Jack,"

"Tell us Carlos," all three voices said simultaneously.

"What now?" they asked in unison.

He couldn't answer them. Wanted to, but couldn't speak.

Wanted to, but choked on his own desperation, instead. Wanted to so badly, but knew his voice had been drowned by fear.

They closed their eyes then, relieving Jack from his suffocation. He gasped hard, as if finally reaching the water's surface after a long, deep dive. With their eyes closed he could tell them everything. He admitted to all of the details as if they had been beaten out of him, leaving him winded and whipped from the chest up.

Jack's spine fell limp. He brought his hands to his face, fingers spread so wide that they covered his entire face. He held his face for a while. Sobbing. Then his sobs turned into frightened wails. His wails became muffled screams that went on and on like an avalanche without restraint. Their eyes opened again, slowly, and he felt their gaze fall upon him warmly.

"Do you see now?" he asked through the spread of his fingers. "Do you finally see?" The three men looked liquid through his tear-rippled vision. Their faces were pink blotches, like clots of watercolor paint missing the details. Jack pressed his eyes shut, and a tear curved out of the corner of each, meeting at his chin.

When his sight cleared and the details formed back on their faces, their expressions held no emotion.

"You don't believe me?" he asked breathily.

"We believe you," they said together, forming a single, rounded voice. Then David and Adren shut their eyes, death plaguing both of their countenances, and Jack understood that they *did* believe him after all.

"Then will you tell someone? Will you save their lives?" Jack couldn't contain the relief from his voice.

"No," said Victor.

"No?" he screamed, and now his hands clutched at the pant legs of his silk pajamas.

"We're not here to discuss salvation, Jack."

"But thousands will die! Why won't you?"

"'Who is like the wise man? Who knows the explanation of things?'"

"Don't give me your sage bullcrap."

Their voices were a contrast to one another. One man's screaming, the other man's soothing. "Don't you come in here and call me 'Jack' at the first chance you get, make me reveal myself to you, make me reveal my horrors, and then stand there without even a single care for any of it!"

"This is the catastrophe by which all others will be measured."

"What's that even mean?"

"Maybe it means that it's meant to happen. Maybe all of these catastrophes are meant to happen. That's why no one stops them."

"No, it can't happen. That's too much. Too much to bear."

"Then stop making excuses, and save those people. We weren't sent here to do your job. We came here to make sure you've received your call. It's up to you to change it. Quit blaming us for something you should do yourself."

"No," he told them. "I can't. No one will believe me. Who would believe me? You *have* to do it!"

"The visions didn't come to us," Adren said opening his eyes while Victor closed his. "Stop making excuses for yourself and do your job. Men like you have been given this gift to stop these catastrophes, not to wither in fear from them."

"Freaking David Booth," Jack screamed, wrenching the name and twisting it within his lips. But he wasn't cursing the name; he was cursing the fact that he would become like Booth, forsaken and blamed. "It's too late. It's going to happen tomorrow."

"If that's what you allow."

"I'm not the one to blame here! I'm not the one responsible for all their deaths."

"Is that what you believe?"

"I know it," he shouted, as if making a plea to convince himself.

"Even if a wise man claims he knows, he cannot really comprehend it," Victor said.

"Will you stop that," he demanded, his words shaking like loose boards being run over. "Just stop it."

"You've been lucky so far, Jack."

Jack's face became complex with disbelief. He stammered a laugh that felt like a cold, strangled cry. *Lucky?* he thought. *How can you call me lucky?*

"So far it's been only the death of others you've seen, and not your own. It would be quite a conflict if *that* were to happen. I don't believe you would save your own life if such a vision came."

"Anyone can see his own death if he chooses. It's called suicide."

"Foresee it, yes. But save it? You couldn't even save that woman at the bar. You allowed it to happen, and that's no different than *making* it happen. The difference between you and David Booth is that he actually *tried* to save Flight 191."

"I was put in jail for that woman! How can you tell me I didn't try?" Victor's eyes closed.

Slowly, he turned and stepped towards the door.

David followed.

Then Adren.

"Don't leave me," he begged. "Don't leave me here alone with this."

But their ears were just as shut as their eyes. With the click of the front door closing, the room became as quiet as death.

The next day, he sat, eyes glued to his flat-screen television, watching replays of the planes crashing, watching the fear in the eyes of the news anchors, listening to the estimates of lives lost.

It was almost three thousand now.

Jack Carlos contemplated suicide that afternoon, plagued by the riddles of life and the paradox between *making* and *letting*.

How much control did he have over those planes? How much control did he have over the manifestations of his dreams? How responsible was he for his inaction by allowing those events to unfold?

After the plane crashes, he tried to grab hold of a vision of how he might die. He tried to envision the method of his suicide. He didn't own a gun. A knife would be too bloody. Hanging seemed unreasonable.

Which way am I to die? he contemplated.

He tried to picture the many ways. Hit by a car. Leapt off a building. Struck by lighting. Drowned in a lake. But none of those visions would come to him. And so, he couldn't let any of them happen.

The Problem with My Shoes

The more I tried running, the more they'd appear,
"Come closer," they said; they prickled my ear,
Somehow they forced me to sin every day
I wish, oh how I wish they'd just go away,
So I placed this here gun to my ear and I said,
"I give you three seconds to get out of my head."

—Marco G. Sauret

I knew I was in trouble when my shoes started talking to me. That sort of thing isn't supposed to happen. When inanimate objects talk to you, you're supposed to ignore them. If your couch says, *Get off of me*, you sink your ass down even more. When voices speak to you at night, coming from the darkness, coming from some hole in the wall or from the drain in your sink, you run like hell. You either run like hell or you pretend like it's not happening. Never,

ever, do you talk back.

That was my mistake with my shoes, I guess: a pair of beat up old Airwalks—the kind you'd see skaters sport back in the eighties. I began to wear them more and more as my other shoes started to disappear. In the end I was left with either the Airwalks or a pair of sandals with the straps chewed to ribbons. So when the day came for my job interview, I slipped on the Airwalks, matched with a two-bit business suit I had hanging in the closet, and drove to downtown Chicago where the office was located. The guy interviewing me took one glance at my shoes and looked as if he could have jumped through the ceiling.

"Nice," he said. That was it, but he said it as if his head could've exploded.

I said what?

"The shoes. Shows creativity…" He was searching for a name.

"Scott," I told him. "Scott Myers."

"We need someone like you around here, Scott. You applying for the job?"

"That's right."

"It's yours."

"Don't you need to see my résumé? My credentials?"

"Naw, it's all right. I have a feeling 'bout you."

"My portfolio?" I persisted.

"I've seen enough."

You've seen my shoes, I thought. Nobody gets hired because of their shoes. Why not my suit? I bought it under a bridge from an Arabian guy who sold them out of a cardboard box. The pants are stain repellant.

The guy himself knew how to dress to impress. He wore a tie loosely bound around his neck over a T-shirt that read, "Soccer mom—watch out." His hair was all messy, as if he detached his head from his shoulders, tossed it in a Laundromat washer, and then stuck it back on. His eyes blazed with vigor, and when he shook my hand I thought he'd take it with him.

"I'm Dave, by the way. They call me the Chief."

Nobody calls you that, I thought, but instead I said, "Why the Chief?"

"I'm the editor in chief. I read everything that goes on under the roof of this office, and I get to say what goes to print and what doesn't. You know what your job is?"

"Yeah, well, sorta."

"That's better than nothing. You're now our new writer for the 'Lost Unfound' column. It's sort of like the Unsolved Mysteries section of our magazine. You can cover stories right here in Chicago or wherever you want. Whatever goes on out there that's strange and doesn't quite make sense, you cover it, and we print it."

"Got it."

"Good. Susie there—she's sort of like the orientation specialist around here—she'll help you with any questions you got."

I got the general rundown, and I'd be back the next morning for my first day of work.

Two weeks later, I hadn't gotten my first paycheck yet, and I was already three weeks overdue on my gas bill. It was going to get shut off within the next five days, the delinquency letter read. The phone had been gone for a while already. Water and electricity were the only things left. I intended to keep those.

So I wrote a few columns: Missing grandmothers, alien sightings, gifted children— that sort or thing. When the first check finally came in the mail I paid rent and bought a pair of Vans that were on clearance. The next day at the office, when Dave saw those on my feet instead of the Airwalks, things didn't go so well.

"Who are *you?*" he first said.

I gave him a blank stare, but when the confusion failed to leave his face I realized I'd have to give him a hint or two. "Lost Unfound?" I said, wondering if that would light a bulb.

"Oh, oh. Right. What are you doing here?"

"I work here. You hired me."

"It's Tuesday," he said, as if already I was breaking rules and schedules.

"I work Tuesdays."

"*Do* you?" he asked, as if I were trying to pull a fast one on him.

I ignored the question. "I got that new story if you want it. About that underground organization that stalks out visionaries."

He took it from my hand briskly, scanning it with his eyes darting across the page.

He shoved the page back to me a minute later. "Yeah, well, it's crap. 'Specially the title."

"There is no title. You post the title, not me."

"I don't know. There's just something wrong about it. And you. You're different. Just go home today, and come back when it's Wednesday."

So I came back the next day wearing the Airwalks. By now I had worn them so much that their soles were turning into a pair of flapping lips. In all, they were still the most comfortable shoes I'd ever worn, but soon they wouldn't look any better than my sandals.

Unhesitant, I walked into Dave's office, if you could call it that, swatting down the same story on his desk. Unedited. Unchanged. Untouched. And still without a title.

He took a glimpse, placed it neatly on one corner of his desk and said, "Great."

"So you're putting it on this week's issue?"

"Course I will. Why wouldn't I?"

"I haven't touched it since yesterday."

"That's all right, I'll think of a title."

"No I mean—nevermind." With that I was out of his office, shoes flapping beneath me and my tonsils scouring in my throat. Damn shoes.

On Thursday, Dave wore a pair of black dress shoes that shined like glass. The rest of him was in jeans and a T-shirt. He titled my story, "The Black Suits Among Us" and ran it through the print. The issue would be out the next day.

Friday was when things started to go wrong. Friday was when I knew there'd be trouble.

I was at my desk, a creaking metal thing hidden beneath stacks of papers and piles of trash, when suddenly I realized I wanted a glass of milk. No logical thought pattern had led me to that conclusion. No preconditioned stimulus had inspired that specific craving. I just wanted milk. It was one of those random cravings that first hits your brain, and then works its way down to your stomach. The thought of chocolate had often done that same thing to me before, but milk?

I tried to dismiss the thought, knowing that a lunch break would come soon enough, when suddenly I heard a snickering beneath my desk. I pushed back my chair, swiveling on its rolling wheels, looked underneath, but saw nothing. Just cable wires that ran from the back of my computer up to my monitor and printer. I scratched my head, it itched, and pulled myself back to the desk.

Right in front of me, was a glass of milk.

Not orange juice, not water, not a chocolate smoothie. Plain, simple, white milk. And I had a feeling that it wasn't soy.

I screamed—sort of like a mix between a gasp and a yelp, but it was still a scream all the same. A girly one at that, too. I looked around trying to find whoever might have left the glass behind, but the closest person was Susie, staring at me from her desk by the window.

Her one eyebrow cocked, questioning in her own silence why I had screamed. I pointed at the glass of milk. Her look of distrust turned only more suspicious.

Where the hell did it come from?

"Just drink it," a voice said, roughed and bossy. It came from under the desk, and as it spoke I felt a tingle rise from my right foot.

What the hell?

"Quit being such a sissy girl and drink your mystery milk." This was the sort of voice you were supposed to ignore when you heard it. It was the sort of voice that you ran like hell from. Instead, I picked up the glass, pressed it between my fingertips and drank. I downed that milk in half a dozen gulps, taking no breather until I swallowed the last drop. It wasn't like the voice was telling me to commit mass murder or jump off a cliff. It told me to drink the milk, so I did. Something I had wanted anyway.

After I was done, I looked under the desk again and saw nothing still.

I imagined the voice, I told myself while backing away from the desk. But if that was the case, then I imagined the glass of milk, too, and I must have imagined drinking it.

That can only mean that I'm either delusional, or schizophrenic. If I imagined that glass, now empty on my desk, then it doesn't exist. No one else can see it but me.

I held the glass in my hand, palming it and turning it around with my fingers. Susie watched me from the corner of her eye, trying to do so without being noticed. *Except she doesn't see the glass,* I thought. *She can't see the glass it doesn't exist. In her eyes, my palm is empty, my fingers spinning nothing but office air.*

I tossed the glass up in the air and caught it back in my palm, feeling its weight and shape. Sure *felt* real. Still, following logic, glasses of milk don't just appear out of nowhere after a simple crave.

Without thinking twice about it, I launched the glass across the large, overall office room, over desks, over computers, over heads. No eyes traced its flight except my own because that glass didn't exist. Just like that voice under the desk didn't exist.

But then—

Crash!

The sound of glass exploding cut through the noise of keyboards tapping and useless chitchat filling the room. Faces snapped at the burst of broken glass, lying at the door of Dave's office. Then the faces snapped back to me.

I stood there, watching it all the same way you watch a magic trick gone horribly wrong. The kind where the vanishing elephant gets pissed off and goes on a rampage.

"What'd you do that for?" someone asked.

"Yeah, Scott, what in the hell is wrong with you?"

"There is no glass," I told them.

Dave's office door opened. He wore a shirt plastered with glued-on macaroni. "Brilliant," he said, "Better that glass than a computer screen, at least. Whoever threw this, why don't you clean it up and get back to work."

Except he was looking right at me as he said this. If it hadn't been for my shoes, who knows what he would've said instead.

As the weeks went on, those shoes became more and more worn. I couldn't even walk in them without the soles smacking at each footstep. And I had no other choice but to wear them. My left shoe from the pair of Vans went missing the day after the milk incident.

And the right shoe, well…

It hung itself.

The next morning I found it hung from the ceiling fan, spinning, using its own laces for a noose.

Then the craziness just went on snowballing, piling up with more insanity as it went along. Nights would come that I'd hear incessant snickering from the closet. "We're the booger monster," one of two voices would say, choking up with laughter at each word.

"We're coming to eat you, Scott," the other would add.

And I knew it was them by now. The shoes. A pair of two wise-asses who had nothing better to do than keep me up at night and distract me at work during the day.

About a week later, my car broke down and I was forced to ride the bus to work. Those random misfortunes always seemed to happen to me. When I had the car towed to a mechanic, some grease monkey holding a Bud in his hand told me the engine was blown.

"How can the engine just blow? I was taking care of it fine."

"Stuff happens I guess."

Coming out of my apartment the next day, I turned to lock the door behind me, and when I turned back, I tripped, smashing my face against a wall. My shoelaces were tied.

"What'd you do that for?" I asked my shoes. Some guy walked past, looked down at me, and walked away shaking his head.

"We're just holding hands," my left said.

"I ain't no queer. Don't look at *me*," said my right.

Downstairs, in front of my apartment building I caught the bus to work. Sitting across from me, some guy was talking to his umbrella. *What a whacko*, I thought, and I told my shoes to shut up. They were telling dirty jokes to one another.

I caught a man staring at me. When I looked at him, he didn't look away. He just kept staring. I saw myself in his eyes for a moment. I didn't like how he was judging me.

I wasn't crazy. It was the shoes. They were making me look crazy.

At the office, I greeted Susie before going to my desk.

"Good morning," she said.

"Hey there lady," my right Airwalk added.

"She's a cutie," Leftie chimed next.

I walked away kicking things and stomping my feet. Lefty and Righty yelped in pain. I can't say that I didn't enjoy it.

"Will you stop that?" they screamed up at me.

"Not until you two decide to shut up," I snapped down at them.

"All right, all right," they both said together.

"Okay, good."

Three staff members stopped what they were doing to stare at me.

"Morning—" I pitched quickly, and ran to my desk.

The annoyances didn't stop that day, though.

"What's better than stapling fifteen babies to one tree?" Lefty asked the next week, right when I was in the middle of revising my latest article.

"That's disgusting. I don't want to hear it," I snapped, pushing back from my desk to glare down on them.

"What? It's a funny joke."

"Quit telling these disgusting jokes," I shouted at my feet.

"You're not the boss of me," Lefty said.

"Yeah, me neither!" Righty added.

I ripped my shoes off my feet and whacked them against my desk, one in each hand. Each hit delivered a hard smack.

"Just die!" I screamed after I had delivered enough whacks to shut them up.

The office place froze.

Everyone was staring at me.

I looked around, holding my shoes at eye level.

"Spiders," I said. "I was trying to kill a pair of spiders on my desk. But I got them. So we're all safe now. We can go back to work."

They just went back to whatever they were doing. The rest of that day, neither of my shoes spoke again.

A week later, I decided I'd had enough. I looked up a few numbers, and I voluntarily admitted myself into the Department of Psychiatry at the University of Chicago. All I had to do was fill out an application online and a meeting would be scheduled. The next day I found my way to the front desk. I told the girl behind the counter I might possibly be schizophrenic. Her nametag read, "Pricilla."

"This is financial aid," she said.

"Oh."

This wasn't even the right building.

I asked for directions and she went through them with me, the whole time my shoes telling dirty jokes to one another. I found out what the President and the Pope have in common when they fly a plane while Pricilla drew lines on a campus map. I snatched the map, said thank you, and ran. The whole time my shoes following beneath me.

You don't exist, you don't exist, you don't exist, I kept repeating to myself as I ran. They just laughed, really enjoying it all.

"Go to hell!" I screamed at them. "Stop laughing!"

Every person within a block turned to stare at me.

"I'm schizophrenic," I told them, as if to explain, and I ran away.

At the psychiatric department I was placed on the third floor, sandwiched between the bipolars and the Alzheimers. I was assigned to Dr. Goldman, whose face reminded me of a dry, wooden plank—flat and lined with wrinkles. When we met, he too was quite drawn to my shoes. Often he'd be talking to me but looking at them, and I explained to him that they were the problem. Those damn shoes.

"The problem isn't with the shoes, Scott," he told me. "Those shoes aren't actually talking. They don't have lips that move or vocal cords to speak with. They're inanimate objects."

"So the problem is with me, you're trying to say."

"I was easing towards that, yes."

"Then the first step is to get rid of them," I said.

"Not at all," Dr. Goldman said soothingly. "When patients with extreme phobias come in here for treatment, the last thing we do is remove the cause of their fear from them. Otherwise, they'll never overcome them. Instead, we embrace the two together; often lock them in the same room."

"But I'm not afraid of my shoes."

"No. But 'they' are the reason you're here. Until you bring your mind to realize those shoes don't actually talk, you'll never be relieved of them. Who knows what will start talking to you next if you just get rid of the shoes now. Therefore, those shoes are the only ones you'll be allowed to wear in here—shoelaces off of course, just like the rest of the patients."

"That's ridiculous. I'm not going to stand for this. I'm not staying here."

"You really have no choice."

"What?"

"You've already signed yourself in, and although that was a voluntary choice, you can't be released in any way without my consent. You're here to stay for at least two weeks, at which time we'll go through your first review. Then we'll see how much longer you'll need to stay. You'll be compensated for your sojourn, of course."

I slumped in my chair, thinking about all this.

"What if I just left?" I asked.

"Without my signature? You could very well be arrested and brought right back here."

My shoes started snickering.

You don't exist.

They laughed only harder.

Being locked on that floor made me realize how much saner I was than the rest of the loonies. The umbrella man who used to ride my bus was roomed next to me, his umbrella stuffed in his pants and a big grin plastered to his face everywhere he went.

The umbrella's name was Lisa.

Some other guy named George thought he was covered in feathers. He was constantly plucking them off his skin. Except what he was plucking was his arm hair and leg hair and chest hair, and it was just too painful to watch.

Then this guy named Jean, everyday before even touching his food at breakfast, lunch or dinner, he sang the Head, Shoulders,

Knees and Toes song. In French.

He sang that song so each time he went through the words, he'd say them faster and faster, not stopping until he collapsed on his bench from exhaustion. Then he would eat.

"Tête, épaules, genoux et pieds. Genoux et pieds," Jean was singing on my third day there, and already I was getting sick of it.

"Shut up you freak! Shut up!" my right shoe screamed at Jean.

"Now you know how I feel," I told him.

"Whatever. You don't even know what any of this is about."

"What the hell's that supposed to mean?"

"You don't even know why you're here."

"I'm here because of you two," I shouted between mouthfuls of stuffed cabbage. "You *put* me in here."

"Oh *we* did? We forced you to run in here and sign yourself in?"

"Pretty much."

"Don't start this." Lefty tried to reason with Righty, but he would have it no other way.

"Look at this place," Righty said. "Just take a look at these people and what they're doing. *Really* look at them."

"I've *been* looking at them. For the past three days. They're nuts."

"No, they're spoofs."

"Spoofs? *You* two are spoofs. You don't exist."

"And yet you keep talking with us. And you listen to us. I don't think you're making much progress," said Lefty, realizing that the game had begun and he might as well support his side of the team.

"Will you shut up?"

"Not until you realize why you're in here."

"To make you shut up!" This time I screamed the words,

clutching my ears in my fists. George squawked a crow's screech and scampered away. Then, for a moment, I could actually see the black feathers on his skin, patches of them missing like a reverse Dalmatian.

I looked at Jean and realized why it made sense to sing that song before every meal. He was being thankful for his body, which was fed and nourished by the food he was about to eat. I could even hear Lisa's voice, the umbrella, reciting beautiful poems of rain to her owner.

But then it all vanished. It was like waking up from a dream, where the surety of its existence fades and you return to the real world. I was covered in sweat.

That brief experience had left me feeling warm and uncomfortable. But then everyone was just another loony again.

"None of this exists, Scott," Lefty said to me then, calming my nerves just the way a mother would after her child screamed his way out of a nightmare. "It's not real."

"And you're pointing the finger here? You're judging those guys' sanity while there you are, wearing shoes without laces, talking to me? A talking shoe for goodness sake! You're right. None of it exists. *You* don't even exist."

"Not anymore than you do, I guess."

"Cut it with all your riddles and say what you need to say."

"Just think it through for a moment, Scott. Think about how you ended up here and all the events leading up to this."

"Like what?"

"Like the glass of milk for example."

"You put it there. To mess with me."

"How could we? We don't even have *hands!* It just appeared. Glasses of milk don't appear out of nowhere. It defies logic. But you were right even in the beginning. People *don't* get hired because of their shoes."

"Yeah, you damn punk," said Righty, chiming in at the first chance he could get.

"Shut up a second, Righty. I'm talking." Then to me, "Look at these people around you."

"They're insane," I whispered, keeping my comment under my breath.

"No. They're stereotypes. *Real* schizophrenics are not this oblivious or obvious. Like Righty said before, they're spoofs. Everything is here just to surround you, and everything is the way you'd imagine it. It's like a stage fit to the actor, and you're the only one actor. No one else even exists."

Little by little, the loonies left the lunch table, disappearing towards the only door in the room. None of them looked back. A few moments later I was alone with my shoes in the luncheon.

"So I was right, you *don't* exist," I told them.

"And in a way, neither do you. Your view of existence is based on the fact that you're surrounded by other people, by scenes and objects that you directly link to their own existence. But it's not like that. You might as well be just words on a paper, or a stick figure for which everything is drawn around. Every single scene, to the last detail, is nothing more than a doll house for you to play in."

How do you respond to that? What kind of claim was this?

"No, I'm sorry that doesn't make sense."

"Then why do you think everybody left, in perfect timing, for you and us to be alone?"

I looked around. He was right. We were alone. And yet, I felt watched. It felt as though someone was watching over me. Penetrating my thoughts. Molding my emotions, even.

No.

That couldn't be.

That was a kind of paranoia that went beyond talking shoes.

"Jean had barely finished his 'Head Shoulders Knees and Toes' song. No one eats that quickly."

"So everything that happens is pre-planned, is that what you're saying?" I questioned.

"Yes. From your car breaking down to you ending up in here. All of it is happening *to* you. Everything, every single bit of it, is *for* you."

"What about *me*, then? Don't my actions matter? Don't I affect the outside world with my behavior?"

"You would if there was such a thing as an outside world. But there isn't. It's all in your head. Everything you do, everything that happens is preconceived, pre-plotted, pre-organized."

"What about free will? Can't I do, say and think whatever I want, though?"

"That's what you believe," Lefty objected. "But how do you know that someone isn't *making* you do these things? Meanwhile, you take credit for these actions and you call it free will."

"Who could *make* me do these things then, huh? I chose to come in here, didn't I?"

"Sure you did. You signed yourself in, but isn't it funny how you can't get yourself out? You're in here to embrace your existence, or the lack thereof, at least. All of this—the entire charade— was for this moment."

"What do you mean 'charade'?"

I didn't know what to think. I wasn't sure what kind of mind game they were trying to play over me.

The walls around me felt like they were made of paper. I could see words scribbled all around me. What the hell was this? My visions were becoming more and more out of control.

I wanted to regain control. I didn't want to get lost in my own insanity. I didn't want to listen to the shoes' absurdities and conspiracy theories.

"Nobody is making me do anything I don't want to do," I told the shoes.

"Your *creator*, Scott, that's who makes you. He's the one who decides everything you or anyone else does in this ploy of his. Everything else is an illusion. You're nothing but a figment of his imagination."

"You have it all wrong. *You* two are the figments of *my* imagination, and now that I'm trying to get rid of you, you're trying to pull the spin on me. Isn't that right?"

"Prove to us your existence, punk," said Righty.

"*I'm* the one wearing the shoes here, all right? You got me? You're not in control, *I* am."

"In control of jack, you asswipe."

"I've had enough of you!"

I ripped Righty off my foot with both hands and launched him across the room, harder than I ever launched that glass of milk, with more hatred than I ever had for anything else in this world. I watched that shoe hurl through the air, spinning, my eyes not missing a single frame of its motion. Then, a terrible fear struck me.

No one was watching that shoe because I was alone, but suddenly I knew it would be just like that glass of milk: unnoticed until shattered. I knew then that as soon as that shoe hit the wall it would burst into hundreds of pieces, like a porcelain vase. Because it wasn't a shoe. It was a figment that existed outside of the laws of physics or the rules of logic. It would hit the wall and shatter. I knew what it would mean.

I could see it happening in my head already – that shattered shoe – just like I had seen the feathers on George, and had heard Lisa recite those beautiful poems. All I needed was to hear that crashing sound. All I needed was for the bittersweet doubt of my existence to be slapped in the face. I closed my eyes.

Thump.

The shoe bounced off the wall, and dropped to the floor. No shards of broken pieces. No loud crashing sound. Not even a scream of pain from my shoe.

Relief filled me. Mounds and mounds of impermeable relief. I erupted into a laughter that shook me from within. I looked down at my left shoe, and it said nothing.

It just wrapped around my foot like a shoe is intended to.

"Are you there?" I asked.

Nothing.

"Are you alive?"

No response.

"Do you exist?"

I didn't expect that silence to last much longer. I thought that perhaps my shoes would wait things out, before they would ambush me again with dirty jokes and philosophical inquisitions. I waited some time in silence, expecting them to break it.

I took my left shoe off. Then I took off my socks. I curled my toes and walked around the room barefoot for a little while.

I wasn't sure whether I felt the same or different or changed. I wasn't sure if I was a better person then or a worse one.

I just knew that my shoes stopped talking.

"Then…" I said, whispering to the empty room. "Do I exist?"

Rolling Down the Mountain

Simon whipped the Buick around a light pole, the tires, near bald, skidded, and he parked his tank of an automobile at an angle, taking up two parking spaces instead of one. There were only a few cars in the lot, all of them facing the same dimly lit pizza shop.

From across the Allegheny River he could hear the dim cheer of Pirates fans screaming. Perhaps a home run. The night air fell around him. It was the kind of air you could float through.

Few stars winked an eye down from the sky, and no moon glowed from high above. A warm breeze swept through, but Simon slipped on his hooded sweater anyway. It made him feel cozy and it hid his fat body from himself.

He struggled with his weight as he stepped out of the Buick. The car's suspension rose by inches once he finally lifted himself out. The Buick was the only car he knew of that had a driver seat big enough for his body. From the passenger seat his sister, Grace, looked up at him with a meek smile, younger than him by a year, but thinner by at least a hundred and fifty pounds.

"Wait for me here one minute," he told her.

"How long are you going to be?" She wore a Grumpy the Dwarf T-shirt, and her dark wavy hair fell to her shoulders in jagged layers. He envied the fact she looked so pretty. His own thin sister. He loved her as a sister, but hated her easy beauty.

"I'll come right back out," he said, almost bitterly.

"Simon."

"What?" his voice pressed with annoyance.

"What's this about?"

"I can't tell you, yet. Maybe after tonight."

"Is it the Brotherhood?"

"I know nothing about that," he said, shut the door and turned away. The door made a rusted, clunky sound as he closed it—the music playing from the car speakers muffled. The song remained in his head though, and the same verse repeated itself in his mind.

"Who needs sleep?" the Barenaked Ladies' song asked over and over again. Not him. Hell no. He was blazing with energy. He was pumped.

Let's do this, he thought. *Let's do this.*

He felt ready for anything tonight. Anything.

Simon hopped left and right in sync to the tune playing in his head. His body was the size of boulder, but right now, this second, he didn't care. He made quick, jagged steps that formed a half-fast, improvised dance. With each hop, his wide belly bounced, his swollen cheeks quivered, and the hood of his sweatshirt bobbed up and down.

He stepped toward the pizza shop entrance, a flat-faced building with neon beer lights glowing up against the window. With a quick tug, he pulled on the handle, and the door swung open. Inside, the place held a long bar that curved around the corner of one wall. Chairs in faded Bordeaux were scattered around the rest of the tidy dining area. The floor was riddled with old stains.

Simon stopped humming the song and found himself surrounded by a few dozen guys, all standing around facing the front counter. He pulled the hood back and the crowd of guys parted a little for him to move forward. He excused himself, keeping his head low. A few of the guys patted him on the shoulder as Simon made his way forward. It made Simon feel welcomed. Accepted.

"Good, we're all here then," a sturdy young man said. He had short, cropped black hair, and he sat on the front counter with his legs dangling. He had a strong frame, and his bright face held a brimming smile and the jawline of a Roman god. He was a bit of a legend among these men.

"I was starting to think you weren't gonna' come, Simey."

"Couldn't miss this," Simon said low, his eyes downcast and sheepish. As he spoke, a rush of eagerness sunk into his throat, pounding back at his beating chest.

"Good to hear," the other man said. Then he redirected his attention to the rest of the group. "Now, I see we got some new faces tonight. Good. We're in for some fun."

They all listened quietly as he spoke, watching.

"You guys have it easy tonight. Much easier than when some of your senior brothers and I had to go through initiation. Tonight's your only test. You pass, you're in."

Simon's cheeks burned red with anticipation. He was finally going to get the chance to prove himself worthy of the Brotherhood. *Brotherhood.* He liked the sound of that word. It formed a sense of unity and strength inside his head. The sound of the word spoke of acceptance. Better than family. Better than fraternity.

Simon thought of fraternities as a gathering of village idiots, wanting to create their own social hierarchy. This was different. This would be a group of brothers he could call his own. Friends. That word, now—yes, friends—that word made his belly soft. Of course, college frats had room for chubby guys like him, too. Except the role of a keg-guzzling drunk didn't appeal to him. No. It would be hard to fit in a fraternity without the beer.

For Simon, joining the Brotherhood was still only a fuzzy fantasy. He was still wrapped up in the word. He knew nothing about it except of what he had heard from a few rumors. Every year the Brotherhood of the Breath recruited new members who would have to pass a test to join. A few years back, Simon heard, those who joined had to battle one another inside a bamboo cage. Man versus man. He felt that if he could do something like that, if Simon could battle in a cage or overcome some kind of gladiator test.

In truth, he didn't know what that would mean. It was fantasy. It was glory, somehow. He had no idea of what the Brotherhood would offer him in the future. But it was this very unknown that attracted him most. It was having this open-ended possibility that he could mold inside his mind. The Brotherhood gave him a chance for acceptance.

Dan Pietro was their leader, sitting calmly on the bar with his feet dangling back and forth. He was the Brotherhood's elder. He spoke to them now of overcoming fears and the self. He spoke of spiritual strength, and overcoming one's inner struggle.

"Tonight is about you," Pietro said, roaming a finger across their faces. "If you don't think you're ready, step out now. Tonight you become brothers. Brothers of this very earth. Formed of mud turned to flesh. Tonight we'll find out if you've got the lungs to breathe in the Brotherhood."

"*Brotherhood of the Breath! Brotherhood of the Breath! Brotherhood of the Breath!*" they all chanted, as if in response to a eulogy. At each chant, they pumped their fist on the shoulder of the man beside them. Simon felt the fist, felt the breath of life surrounding him, felt the anticipation of blood wanting to surge.

"Last chance to step out now," Pietro said, looking at each one of the guys in the face. None moved. None flinched. "Alright then. Leave your cars here. We're going for a ride. But first, bow your heads."

They all lowered their chins to their chests, holding their fists in front of their chests, touching at the knuckles. They recited the Brotherhood's Creed, memorized by verse and rote, repeated through sleep and day, carved into each of their minds like a battle scar.

> *I stand united with my Brother's breath*
> *None is truer than the Brotherhood self*
> *My flesh, my mud, is within their skin*
> *Their dust, their dirt, is within my own*
> *Creed with sweat, and cry our blood*
> *Through eyes that see no other cell*
> *Breathe my life, and see no death*
> *Through sand or storm my back holds strong*
> *Sustaining firm my Brother's lungs*
> *For wind nor gust will make us fall*
> *We stand united in the Brother's breath*

Simon loved every word of the creed. He spoke each word with firm relief. Speaking those verses made him feel like standing still under the sky's clouds with gusts of wind passing through him. It was like learning to breathe anew.

"Let's ride," said Pietro.

Ride. To Simon the word sounded mysterious and adventurous. A band of brothers going out for a ride.

They all stepped out into the warm night. Simon could barely feel the air around him, it was so close to his own body temperature. A large cattle truck pulled in front of the pizza shop, rumbling with its hinges creaking. Its mechanical grinding ruptured through the hollow silence of the empty parking lot. The guys laughed and hooted at its sight.

"What the hell is this?" Simon's sister asked him as he ran back to the car to tell her she could go on without him. She looked at him with glossy and quivering eyes. Did he see fear in them? Nonsense. Nothing to fear.

"What's going on, Simon?" Grace asked again.

"Don't worry about it."

"Where you all going?"

"For a ride," he said, trying to sound the way he felt inside, but fell short of expressing the rumble that ran down his chest. He shot her with some directions to get home and then turned away toward the truck.

"It's easier if you go through Oakland. Avoid the construction that way," he said.

"How are you getting home?" she shouted after him.

But he was already running after the back of the cattle truck and hopped onto the trailer with the rest. The metal trailer stank of country life and cattle dung. Shreds of hay were scattered across the floor, along with a few puddles of urine. Simon and the rest of the guys tried to avoid stepping on anything liquid. Some of them brought their shirts over their noses to filter away the smell. The only one not bothered by the stench was a thick-boned kid with a neck the size of a barn. He wore a flannel shirt and worn, leather boots.

He looked at everyone else and chuckled as they tried their best not to choke at the smell. He took in an exaggerated, deep breath and exhaled as he said, "Smells just like home!"

"Howdy-ho, Hillbilly!" someone joked. They all laughed and punched each other on the shoulder with a fist. This was their thing. This was their sign. They knew one another by it. Simon held himself inside the moment, watched the faces around him with a sense of longing. He had never had this. He had never had a moment with friends where nothing mattered. Here, inside this universal instant, it didn't matter to Simon that he was on the verge of obese and had never had friends before this night. His own sheepishness felt distant. He was here. He was now. Breathing the breath of each second. Everything was on the outside right now, and he was on the inside… untouchable.

Two of the Brothers at the end of the trailer shoved each other back and forth, trying to make the other step on the big puddle of urine, laughing, throwing ridiculous insults at one another.

"Come on piss stain."

"Shut up you lard ass."

It was great.

As the truck sped down the highway, Simon couldn't help but wonder, though… Where in the hell had they gotten this truck? Where were they going? He wondered these things without really needing an answer. It wasn't relevant. They were going for a ride.

That's what mattered. The trailer and hinges jostled and squeaked back and forth. They all hung onto the holes in the trailer as the truck rumbled on.

The engine made a deep, grinding sound as they took a sharp exit that knocked them around.

The landscape changed in one sudden turn. From city to hillsides, in just a few miles of road. They were heading south toward West Virginia, Simon realized.

Simon watched the hills pass and the twining roads twist away through the trailer's holes. Back in Pittsburgh the sky had been clear and warm, but clouds were already forming in the stretch ahead. Small droplets of rain hit the roof of the trailer, and the farther they drove, the heavier the rain became. The raindrops sounded like fingers tapping, then knuckles knocking, then fists pounding. The trailer was like being inside a hammering drum. It felt like they were entering another region of the world.

An hour later, the truck's tires rumbled over a gravel road that cut through a field of trees. The transmission pulled hard in low gear, trudging up a hill, then down again, and twisting around a tight bend. Inside the trailer, Simon and the rest of the Brothers tried to hold on, but they were battered against the inner walls of the trailer. They were in the heart of the Pennsylvanian country side. Out in the dim distance, Simon could see a field of corn spread like savanna grass, spreading out to reach eternity.

"We in the boonies, boys," someone said, taking his best shot at a southern accent.

No one laughed. There was a sense of wonder in that tin can silence.

Then the trailer door split open, creaking as the heavy hinges swiveled. Dan Pietro and some other guy stood looking up at them.

The second man wore a pair of padded working gloves and a parka that draped down to his feet, as if he had known it would rain.

"All set?" Pietro asked the other.

The guy in the parka pointed out somewhere—pointing high. Simon couldn't see from behind the crowd of guys. Pietro looked in that direction for a moment and nodded. Good, he seemed to say with that nod. Then he waved at the rest of the Brothers inside the trailer, calling them to come down.

They all climbed out, hooting and yipping once again to kill the silence. As Simon stepped off, his feet sunk an inch into the mud. The gravel had ended about fifty yards back. Thunder struck to light the world around him. For a short moment he saw everything as if holding a panoramic view. To his left, the line of trees cut off, and the land precipitated into a black hole. The savanna cornfield to his right seemed to blend right into a hillside. The hill itself, though, shot straight up into the sky. It was like staring up a wall of dirt and grass. The angle of it was impossible. Its muddy, rocky land jutted forth, subdivided with patches of sporadic grass growing like long turfs of hair. The falling rain melted right into that hill, absorbed by it.

Devoured by it.

In the wavering glow of lightning, that hill seemed to be breathing. Like one enormous lung. Simon stood there, facing the hill, not realizing he was breathing at the same rhythm of that hill. Breathing alongside his Brothers.

The guy in the parka had pointed to the top of that hill. But no. This was more than just a hill. This was a mountain.

"Gentlemen!" Pietro shouted, the word barely making it through the air, now thick with humidity and falling water. His arm shot up to the hill, but his eyes were fixed on them. The Brothers all stood surrounding Pietro, a large huddle of them in the splashing rain, looking like small boys compared to the mountain that towered over them.

From the blackened sky, another thunderbolt flashed, making the clouds around it appear for a split second. They waited for the sound of thunder to reach their ears, and when it did, it sounded like the roar of the ocean crashing against rocks.

"Whoa," they exhaled in unison, dazed.

The rain increased, drenching their clothes. The splat of the raindrops hitting the ground made it hard for them to hear much else. It sounded like an auditorium full of kids battering their feet on the floor. Simon pulled his slick hair back, and blew air at the water that ran over his lips.

"Faith and allegiance to the Brotherhood are not enough," Pietro shouted over the rain, pointing to the incredibly steep hill. "Action speaks louder than faith. Louder than allegiance. Without action, the rest is hollow, meaningless and empty."

His words vibrated against their ears. Against the rain. Against the mud and their faces.

He went on.

"This is 'The Mountain.' Do you all see that white flag at the top? When you see that flag drop, that's your signal to start climbing. At the top of the Mountain you'll touch the flagpole. You do this…" he paused, watching them, "and your breath will bleed with Brotherhood."

"Ain't we gonna' be brawling 'gainst one 'nother?" the hillbilly guy asked, his hair glued to his brow.

"No," Pietro said. "You're not fighting each other to see who gets in. You'll be fighting yourselves. You'll overcome your own doubts and exhaustion and fears. Action, my brothers. Without action, your faith is nothing to the Brotherhood."

He waited for those final words to settle, and then said, "I'll meet you at the top."

With that, Pietro hopped on the truck with the guy wearing the parka and drove off. The truck rumbled, following a steep and narrow road that circled the other side of the mountain.

The Brotherhood recruits faced the steep hillside. Their necks tilted all the way back just to look at the top. A white light shone at the fluttering white flag strapped tightly to the top of the pole. The seconds passed. They watched and waited. Simon's stomach was filled with a fluttering, and his muscles twitched with anticipation.

He was scared, he realized. *What if I don't make it? I'm too damn fat for this.* Breathing heavily, his wide chest expanded and contracted. He could *feel* his own weight right now. He could feel his bulk. There was no way he could make it. His wet, sticky clothes clung to his skin like tape.

Then the flag dropped. Simon let out his breath. They all charged the base of the mountain like soldiers fighting to gain ground at Iwo Jima. It wasn't a race. It didn't matter who climbed to the top first, nor who overcame the mountain last. All they had to do was reach that flag. All they had to do was overcome this mountain. Overcome this monstrous, breathing thing that screamed with every flash of lightning.

Simon ran as fast as he could, but he couldn't keep up with the others. The base started off impossibly steep, and the men charged it at an angle, cutting into the slope with their legs. Once they gained some ground, the hillside took gentler curves. As Simon reached the slope of the hill, he grappled the ground with his hands and feet. His fingers dug into the soft earth, slicing through as if it were clay. With the first kick of his legs, trying desperately to hurtle himself up, his sneakers slipped on the grimy soil, and his face smacked into the mud.

Nose first.

It smelled of earthworms and stale rain. The sludge of mud covered his face in brown patches, resembling war paint. He groaned aloud, and rolls of dirt flowed into his mouth, forming clumps around his teeth. He spat out the dirt and gave a shriek of determination. He would do this. He would overcome this bulk.

Simon's nickname as a kid was "Firestone" because you could roll him like a tire. The insults had grown only worse throughout high school. It was for the ghosts of these teasings and jeerings that he would do this. It was for those faces who spat insults that he would overcome this mountain. It was because of this earth. Because of this world. No, the hell with the world. This was him. It was just him and the mountain. Nothing else existed under the thunderstorm of billowing clouds and laughing rain. He alone would defeat this.

Using his fingers as claws, he forced himself up the slippery ground. After only a few yards, his muscles started to ache. He pounded his knees to the ground, and kept kicking up. The rain fell in his mouth as he gasped for strength. He climbed upward through an ocean of mud.

With his fingers, he grabbed whatever he could reach. Patches of grass tore away in fistfuls, each time making Simon lose leverage. Looking up, he could see that most of the other guys had already made it halfway up. *The hell with them for leaving me behind. Damn you brothers. This is my hill.*

Between his fingers, layers of mud flowed around his knuckles, turning his hands into webbed palms. Every inch of his clothes was already drenched, and patches of mud spread over him like blood stains. Simon leaped for a root sticking out of the ground. It was gnarled and wooden. Just as he reached for it, a skinny guy ahead of him with long chicken legs slipped. As the boy lost leverage, he came sliding down toward Simon, his one foot slamming into Simon's jaw. Simon's face jerked back, a burst of pain hanging on his lip. He held on to the root, praying it would support his bulk.

The other guy hung onto Simon's hoodie, which clung to Simon's wide body, who gripped onto the root, which held onto the mountain. Everything connected. No chances or coincidences here. Either the root would hold, or it would snap from the mountain. The mountain, their enemy. Everything seemed flipped somehow. With his free arm, Simon grabbed hold of the other boy and tried to help him up again.

He shouted something to Simon, but it got lost in the rain.

A few feet ahead, Simon saw another vine-like plant that burst out from the ground. He grabbed for it, meaning to pull himself up, but as he tugged, the roots tore from the soil, and he was flung backwards. He went tumbling over his spine, crashing down onto the nape of his neck with his legs up in the air, then flipped once more back on his barreled chest. The slam winded him, and a rush of pain spread out from his chest like a rose with fish hooks for petals.

He was at the bottom again.

For a moment he could not breathe, and took in only dry gasps of air. His every breath wheezed into his lungs like a bad cramp in his chest. He looked up one more time, seeing the rest of his Brothers minutes away from reaching the top.

But then, something happened.

The Brothers leaped aside, dispersing left and right as huge, boulder-like object came rolling down the mountain. A scrawny kid jumped out to the side, almost clashing into someone else, as one of the boulder whiffed past him. Two more of these huge rolls pushed off the top of the mountain and came rushing down, eager to hit any one of them in their path.

Another boulder tilted over the edge, hesitated, then plunged down like the rest. It swooped off a small incline that stuck out from the ground, flipping high as if flew off of a launching pad into the air. The boulder was airborne. Spinning. Holding. Hanging there for the longest time. But then it came down fast. Faster than it ever went up.

By this point Simon had lost all track of his body. Lost all hold of his senses. He didn't even realize he was halfway up the hill once again, until one of those whizzing, rolling things bounced right for him. He ducked, hugging the mud, and the thing just missed him by a foot or so. Most of the guys had slowed down or slipped back to avoid getting hit, and now he was nose-to-nose with most of them. Then… finally it happened.

The heavyset cowboy dove out of the way of one tumbling roll, but instead leapt right in front of another. The boulder-like object smacked him like a bag of flour exploding. No, not flour. Like fine strands of hair. Those things rolling towards them, eager to pulverize every body in sight, weren't rocks at all. They were bales of hay.

Simon watched the cowboy fly back twenty feet down the hill. He slammed his shoulder blades against the trunk of a misshapen tree. As Simon stopped to watch, one of the bales whisked past him, scratching his cheek.

One by one, the rolls of hay struck the Brothers with deadly accuracy. Their bodies flung like rag dolls and spun in the air, only left to slam back down onto the muddy earth again.

Simon rolled to the right as one of the boys came skidding down the slope. Then he dodged to the left again as another bale rolled towards him. Then another. His fingers dug into the ground and he scampered away again, but came across another boulder's path. The rolls of hay came from every angle. There must have been at least a dozen of those bales coming down at every moment. The stream of them never ended. They filled the sky as they tumbled down at them. Simon ducked behind a large rock that stuck from the ground like a hangnail.

The hay kept coming. The rest of the boys were now scattered across the land. They were separated. They were alone. Each of them on their own. The only sound Simon could hear was that *whisk-whisk-whisk* of rolling hay. Like nails scratching dandruff. Even thunder heeded to those bales in sound.

Simon came out from behind the rock and started climbing again. He didn't know where the pole was anymore. He felt disoriented and for a static moment he didn't even know if he was climbing up or down. It was that sense of vertigo he often got when watching the road swoop past him while riding in the car. Was he swooping past or sitting still? Reaching skyward, or scampering downward?

Another roll sped toward him, but on its way down it smacked a tree stump. The large mass of hay spun like a coin, flipping around and round sideways. Turfs of hay tore away from the bundle. In mid air, the twine holding the roll together snapped, and before the entire mass could hit Simon, it turned into a confetti mist of yellow hair.

He felt a sense of laughter inside him, which wouldn't come. He felt like he'd escaped death. The snips of hay came down around him like ashen flakes from the sky. All slowly and in swooping zig-zags.

He resumed his climb. The crawl became a trot, the trot became a rush, the rush became a sprint… all the while skipping and dodging the rolls rumbling past him. Webs of pain stretched along his arms and legs. His muscles felt like meat gnawed by rabid dogs. He couldn't take it any longer, but now the ground had started to feel less slippery beneath him. Stealthily, he kept his body low to the ground. He looked up for an instant and caught a glimpse of another tire of hay pouncing down towards him. He ducked back down, pressing his chin to his chest and his nose to the earth. The hay rolled over him without leaving a scratch.

He went on climbing, but every reach with his arms made his muscles stretch tighter.

A few more reaches—

A couple more—

His hand fell flat on the top of the mountain. Like that. In an instant. At the top, as if the climb had never happened. He lunged his body over the plateau's lip. *Welcome*, said that ground. It spoke to him. He would've kissed the hilltop if only it had a mouth. The breathing stopped. The world was flat again. Simon settled for a hug instead, arms outstretched to his sides and his palms squeezing the dirt.

Another lightning flashed in the sky, and the flagpole appeared before him. Then the flash was gone, and the pole disappeared back into darkness, hiding amidst the cascade of raindrops.

Touch it, he told himself. Or maybe it was the mountain speaking to him. The trees and rain and clouds shouting to him at once. As if in a single voice. A single language.

All his energy had escaped him, down the hillside slope, and now Simon didn't have a single spike of adrenaline left in him to finish the sprint. But he had to get to that pole. He wanted it so badly that hugging this ground wasn't enough to remind him he was alive.

With his flabby arms, he pushed himself up. His legs slid again down the slope, dragging his torso down with their weight. He was going down the hill again. He tried to push with his legs, but each of his kicks slipped. His fingers traced trails on the mud. He was sliding backward.

He knew that this had been too good to be true. He knew he didn't deserve to be in the Brotherhood. That he would tumble backwards and smack the ground and hurt himself to the point of needing a trip to the hospital. Or worse yet, to the point of giving up.

But he caught himself.

With his elbows and knees he crawled low to the ground. A movement of inches. Determination was the only manna that could feed him. Was anyone waiting for him by the pole? Was there anyone in the vicinity of sound or pain? Yes, his Brothers were all there. They were all waiting for him around the pole. Waiting and cheering him on.

But what if he failed to reach the pole? What if he gave up? Would they abandon him and forget his existence?

He didn't want to find out.

He moved forward, crawling toward the pole. So this is what muscle failure felt like. Pushing and pulling. Moving closer. Reaching, stretching, scrawling pathways in the dirt. Drawing history in the mud. And once he reached the pole, what he saw was simple: his Brothers, standing around him, covered in mud. They were of this mud. Made of this dirt. Made of dust and returning to it.

He had looked forward to this day for a long while now, and now he had it, but he was covered in mud and so were they.

The word lodged in his mind.

Mud.

He thought it again.

Mud.

In the end, this is all they were. There was nothing magical about this brotherhood. Ashes to ashes, and dust to dust. That was all.

Was this what he had crawled up a mountain for? So he could be surrounded by mud? United with dirt?

Their faces cheered him, picked him up with as many arms as it would take to lift his bulk. His slippery, heavy body escaped their grasp several times. They shouted for him, and laughed with his cries. They were one with the earth. Of the earth. Of a single breath. United under this darkness. No more lightning dazzled the sky that night. Brothers, they were, but of what substance and value, Simon did not know.

Chase

This was the night Rob would chase the deer. He would later deny the event had meant anything to him. He would later remember it as a silly event not worth discussing with anyone. It wasn't the type a story you would tell your buddies at the bar and have a big laugh about it. He was a little buzzed from the beer and it was just a foolish, spurt-of-the-moment thing. The chase had meant nothing to him.

It was all silly, really.

A story not really worth telling.

He sat down at a pavilion tucked in the woods behind his house. He wasn't sure to whom the pavilion belonged. Nobody took care of it. The wood was weathered and splintering in certain spots.

He sat the six-pack down next to him and stretched out in his seat. He felt his muscles tighten like twisted twine.

He finished his first beer in solitude. Then his second. Then his third.

He was down in the valley of the woods, but up on the hill he could hear late-night traffic rush by.

The ache in his muscles rose in waves up his back and shoulders. He felt the knots tighten under his skin as he massaged his neck with his hands. He closed his eyes and tried to breathe in the cool night air. It smelled of dry leaves. He kept massaging, trying to forget his surroundings and fill himself with that smell.

Dried leaves, he kept thinking to himself. *Man, I love that smell.*

"I hope it doesn't rain," he said. The rain would ruin that autumn smell. It would turn the leaves' odor drenched and choked.

He began his fourth beer and tried to drown the pain of a twelve-hour day of carpentry and construction. He worked for his father. A business he couldn't abandon. Even when Hailey told him the news, the fantastic news of her job offer in New York City, breaking into fashion with some major high-end clothing line. He didn't know fashion. He didn't know clothing. Those details didn't matter to him. What mattered was that she was moving eight hours away for some job.

"Not just a job. This is big. This could be it. It could define my career," she had told him.

"It's clothes," he'd told her. "You can design clothes anywhere. You can just do your designs from here and, like, email them."

"And *you*," she had said playfully, hopping on his lap, kissing his forehead. "You can do construction work anywhere. Even New York. Heck! *Especially* New York."

But he couldn't do that. Couldn't abandon his father who was in poor health and depended on Rob to steady the ship. Their contracting company was called *Herald and Son*. If he left for New York, the business name would just be *Herald*, and then Herald would die and then it would just be… nothing.

So he'd let her go to New York. How did the saying go? If you love them you'll…

Chase after her. That's what he *should* have done. He should have gone after her.

He slammed the bottle down next to him. It startled him. He didn't realize he'd brought it down so forcefully.

"Damn," he said.

What time was it? He didn't have his watch. Didn't have his phone with him. He was alone in the woods in some half-dilapidated pavilion, finishing his fourth straight beer, thinking about her again.

At least they hadn't lied to each other. At least he hadn't said, "I'll come visit you," knowing well that work and the distance would prevent him, and at least she hadn't said, "I'll wait for you," knowing well the city life and the crowds would have tempted her. Those lies would have made their split unbearable. Truly unbearable.

"Yeah, sure," he said to no one. "Because this is so much better."

He finished his fourth and popped open his fifth.

He brought the bottle to his lips, but a rustle of leaves stopped him.

Under the cool moon, he watched the trees around him. The air seemed to cut right between the branches. But it wasn't the breeze that rustled those leaves. At first, he saw nothing.

Then… his eyes adjusted to the figure ahead. He wasn't sure how long she had been standing there, but it felt to him as though she had been watching him for a while. He had an urge to shoo her away. He wanted to return to his solitude and drinking and be left alone to his thoughts.

But something appealed to him about that figure.

She stood there, watching him. Then, as soon as they had noticed each other, she lowered her neck and grazed the grass.

An urge rose in him. A very strange urge to walk up to her and pet her.

He took a long gulp of beer and set the bottle back down.

She raised her head again and they found themselves staring into each other's eyes. How weird it was to stare at wild nature in the eyes like that. And to have it stare back at him with both intent and awe.

"That's…" Rob began, cleared his throat, and tried again, "That's a deer."

His words seemed distant. He didn't recognize them as his own.

Rob's lips parted, but he would never find the words to explain how he felt that moment.

A strange tingle rose in him. Like getting flicked in the ear, with a warm afterglow following the initial sting.

He stood, slowly, very slowly, and he remembered his body's aches. A joint popped into place, felt like his knee, and the deer twitched at the sound, but then held her ground.

What does she want?

The deer took a step. Paused. Then walked casually closer to the pavilion's entrance.

He was no deer whisperer and certainly not an animal expert, but he'd never seen a wild animal in his entire life walk so casually up to him like that before. Nobody would believe this.

The moon's glare skimmed off of her coat, outlining the shape of her body.

"What do you want?" he asked.

He was actually talking to her. And that felt so stupid to him, and he almost sat back down to ignore her, but then…

She nodded her head to the side, and he could have *sworn* she was trying to call him to her. *No. Come on. That's ridiculous.*

He thought about Hailey, then. How she had always played hard to get, even from the start. They'd met at a park. He was wearing a flannel shirt, jeans and a pair of work boots. She wore a pair of jogging shorts and a tank top over a sports bra. They chatted for a minute while she stretched, and then casually she'd said, "I'm going to go jogging now. You're welcome to come with."

"Like this?" he had said, pointing at himself. "Not exactly running clothes here."

"The invite's there," she'd said, smiled, and without a pause she turned and jogged off.

He didn't wait. He jogged right after her. They went for three or four miles. His jeans were black with sweat and he had blisters on his feet the size of grapes by the end of it. But he finished the run with her phone number and a date.

They dated for two years and he knew he would propose eventually. He loved her playfulness. She loved how he was always willing to come after her and win her over every time. She was constantly testing him. Even until the end, by moving to New York.

And he had let her go.

Bad choice, man. Bad choice. You know how flirty she can get. You know she'll find some guy at Central Park in no time, entice him for a jog, and then she'll never run back to you.

This was ridiculous. This deer. She was still standing there. Staring at him. Waiting for him to make a move.

"Go away," he told her. "We're not doing this."

But a strange part of him wanted to. He wanted to chase the deer and catch her. If nothing else, for the sheer fact that he could say he did. Anyone could hunt down a deer with a rifle, but who could actually say they caught a deer with their bare hands?

He had a smirk on his face. He could feel it.

He felt caught inside a sort of dream. He wasn't sure if it was the beer or the allure of wilderness enticing him. Inviting him. Could he feel her heartbeat? No. Come on. Of course he couldn't. Could he?

His heart thumped. He felt a cheer in his chest, like the feeling of being inside a crowded stadium and your bones vibrating to the sound of everyone screaming. There wasn't even a steady rhythm to his breathing. Yet, he must have seen at least a hundred deer in his life before tonight. Never had he felt like this. Except, this deer was an object of beauty in a moment of need. He felt held in that moment, like he was hanging there, dazzled by the meaning of this doe staring at him. How long had they been staring at one another.

The entire moment lasted about two seconds.

The Doe took another few steps closer, looking for a fresher patch of grass to graze. Now she stood an easy twenty feet away. His heart was beating so hard and so loudly that he feared it might scare her away.

She took one step back.

And then she began trotting around the pavilion, keeping her face on Rob as if inviting him to a game. Her trotting was so in sync with his heartbeat that he confused the two for the same thing. Even this he would later blame on the beer. Each patting on the ground from her feet held another beat in his chest.

"I want her."

He felt like he was swinging by a pendulum. But who was he talking about? The deer? Did he want the deer? Or was he thinking of Hailey then, wishing he had chased after her all the way to New York.

I'm going to catch her.

She sped around one more lap and then stopped in front of the small pavilion's opening. She tilted her head crookedly, putting her curiosity on display. Everything she did seemed like she was putting on a show. Every gesture was exaggerated and playful. She stood with an inviting look. Her chest expanded and contracted in heavy breathing, and Rob saw that this was his chance.

Rob knew she wouldn't simply allow him to approach her and pet her. This was a game soon to become a chase. Yeah, he would have to run for her.

Standing there, he stuffed his hands in his pockets and looked away, bluffing disinterest.

The doe looked disappointed at his disinterest. She dropped her head and stepped a little closer. Then a little closer still.

He bolted for her. She scrambled with surprise, and her legs tangled for a moment, caught her balance and took off.

The chase was on.

She went around the pavilion clockwise. Rob ran the other direction, meeting her halfway. As they were about to collide, her legs scrambled in an effort to stop. He planted his feet but didn't leap for her. He didn't want to catch her so early in the game. After all, how fun was a game if it ended so soon?

Instead of turning around, the doe shifted her weight and brushed right past him, pulling her body away from him. He could smell her as she went by, and although her fur didn't smell of dried leaves, her coat held an aroma that sparked his nerves. Her smell was full, musty almost, but held a sweet afterglow. Wild nature. As all of her glow took hold of his senses, he turned and stretched his arm for her but grasped nothing but air. He spun around, but already she was out of reach. He ran. It hurt. His legs felt stiff and his joints sore, but he ran all the same.

The doe bobbed in and out, between trees, piercing deeper into the backwoods and away from the road. She tried to outrun him using her agility, but he kept up, dodging the trees easily. Sweat formed on his forehead. The breeze helped him keep cool through the run. Rob felt his muscles straining, but he pushed through. Maybe she was getting tired too, but he didn't know.

As the doe cut in again, she slipped on a pile of leaves. Her legs tripped and she tumbled to the grass.

Rob dove for her.

But he fell short.

She sprung up again from the ground and headed back toward the pavilion. Rob picked himself up. He ran hard, pushing the tread of his shoes into the ground. The muscles in his thighs began to throb, first in a mild heat, and then turning more and more intense. The throbbing spread down to his calves, pulling them stiff.

He ran with all he had left, watching the Doe's tail in front of his eyes, but still too far to actually grasp it. With one arm stretched out, he tried to reach it, but his fingers fell a hair too short. He kicked harder with his legs and then stretched for the tail again. He could finally touch it. He did.

But just as soon, it slipped from his grasp.

Rob panted hard and could feel his whole chest in his throat.

If he wanted to catch her, it had to be now. She could outrun him for days.

The Doe cut low beneath hanging branches, and Rob just plowed through them with an arm to his face. They ran past the pavilion.

By now Rob's legs were giving in, and the Doe was heading up the hill toward the road. He followed, feeling hot and red all over.

Sweat drenched his brow and his shirt stuck to his skin.

That hill was a burn to climb. In another hop, the Doe would be over the hill and maybe gone for good. Rob had just once choice.

Leap.

As he went through the air he knew he would make it. All he had to do was wrap his arms around her legs and tackle her to the ground. Everything turned breathless and still in those airborne milliseconds. Nothing ever moved slower in his life than in that moment.

Her odor was pungent.

Then, real time resumed and one of her hind legs cracked him across the jaw. Rob's neck snapped back to the left. That kick smacked his cheek into his teeth. He could taste the blood before ever hitting the ground.

His head bounced off the turf.

The doe trotted away, looking back for only an instant, knowing that she had won this little game. She hopped onto the road, not looking in either direction, when a gnashing sound cut through the air. It was a long honk, followed by the screech of tires. A bright pair of beams drowned her body. But she didn't stop, and the car—a Ford Explorer—swerved out of the way.

Rob closed his eyes. He couldn't look, afraid that the car might clip the doe in the last second. Then, a crash forced his eyes to squint harder, screwing his whole face into rivers of wrinkles. Once he opened them again, he saw the Explorer smashed against a tree trunk on the side of the road.

Rob looked across the road but couldn't see the deer. No movement showed inside the car, and now he felt too weak to go see if the driver was okay. The pain was all over him. He wasn't sure what to do with himself.

She's gone.

You never stood a chance.

She was gone into the night, and Rob didn't have enough strength to stand again.

A Crown Victoria drove past. The car slowed down as it approached the crashed Explorer, then stopped. An older gentleman got out and checked on the other driver. No. He wasn't exactly old. But the man's hair was bleach-blond, and it had appeared white at first. He wore a dark business suit.

I'm sure he's okay. I'm sure he's fine.

He let a moment pass.

"I'm fine," he said. Slowly he sat up. Sore. His entire body. It was so incredibly sore.

He had one more beer left at the pavilion. He could go back and finish it and let his pain wash away. Or he could go home and go to bed and try to forget his idiotic attempt at trying to chase a deer. What the hell was he thinking?

He wasn't sure which he wanted more: that last beer or sleep. Or Hailey. He wanted Hailey.

He pressed his tongue against the inside of his cheek. He spat out some blood then rubbed his jaw where it hurt the most.

This chase had not gone his way, but maybe he still held a chance with Hailey. Tomorrow he would drive straight to New York. He would call off for a couple of days, and he would drive straight there to surprise her. Hopefully his dad would hold off at least that long. But tonight… Well.

Tonight he would finish that beer.

The Staring Game

I started the staring game because I wanted to see what it felt like to be God. To watch people closely, and judge who they are. To stare at them and develop a commentary about their lives. Inspect their cleanliness. Their demeanor. Their level of self confidence. Their gestures toward friends. Their words against strangers.

The game started when I was shaving in my small Chicago apartment one day. My bathroom window looks out to a back alley that's filled mostly with trash. Drug dealers go back there to do their business. And normally I wouldn't care. There's nothing really interesting in people exchanging money for drugs.

But one Sunday morning I watched a young man and a woman meet a coke dealer together. The girl was beautiful, with wild, dark hair. She dressed like a hippy, with hundreds of bead necklaces and colorful bracelets. The thing that caught my eye, though, was her tattoos. Her body was covered in them.

They weren't your typical tattoos. They were words. At least that's what it looked like from three stories high. Her knuckles, her arms, her shoulders, her ankles... They were everywhere. When I first saw her, I was angry with her. Angry that she would ruin her skin and her body by covering herself in words like that. But the more I saw her coming back, the more I felt compassion for her. She seemed trapped. Trapped in her tattoos and those words. Trapped in this city. Her gestures were jittery and distrusting. She seemed troubled. It made me wonder about her.

What kind of woman covers herself in tattoos like that? Just words. Not pictures or artwork. There was something poetic about it, but also disturbing.

The couple came to pay for their fix on a weekly basis. I watched the exchange from my private window, and I felt a little bit what God must feel like. High and above watching humanity effectively destroy itself.

Then one day, the guy came to pick up the cocaine, but the woman wasn't with him. He was with a little boy. What kind of man brings a boy to a drug deal? And the dealer made nothing of it. Here's your money. Here's your drugs. Okay, have a wonderful addicted life now. Take care. Bye, little boy.

After that, I never saw the couple again. I never saw the woman with the tattoos. But by then, I was hooked. The staring game had taken hold of me, and now I needed my fix.

The rest of the dealer's customers were boring. Just regular junkies. So I had to take my game outside of my apartment.

On my free weekends, I would go to a park, or a coffee house, or a bar at night, or anywhere crowded, and I'd pick a person and stare at them for a while.

There's a coffee place by the lake where the girl barista has a tattoo of a flying crow on the back of her neck. She never smiled at women with children. She looked disgusted by their motherhood.

The businessman who walks his terrier in the park carries a green baggie with him, but never actually uses it to clean after the dog. He carries it in hand just for show. The terrier seems old. He lets the dog off the leash most days even though there are signs that prohibit it. He cleaned up after the dog only once, and only because he noticed me staring at him.

There's a dago-looking dude at the Irish pub on the South Side who will drink nothing but Jagerbombs and Yuenglings. He never buys anyone a drink. Ever. He always leaves three dollars for a tip regardless of who is with him or how much he's had to drink. He comes and goes with a different woman every week.

I thought I'd begin hating people rather quickly when I started this game. After all, if God exists, he'd hate us for sure by now. What else can you feel toward a people who ignore you for centuries, and whose favorite activities are consumption and self-gratification? What else can you feel toward a people who murder, lie, steal, rape and abuse their own bodies? Then they blame you for everything that's wrong with this world.

But in playing my staring game, I didn't get the benefit of watching people in their most vulnerable settings. In order to avoid getting caught, I had to play the game in thick crowds. I rode the public bus to work just so I could watch people during the week. There's a man who thinks his shoes are talking to him. He's young and handsome, and if he didn't talk to his shoes, he'd look like a regular guy. From the look of it, his relationship with the shoes has gone sour. He does a lot of shouting.

But as the game went on, I was less interested in being secretive. In fact, most times I *wanted* people to feel watched. I wanted them to know I was there, judging their actions, decisions, discomforts.

I felt more a sense of amusement than hatred toward these strangers. Some of them were truly despicable people, sure; like the number of guys at the bar who got young women wasted just so they could drag them out to their car, practically carrying their drunken bodies on their shoulders. Or the drug dealer in the back alley, who will sell to anyone, even children. One time I watched him beat an old junkie to the ground and stomp on him because he owed him money.

What kind of God just watches these things happen and doesn't intervene? How passive and removed can you possibly be from our suffering. It made me question whether he exists at all.

I watched the junkie lie on the ground for a long while.

God, do something! Help him out!

I'm not sure if that was a prayer or what. Did God enjoy watching the man suffer? I felt repulsed by it. Saddened.

I thought I was going to watch this man die right before my eyes, but several minutes later, he stumbled away. He was okay. He was alive, at least.

No. It wasn't hatred that I felt toward these people. Perhaps a sense of pity. But who was I? Just some guy with an office job and a slight addiction for watching people. Who was *I* to hate them?

But I *would* discover hatred. Not my hatred toward them, but their hatred toward me.

That's the first thing I discovered from the game: That people hated the idea of being watched. Of being studied. Judged.

I watched the barista girl hold the biggest grin as she served an espresso to a punk-rocker kid with messy hair, and then dropped that smile completely as soon a woman with a baby on her hip ordered a pumpkin spiced latte.

I spent three hours in the coffee house just staring at her.

At one point, she became noticeably tense. The place was pretty empty, except for a girl waiting for her drink to go. The barista made her coffee, but she tightened her lips and shot glares at me the whole time. I never looked away. I didn't care. This was my game. This was my experiment. I wanted to know what people would do if they knew they were being watched all the time. I wanted to know what people might say to God if they had a chance to confront Him.

The customer got her drink and left.

The girl with the crow tattoo came up to my seat.

"You're going to have to leave, now," she said.

"I like your tattoo," I said.

This paused her, but only for an instant.

"Listen. I don't know what your problem is. But you have to go."

"My problem? I don't have a problem. I'm just people watching."

"Go. Just, get out…"

"Why do you hate mothers?" I said.

She didn't answer me. Instead, everything on her face tightened. Her brow, her cheeks, her chin. Everything.

"Get the hell out of my coffee shop right now!" she screamed. "You insane creep!"

Insane? I wasn't *insane*. I was just watching her. I didn't wish her any harm. I just wanted to study her and make a judgment of her character based on her actions and interactions with others.

This was my first experience with her hatred, anyone's hatred, toward me. And I was quite taken aback by how convulsive she had become; how aggressively she had exploded. When I started this game, I figured that at some point people would confront me. I wanted that. But I thought we'd go into it with a chance to explain my experiment.

I stood, slowly, and she took a step back. She stared me down as I walked out of the coffee shop. I didn't like the feeling of her eyes on me. I hadn't done anything to her.

But that wasn't my worst interaction.

The guy from the Irish pub was worse.

I knew he had finally noticed my staring when he kept making comments at his girl and pointed at me from the other end of the bar. The girl would half-drunkenly pat his chest, trying to tame her man, dismissing his overly exaggerated rage.

I knew he would come confront me at some point, so I ordered a Yuengling and a Jagerbomb. I sat them down in front of me. It took him longer to come up to me than I thought. The beer glass began to bead with sweat.

When he finally came up to me, I said, "Here. I got you your favorites," and nudged the two drinks toward him.

"What the hell is your problem?" he asked.

"That's the same thing the girl at the coffee shop wanted to know," I told him.

He winced at my comment, like he had no idea what I was talking about, which, of course, he didn't.

"What the hell's that supposed to mean?"

"It means sit down, have a drink with me, and I'll tell you what my problem is," I said.

"Dude. I don't want nothing to do with you. Just leave me alone and quit staring at me. I don't like it. I see you looking at me one more time, I'm going to beat your eye sockets into your skull."

"I'm just looking, man. I didn't do anything to you."

"Well, stop."

"Before you go..." I grabbed his wrist. He looked down at my hand, and I let go.

"What?" he groaned the word.

"Why don't you ever buy anyone a drink? Why do you always tip exactly three dollars? Why do you come here with a new girl every week?"

The look on his face was appalled, and I thought maybe I was striking a chord. Maybe we would get to the root of his weekly routines. We might be able to discover something together here.

"Why are you so sad?" I asked, thinking that question might break his silence and we could sit together and enjoy a few beers over deep philosophical matters.

But a rage set off in him that I didn't expect.

He grabbed my neck, and before I could slip away or push him off, he slammed me against the bar. The edge caught my cheek and blood poured from my face. But he wasn't satisfied with that. I was on the ground and he was upon me with fists and jabs and kicks and knees. All I could do was go in a ball, but I caught a look in his eyes that was filled with hatred so pure that the look of it hurt as much as the blows he delivered.

Eventually people stopped him and pulled him off me. But by that point my face had bled down to my shirt and my body hurt so bad that I had to be dragged out of the bar. I didn't make it home that night because I could hardly walk. I hobbled to a side alley and spent the night with my back against a brick wall, crying out in misery and pain.

But despite the pain, the beating, the hatred—I couldn't stop this game. There was still the man who walked his dog at the park in a business suit.

The next morning was Saturday. I regained some strength and made it to the park.

I sat down at my usual bench. As people walked by and saw me, saw my bloodied shirt, my busted lip, my swollen eye, their look of disgust was petrifying. *You don't know me*, I wanted to tell them. *You don't know anything about me. I'm not a bad guy.*

Their stares made me feel exposed. I felt like they could see past the bloodied shirt and the bruises. They could see my inability to keep a girlfriend. They could see me wasting hours on my work computer playing meaningless games instead of doing actual work. They could see the time I ran over a dog and didn't stop to see if it was okay.

Later, I felt bad for that dog. I felt bad for whatever family it had belonged to.

Now I felt like all of my mistakes, my sins, had bled onto my shirt for everyone to see. None of them liked what was there or what I had to offer.

The man with the terrier showed up at nine in the morning, just like every other Saturday. Except, this time he paused, looked at my beaten body and walked up to me.

He sat down next to me with the green plastic bag in his hand, empty.

"What happened to your face?" he asked.

I didn't want to answer him.

"Why don't you ever pick up after your dog?" I asked him instead.

"So you *have* been watching me."

"I have."

"Are you one of them?" the man asked.

"Am I one of what?" I mumbled through my busted lips. My

vision was blurred through my right eye. My brain hurt.

The man opened his lips to say something, sighed, and then thought better of it.

"Never mind," he said.

The terrier sat quietly next to the man's feet. No leash needed. The dog panted as he watched people go by.

"I'm Jack Carlos, by the way," he said, extending a hand for me to shake. I didn't take it.

"I'm no one," I said.

He dropped his hand.

"Why have you been watching me?"

I brought my hands to my face. I tried to massage some of the pain away. It didn't work. A strong gust blew from the lakefront. It almost blew the dog away, but the terrier held his ground and the wind passed.

"It's just something I've been doing. It's an experiment. I wanted to know what it felt like to be God."

"That's perhaps the weirdest response you could have given me," the man said.

"What did you think I was doing?"

"I thought you were… someone else. You haven't been the only one watching me, I think."

Great. This guy was a skitzo.

"I'm not crazy," the man said.

"I didn't say you were.'

"No. But you were thinking it. And I don't like that. I don't like that you would judge me without even knowing me."

There was a pause, and I could tell by watching the man's lips move that he wanted to ask me something.

"Ask," I told him.

"What did it feel like? To play God?"

"Hated," I said.

"Hated?"

"People hate you when they feel judged by you. Even if you're just looking. Even if you haven't figured them out yet. It's like how that saying goes."

"Which saying is that?"

The terrier jumped on the man's lap. Jack pet him.

"Hell is other people. A French philosopher said it, I think. People hate looking at themselves through the mirror of other people's eyes. We stand in perpetual judgment when we feel watched by others. We don't like what other people see in us. It makes us uncomfortable and vulnerable. We feel exposed. Like we have been called out on the fraudulent show we have been putting on. Our mask is lifted."

The man seemed to reflect on this for a moment.

"I know what you mean. When I was younger, like fourteen or fifteen, I met a little girl who was six years old, and she had a stare that could penetrate right through you. Even if you smiled at her, she didn't smile back. She just glared with those wide eyes. It made you feel like she knew everything about you. Every sin. Every fear. Every weakness."

"Maybe that's why so many people hate God, or pretend He doesn't exist," I said. "We can't stand the idea of being under His microscope."

"How can you be sure God exists?"

"I don't know. Sometimes I wish He didn't."

Across the park, three men in dark suits stood watching the lakefront, but at times it felt like they were watching us. Again, I felt exposed. Maybe I should quit the game. It hadn't won me any friends, and my face sure wasn't any prettier from it.

"If you were God," I began, and paused.

"What?" Jack asked.

"Never mind. Maybe the question is all wrong."

"Ask me," he said.

I breathed heavily. I wasn't sure I wanted to talk anymore. I wanted to go back to my apartment and sleep. Or maybe I wanted to board up the little window in my bathroom and put an end to the game completely. I didn't want to watch people's silent suffering any longer.

"Why doesn't He stop this?" I asked. "Why doesn't He stop our suffering if He really is there?"

Jack pondered this for a while. A very long while. We passed that stretch of time in silence, watching people live their lives moment by moment. A man walking his dog seemed to be flirting with a woman walking hers. A mother and father encouraged their child as he made an effort toward his first step. The three men in dark suits were still standing there, shoulder to shoulder to shoulder, looking past us.

"I think the better question is, why do we cause such suffering to one another?" Jack said. "What kind of people are we, setting fires, raping women, flying airplanes into buildings…"

I dismissed that last part because I had no idea what he was talking about.

It was late August, and that catastrophe hadn't happened yet.

"I watched an old man get beat up by a drug dealer last week," I told him. "And I didn't do anything to stop it. I called out to God to intervene, to help the poor man, but I just stared at him as he lay motionless on the ground. I didn't run down to help him off the ground. It's no wonder we hate God. We blame Him for the things we do, and expect him to act when we don't do anything ourselves."

Jack didn't respond. Instead his eyes were fixed on the three men in the distance. I wonder what he found so interesting about them. They began to walk toward us.

"Let's go, Blake," Jack said to the dog.

The terrier jumped down from his lap and Jack stood to go.

"What's the matter?" I asked.

"I'm going to have to go. I think you should stop your game. You're not going to solve anyone's problems by playing it. You're not God. You can't pretend to be God. And you certainly don't want the burden of knowing the things He knows. Have a good life…" he tried to remember my name, but then realized I never gave it to him.

"I'm Eran," I told him.

"Okay. Bye Eran. Have a good life."

With that, he left. He walked away quickly. The terrier's tiny steps scurried behind to keep up.

The three suited men walked the opposite direction and left.

How strange. And perhaps meaningless.

Jack was right. I wasn't God. I couldn't pretend to be able to piece these things together. I didn't know why the girl with the crow tattoo hated mothers or why the guy at the bar got so angry when I asked him why he was sad. I didn't have enough knowledge to judge these people.

Eventually all of these strangers disappeared from my life. I never saw Jack come back to the same park after that day. I wasn't allowed into the Irish pub any more. Even though I wasn't the one who started the fight, I was known as the guy who stared at you. People didn't like that. I walked past the coffee shop several times, but I never saw the girl barista work there again.

They had all escaped from me.

How do I escape your watchful eye, oh God?

When I returned to work, I made a commitment to play less on my computer. I bought a small, dark curtain for my bathroom window. But I was still terrible with women, and I often thought about the dog I ran over and left for dead on the road.

A few weeks later, 9/11 happened. My first impulse was to ask God why he'd let such a catastrophe to happen. But every time that question came up, I remembered the old junkie getting beat up in the back alley. Why didn't I do anything to stop it? Why didn't I help him up off the ground and take him to a hospital?

Those questions silenced me.

They humbled my desire to play God.

Gratitude

Myron walked up the airport corridor toward his gate. He closed his eyes for a moment and felt the wind of people moving past, slicing the air with their bodies.

He had missed his connecting flight to Atlanta so now he was stuck in Chicago on a longer layover. His flight coming here had been held up for three hours due to weather. He checked at the gate to see if he could make the next flight. The attendant set him up with a new seat and told him the next flight would leave in two hours.

Two hours?

What was he supposed to do for two more hours? He had already finished reading his book waiting for his last flight. He didn't have anything else to kill the time.

He passed a newspaper box and thought of buying a paper, but he didn't have any quarters on him. Instead he stopped for a late lunch. He sat at the bar of the restaurant so he could watch NFL highlights.

When the bartender brought his food, he took his time with his meal. A man sitting a couple stools away tried to make small talk.

"Are you coming or going?" he asked.

Until that question, Myron had forgotten he was in uniform. He was traveling on orders for an Army conference.

Most people who saw him in uniform at the airport assumed he was either coming home from overseas, or on his way back. People didn't realize that soldiers traveled from state to state all the time.

Myron swallowed his bite of steak.

"Neither," he said, and grabbed for his water because he could feel the meat stuck in his throat.

"Just traveling on business, you could say."

"So what do you do for the Army?" the man asked.

"I'm public affairs," Myron said.

The man made a face as if to show he found this interesting. But from the man's silence, Myron realized the guy didn't know what public affairs meant.

"I'm an Army journalist. Write stories, take photos, that type of thing."

"*Huh.* How 'bout that. Didn't know Army had journalists."

The guy was a heavier man. He balanced himself on the bar stool as if he were trying to balance himself on a toothpick. He propped most of his weight on his forearms against the bar.

"Yeah. Most people don't."

"Well, thanks for your service."

Myron appreciated this. He did. But he gave a thin-lipped smile and said nothing.

What was he supposed to say? *You're welcome?*

In any other circumstance, those were the right words in response to a thank you. But in this case, the words sounded strange.

He didn't know how to respond to these gestures of gratitude. He'd been deployed to Iraq. He had done his tour. But he wasn't sure that he'd done anything that deserved people's gratitude. He'd lost a year of his life overseas and his marriage was falling apart because of it. His wife had taken his son, Joshua.

He never thought such a thing could happen to him. A Christian man. Called to love his wife as his own self, and yet he felt like he'd failed their marriage completely. The way you fail an exam. Every answer he tried was wrong.

His deployment hadn't been hard. He never saw anyone die. He never felt bullets whizz past his head. And yet when he returned, life moved at a slower pace than what he was used to. His wife seemed to demand more out of him than he could give her. He lost part of his hearing from riding in a helicopter because he forgot to wear his earplugs once.

He came back home with less than what he had left with.

Were these things worth thanking? He didn't deserve anyone's gratitude.

He watched more highlights on TV in silence.

After he was done eating, Myron gestured for his check.

The large man down the bar still had most of his beer and sandwich left, but he adjusted himself in his seat so he could reach for his wallet.

Please don't, Myron thought, knowing well what the man was trying to do.

"Let me get that for you," he said. His fat fingers were fumbling to pinch his wallet.

"It's okay. Thank you, though."

He almost wanted to save the man from the embarrassment of not being able to pry the wallet out.

"No, I got it, I got it," though it was clear he didn't have the wallet quite figured out.

"Sir, I appreciate the gesture, but it's alright. I get per diem."

Every time Myron traveled on orders he received an allowance of roughly fifty to seventy-five dollars a day to pay for food at the expense of taxpayer's money. If he allowed this man to pay for his meal, it would be like asking him to pay for it twice.

"Are you sure?" the man asked. He'd managed to fork two fingers into his pocket and pull a corner of black leather out.

"I'm positive. Thank you, though." He flashed the best smile he could manage.

He paid for his lunch with his government travel card, left a tip in cash, and walked out.

His terminal was on the other side of the moving walkway, so he had to walk the long way around just to make his way across. Myron passed another newspaper vending box. He hadn't kept up with the news in a while now. Ironic, given that his Army profession was that of a journalist. The airport didn't have free WiFi and he forgot to bring along a book to read. It was going to be a long wait alone with his thoughts if he didn't find something to occupy his mind.

He knew where his thoughts might linger if he didn't pick up something to distract him. He didn't want to think about Riana. He didn't want to think about Joshua.

There was a thick crowd of people already waiting at his gate. He caught a few sets of eyes tracing him as he found his way to an empty seat. Again he was reminded of his uniform. Like a stain he'd forgotten to wash off. And yet he liked to travel in uniform.

He had the choice to travel in civilian clothes if he wanted to, but going through security was easier this way. He could jump to the front of the line and didn't have to take his boots off. One time, a female TSA agents actually gave him a big smile and pulled him in for a hug.

"Come heah, sugah. Thanks for all y'all do!" she had said, while hugging him tightly.

And very often, random people came up to him to say thank you. Thank you for your service. And though he still hadn't quite figured out how to answer them, he liked the simple gestures of gratitude. He liked the feeling of being appreciated by complete strangers.

Had Riana ever said thank you?

Right. Thank you. Thank you very much for leaving her behind with a baby boy for a year.

And yet he had deployed for her. For their family.

What gratitude had she shown him after he came home? He remembers coming home on a commercial airplane, and his heart felt so heavy it was hard for him to take deep breaths. He had anticipated the joy of wrapping Riana up into his arms and hearing Joshua's squeals of excitement.

But when he saw Riana, she wore a loose wrinkled shirt, a pair of sweat pants and flip-flops. No makeup. Hair bunched in a loose bundle. When he went for a kiss, she turned her jaw to his lips.

He had to ask to hold Joshua. And even then, she hesitated. And even then, the boy squirmed and wiggled to pry himself from daddy's hold. He was a stranger, one year removed.

They slept in the same bed, but her skin tensed any time his fingertips reached for a touch.

You're so damn ungrateful, he wanted to tell her. He gave up a year of his life for them, and now this was it? This was how she thanked him?

One month. Two months. Three months like this.

She asked for a divorce. She said she wanted to move out.

"I'm taking Joshua," she had said.

Those were her words.

Not: 'Thank you for your service' or 'Let me buy you a coffee.'

He never screamed at her before then. Not like he did that night.

"This is how you thank me?" he kept screaming.

The sound of his voice hit all four walls, hit the ceiling, and came back to slap against his half-deaf ears. That's how loud he screamed. And it took a lot to hold back from hitting her. But he pictured it. And the thought felt almost satisfying. The violence of it.

Later he asked God to forgive him for even entertaining the thought.

She broke down crying, covering her face with her hands. She mumbled something through her sobs. Through her tears. Through her hands.

"What?" he screamed. *"What are you saying?"*

"What about me?" she said.

He had no clue what she meant. What *about* her?

He didn't answer her. So she kept repeating it, as though eventually he would.

What about me? What about me?

What words did she expect him to say?

"Hey," a man said.

Myron turned over his shoulder, twisting in his seat to look back.

A man with a head full of unkempt hair and a grizzled, unshaven face stood behind him. He wore clothes that looked like they'd been stuffed into a plastic bag for several days before putting them on.

It took a moment for Myron to realize the man was holding something out for him.

It was a newspaper.

"Yes?" Myron said, not understanding.

"Here," the stranger said.

"The newspaper?"

The question felt stupid as soon as he asked it. Of course the newspaper. What else?

Myron pinched the end of the paper with one hand, not quite taking it. For a long moment both men held on to it, looking at each other. Like holding up a bridge for passengers to ride through.

The man nodded, let go of the paper and walked away without saying another word.

Myron turned back into his seat and opened the paper in his lap. He stared at the front page without really reading it for a minute or longer. He was trying to shake the idea that this grizzled, random man had been reading his mind. Maybe it was no mind reading at all. Maybe the man had noticed Myron hesitate past the newspaper stand earlier.

Perhaps this was the only way the man knew how to say thank you for your service. He had nothing else to offer but the paper.

Still, Myron was a little creeped out by the exchange. How the man had stared into Myron's face, holding onto his end of the paper a little too long.

What he found to be the strangest part was how neither man had thanked the other. He had almost *expected* the man to say the words. *Thank you.* And yet he hadn't. Though the gesture itself was

full of simple gratitude. He'd always found the idea of one man
sharing a newspaper with another very comforting. Brotherly, in
a way.

Had this been Myron's turn to say thank you for once?

He turned and looked around. He saw strangers involved in
their distractions: conversations, computer laptops and telephone
screens. He didn't see the man in either direction or anywhere
around him.

He read a few of the front page articles. National stories. None
of them about Iraq or Afghanistan. Mostly about the bad economy
and some controversy about suspected racism. How quickly the
soldiers had slipped from the media spotlight. And yet, the people
didn't forget their service. He saw proof of this every time he
traveled.

He read some NFL news. The Bears were making a quiet run
to the playoffs, mostly unnoticed. His Jets were also looking pretty
good this year.

None of the other stories held his attention, so he put the paper
down.

Then he looked up at the television hanging above his head.

Breaking news about a plane crash.

Big deal.

Planes seemed to crash almost every day. But then he caught
the writing at the bottom. Atlanta. The flight had crashed at the
Atlanta airport on a bad landing. The body of the plane had broken
in half.

Oh my God. Oh my dear God.

He felt like his life had just been spared. He was supposed to be
on that plane. He felt horrible now for his initial callousness toward
the crash. Suddenly he pictured the people he was supposed to have

sat next to. Metal shards and sparks and people screaming.

He felt a sudden sense of gratitude, and almost said a prayer to thank God, but stopped himself. How strange it would have been to thank God for sparing his life at the cost of all those others. He wasn't sure what to say to God. He wasn't sure what God wanted to say to him.

Everyone around him stared at the screen. There was agitation in that gate. The attendant at the counter tried to reassure everyone. A line of people went up to her asking the same questions. Will our plane be okay? When was the last time our plane was inspected? Did the pilot have enough sleep?

Some people backed out of the flight. Myron almost decided to cancel his flight, too, but what was he supposed to do? His home was in New York and he was stuck in Chicago. Damn the airlines and their insane connections. How did it make any sense to travel from New York to Chicago just to fly down to Atlanta?

In the end, he decided to keep his seat, knowing he didn't have many options.

Forty minutes later, the airline began to board passengers. Half the seats were empty from all the passengers cancelling their tickets.

Myron threw the newspaper in the trash before making his way to the line. He regretted the gesture right away. He could have passed on the paper to someone else. Hell, he could have left it on his seat so someone else had a chance to read it.

He shouldn't have thrown it away. That was stupid of him.

It was weird how he thought about the paper like that. It was almost like his brain was in a daze, purposely trying to find ways not to think about the flight.

He sat in his seat next to no one. He fidgeted as he waited for everyone to board and the flight to take off.

Myron thought about the man who gave him the newspaper. He wished he had at least said thank you.

But then he thought, *What if the man is mad that I threw away his paper? What if he expects it back? What if he demands that I pay him back the seventy-five cents I threw into the trash?*

He asked himself these questions as though he actually anticipated the man sitting next to him.

He entertained an imaginary conversation with the guy. He imagined the man coming down the isle, look down at Myron and take a seat. He would leave his belt unclipped.

You never said thank you, the man would say.

I know. I'm sorry.

You still haven't said it.

Yeah, well now it's weird because you're expecting me to say it.

A sigh. *It wouldn't mean much anyway, since you tossed the paper away and all.*

I wasn't thinking.

Maybe you ought to have been thinking.

I just… Sorry.

What about me? the man might ask.

What do you mean, what about you?

Well, maybe I wasn't done with it. Maybe there was an article inside I wanted to return to, or give it a second look. Maybe I wanted to give it to somebody else after you were through with it.

Maybe you should have just kept the paper, then, Myron thought. But even in his imaginary conversation he couldn't work up the audacity to say those words to him. That would have been a little blunt.

Thank you, he said. *Thanks for the paper. And I'm sorry for throwing it away like that.*

Well alright then. That's all I wanted to hear.

In his mind, Myron watched the man get up slowly from his seat, walk up the aisle to the front of the plane and walk off.

Myron fidgeted with the air vent knob above him. It was cranked all the way open, but no air would come out. He felt the uncomfortable, stuffy warmth linger underneath his uniform. His boots were laced tight, and his pants were bloused to his calves. He unstrapped the wrists of his uniform jacket to loosen some of the hot air. He even tugged at his uniform blouse to fan himself.

Passengers boarded the plane. He waited. They pushed bags into the overhead compartments and excused their way to their seats.

Nobody took the seat next to him. It was one of many empty seats on the flight. The newspaper man never appeared as he imagined, and he felt a little silly for the conversation he'd played out inside his head. Still, those were words he had wanted to say. *Thank you. Thank you for the newspaper. Thank you for offering to pay for my meal. Thank you for your kind words of support. Thank you for your prayers.*

Thank you for raising our boy while I was away.

Maybe those were the words he had failed to say. Of all the words he had screamed at Riana, those were the words he was supposed to say all along.

The airline hostess gave her safety briefing from the front of the plane. She asked all the passengers to turn off their mobile devices. He fidgeted with his phone. He contemplated calling Riana before it was too late. He wasn't sure he could do it. Dial her number, wait for her to say hello, and then, what? Just say thank you? Just like that? It didn't seem so easy, and yet he felt the need to say those words to her.

What the hell. What could it hurt. He couldn't possibly ruin their marriage any more.

He dialed her number. It was one of the few numbers he had memorized.

It rang. A long wait. It rang again.

"I can't talk right now, Myron. Joshua is throwing a tantrum."

Her answer befuddled him. Why had she picked up the phone just to tell him she couldn't talk? All the misfires and old tendencies from their marriage rushed back to him. *Forget it*, he wanted to say, and hang up on her.

He heard Joshua scream in the background. And as shrilly as that sound was, it actually caused his heart to go tender.

"Listen, Riana. I just need to tell you something."

What was he going to say to her? Should he tell her he could have died today? Would that make a difference to a woman already committed to leaving him?

"Can this wait? Right now is really not the time."

"It'll be quick, I promise," he said. "I don't have much time anyway. Flight's about to take off here."

But as soon as he said that, he found himself stuck, not knowing how the words were supposed to come out.

Already he saw the flight attendant make her way toward him. She was only a few seats away, asking passengers left and right to put their devices away, fold their tables, bring up their seat rests.

He heard Riana sigh. Joshua was screaming in the background. Man, he could scream for a two year old.

"Myron, what is it?" He felt her impatience like it could touch him.

Just say it. Just say the words and hang up. The rest can be explained later.

"Sir, I'm going to have to ask you to put that away now. We're about to take off." The flight attendant was already upon him. She looked down at him with a mannequin smile.

"I'm sorry, M'am. Can I just—"

She held that waxy, insistent smile. Like a polite command.

"Oh for goodness sake. Riana, I'll call you back when I land. I'm sorry. I just wanted to say something quick, but maybe this isn't the way."

He hung up, and the sound of Joshua's screaming stopped. *What did you expect, Myron? Did you expect you could just say thank you and everything would be fixed?* He started to doubt himself. He started to doubt every thank you he had ever heard. Did these people actually care or were these just words to them when they expressed their gratitude? If they were so thankful, why didn't they enlist their own sons and daughters to go fight this war?

That was bitter of him. He tried to stop the thoughts. He was angry and he knew he wasn't being fair.

He scrambled for a piece of paper and a pen. He couldn't find any paper, but he fished out a napkin out of his cargo pocket. He used a magazine as a surface and he wrote on his lap.

Dear Riana, he began. Then nothing. He was a journalist—a writer—and he couldn't think of a single word to follow.

He should just wait for his flight to land to call her.

No. He shouldn't. Because this moment would pass. These feelings and this sudden realization would fade, and he would be left feeling groggy and confused. The same way he felt when he tried to write a poem and he put it down for a while to return to it later. None of the original emotions would be there to propel him to finish his writing.

What if he died on this plane and never got a chance to talk to Riana again?

He had to write it down now.

Dear Riana. I love you and I miss you and I'm sorry. I'm sorry for demanding so much and for never telling you what you deserved to hear. Words I hear all the time when I'm in uniform and yet I've failed to share with you. Thank you. Thank you so much for taking care of our home for a year. For loving Joshua and helping him grow while I was away...

He wrote with a sense of urgency. He was careful so the pen wouldn't scratch into the napkin. He didn't have much space to work with so his writing became tinier and tinier, doing his best to fit everything in. Writing by hand was taxing. It was something he rarely did anymore. He grasped the pen so tightly that, as he scribbled, soreness grew up his wrist to his forearm.

Once he was done, he re-read every word. Then he read them again. He felt good about this. It came across a bit like a love letter, but perhaps that wasn't such a bad thing. It was addressed to his wife, after all.

It was finished, and he felt exhausted. Like he'd just sprinted a mile. He had been so emotionally charged to write those words that now he was left drained. It was a cathartic experience. It had all gushed out of him. It felt good.

A while later, passengers were cleared to put down their tray tables.

He ordered a tomato juice and placed his letter upside down on his table. He chugged the juice and placed the empty cup on his letter. The warmth of the plane and the sun shining through the window filled over him. He leaned back in his seat, and he fell asleep. He dreamed of Riana and Joshua. It was an abstract dream of forgiveness. A typical dream patched and stitched together by strange scenes. More emotional than logical.

When he awoke, he felt dazed but pleased. It was a nice long nap. He awoke to a sense that things had been fixed between Riana and him.

Everything's okay, he thought. As the grogginess faded, he amended the statement. *Everything will be okay.*

But when he looked on his tray table, the empty plastic cup and the napkin were gone.

He looked on his lap. On the ground. It wasn't there.

He paged the flight attendant.

"Yes?" she said when she arrived.

"My napkin…" he stammered.

"I can get you a napkin, sir."

"No. My napkin. I need my napkin back."

Her eyes went blank and her lips pursed.

"It's important. I was writing a note on it. I need my napkin back."

"Sir I'm sorry. I threw it away."

"Can you look for it? Please?"

"I—Sir… It's gone."

"I'll help you find it. I'll go through the trash. I just need it, m'am. I really do."

She either found him crazy and didn't want to argue with him, or she saw the desperation in his face.

"I'll go look for it, sir."

He unbuckled his belt.

"Please stay seated sir. I'll go find it."

He caught a glimpse of her frustration as she turned away. It was a look that said, *I can't believe these people.*

She returned a few minutes later with the napkin pinched in her fingers. She held it out from her body like a dead rat. It was soaked.

All of the excitement that had been there before blew out of him. He brought a hand to his face to keep himself from cussing. He watched her place the napkin down on his table like it was a favorite pet. Drowned to death.

"Thank you," he said, but he didn't look at her.

Every word was blotchy. It was a miracle that she had found the napkin in the first place, but now it did him no good.

He stared at it for several long minutes.

He tried to recollect the words in his mind, but he couldn't. It was just as he feared. The words were gone. The passion and emotion had faded. People didn't realize that writing was like taking a photograph. If you lost a photograph, you couldn't just recreate the lost moment. The same thing was true now. Those words were lost.

Once the plane landed safely, everyone clapped. Even he did. He felt a huge relief for living another day, but just as quickly he felt miserable again.

In his mind, he tried to rework the letter he'd written. Nothing.

He stepped off the plane, and after some serious contemplation, he decided he would call Riana after all. He had nothing else to lose. He couldn't make the situation any worse.

When she picked up, he felt like he was about to tell her he'd lost his wedding ring.

"Hello?" she said.

"I'm sorry," he managed. But now he didn't really know what he was sorry for. Did he actually intend to apologize or was this simply the easiest words he could muster?

She was silent, which made it more difficult.

In his mind, all he could remember was her sobbing and crying, *What about me? What about me?*

He twirled his wedding band around his finger. Three crosses etched into the metal. Why did he still wear this? There was a period when things were so bad that he left the wedding band in his car.

"If you have something to say, say it."

"Riana, I had the perfect words written down of what I wanted to tell you. But now I don't remember what they were."

"I don't think an apology can fix us right now, Myron."

"I'm not apologizing," he said.

"Of course you aren't. What's there to apologize?"

"Don't be coy right now, Riana. I'm trying to tell you something."

"Then tell me."

"I'm trying, okay? I just can't remember the words."

Were they seriously having this conversation? He couldn't believe how unprepared he felt for this. Like he was attempting to deliver a presentation and he'd forgotten to rehearse.

"I love you," but that wasn't it either. Not at all. Not even close enough.

Why the hell was this so difficult? What in the world was wrong with him? What a bumbling idiot.

"Is that it?"

"No. I—Listen…" He exhaled. Frustrated. "I just wanted to say thank you. Okay? Just thank you. I thought that you deserved at least that much from me."

There was a moment of feeling stunned. Taken by surprise by his own gush of emotions. And then it came tumbling out. The gratitude he had failed to recognize. It spilled like a glass of wine. The blotchy words from the napkin weren't there, but he had something similar, and that was okay.

As his momentum built, as his words came splashing out more rapidly, tears came from his eyes. He had to constantly wipe them away with one hand. There were so many tears that his lips were wet.

He decided not to tell her about the plane crash. He didn't want to use that event to coerce an emotion out of her that she might not have felt otherwise. He wanted her to know he appreciated her. Period. Not just because he could have died in a plane.

When he was done, there was silence.

"Maybe we can talk more when you get home okay?" she said. There were tears on her lips, too, he could tell.

"I would really like that."

He wasn't sure how much he had fixed with this one phone call. He didn't know whether Riana would remain his wife. Whether he would have to try to write another love letter on his flight home. But at least he had said thank you. At least he had done that.

Before leaving the airport, he stopped at a bookstore and bought a newspaper. He walked to an area with a crowded bench and looked around. Most of the crowd was busily wasting time on their cell phones and laptops. He walked over to a man who was sitting by himself. The man looked immersed in his own thoughts.

Myron extended the newspaper toward the stranger. They both held it for a long second, and then he let go. He walked away without either man saying a word.

Black Coats at the Cheyenne Diner

The three men sat at the diner booth wearing matching, two-button black suits. They were not businessmen, but they looked like men who meant business. The Cheyenne Diner was a good twenty miles south of Oklahoma City, just where the highway stretched beyond the reach of city lights.

The place was decorated for Easter, with paper eggs hung and stuck here and there. It gave the place a cheap and dated décor.

Brown booths lined along the windowed wall. There were no coat hooks to hang up their jackets. It was two in the morning and the place was mostly empty.

Tonight, people would die.

A young couple sat at the other end of the diner chatting, downing glass after glass of root beer float. An older man, haggard looking, sat at the bar hunched over his mug of coffee. The diner's cook had spent a long time at the bar talking to the man, but then finally retreated back to the kitchen. The man at the bar looked disgruntled, and at times he shot glances back at the three men, as if expecting them to come over and talk to him.

They would, but it was a matter of timing.

Distinguishing the three men apart would have been difficult if not for their hair. The tallest of them had spiky blond hair. The one next to him had a bright orange cut that came up in a wave. The third man sat across the other two, a black-haired youth scribbling a string of letters on his napkin.

DTP DTP DTP DTP DTP...

He was writing furiously—without really feeling the pen scraping the paper.

"Sometimes I feel like we're..." the black-haired youth said, stopping his scribbling for a moment, but he didn't know how to finish the thought. His hair fell over his eyes like lush grass, cascading around his head like a thick curtain.

"Healers?" the blond man finished for him, who was much older. Looking at him closely, you could see grooves in his face that showed his age. His hair looked bleach white as he shifted beneath the overhanging lamp.

"No, I mean like..."

"Yeah, *healers*," the red-haired one said, excited at the sound of the word. "Like healers!"

"*Leeches*," the black-haired youth blurted out. He said it like a sneeze, spitting out the word as though he couldn't hold it back. The young couple turned to him; the older gentleman remained hunching, unfazed, murmuring. "Feels like we're damn leeches sometimes," he said quieter now.

"Come on, Adren, you sound so morose when you talk like that," said the blond one.

"It's just… we're not *doing* anything. Nothing good comes out of what we do."

"We try. We do our best. We do our job, and whatever comes of it, comes of it. Isn't that right, David?" He enunciated every word crisply, his tongue hitting every consonant.

"Damn straight," said David, the red-haired one, flicking a straw wrapper he had rolled into a ball. The ball landed into Adren's hair and became absorbed. Adren didn't flinch.

"Okay," Adren began. "But you have to admit that when we talk to these people… When we do what we do 'our *job*' they just—"

"You three out from a weddin'?" the waitress asked, coming over to them and gesturing to the suits with her notepad. Her southern accent meshed her consonants together. Her face was aged, lipstick staining just outside of her lip line, and her face was dimpled and leathery from smoking too many cigarettes, but her body held firm otherwise. She wore blue jeans that came high on her waist and a low cut collar shirt that exposed her cleavage.

"No, M'am. The suits are just part of the job," the blond man said. His voice was charming now, but his face unsmiling. He never smiled around attractive women.

"You three brothers?"

"We're… associates. We travel."

"Hmm," was her response to his nonchalant, mysterious answer. "I've seen gunmen dressed like 'dat before. You know… in the movies." She said this with a teasing smile, tongue in cheek.

The blond man chuckled. "No, no. Don't let your imagination get the best of you. We do the Lord's work. In a sense."

"And what sense would that be?"

Before the blond man could answer, David cut in.

"What are the specials tonight?" He asked this holding a boyish grin, chewing on a straw. He was staring at her chest.

"Those ain't on the menu, Bud. Up here." She pointed at her face, though she seemed pleased by the attention. She liked the mood of these guys. It was a nice change from the late-night truckers who threw change on her tables and called it a tip.

"I dunno," said David, his boyish grin as big as ever, "They've got 'dessert' written all over them to me."

"David…" the blond man said in a reserved and calculated tone, like a father trying to correct a child.

"Victor…" the red-headed David said, responding in the same serious tone, forcing a mock-concerned look on his face. This made the waitress laugh. "See? She likes me."

"It's the suits. Anybody else I'd pro'lly woulda slapped him," she said but was still smiling. "Any case, what can I get you?"

"I'll have a cappuccino if I may. I'm afraid it'll be a long night," Victor said, pronouncing the drink crisply, in perfect Italian pronunciation.

"We don't have any cappacheenos here, sir. Just reg'lar coffee."

"All right. Just give me your finest, and a small dish of whipped cream on the side."

"Will do. And you… uh… David?"

"Dave if you want. I'll have a glass of cow juice."

She looked at him, uncertain, her pen half-touching the pad.

"He means milk," Adren said, a voice as dry as falling leaves, but just as gentle. He was leaning back in his booth, with his hands wrapped on the back of his head, elbows out. His eyes, the waitress noticed, were of a placid blue color. She could have dipped into them. He had irises like halos.

"And you?" she said to Adren, her breath hesitant.

"Wait, woah, I'm not finished," David said. "Ask the chef if he can stack me up a pancake on top of two Belgian waffles, butter in between, syrup on top, and three sausage links and bacon strips— extra crispy—staggered above it all. Powdered sugar too if you have it. It's good with the cow juice."

"I'll just have a toasted bagel with cream cheese and a water. We're not all freaks at this table," said Adren. Then added, "Thank you."

She turned away, laughing to herself, and David watched her breasts bounce as she spun. Then he stared at her rear as she walked away.

The Lord's work, Adren thought. *Right.* He was starting to doubt that idea more and more the longer he stuck with this… this line of duty.

Victor was staring across the diner at the old man sitting at the bar, who was still sipping on his mug of coffee. Adren watched Victor watch the man. He was their guy. He was their "visionary." Adren knew this without Victor saying a word. It always felt like the three of them knew one another's thoughts, somehow. Knew each other's ideas, opinions, and mental advancements. Yeah, the man at the bar was their guy, and they were his… leeches.

They had been clinging to him like duct tape, following and watching him for over a month now. Except, tonight was the first time they had come this close to him. For the past month of watching, they had kept their distance, keeping an eye on his behaviors to make sure he really was a visionary. Adren had been left out from most of that work, from most of the watching. "You're still too young," Victor had explained. So tonight was the first time Adren had seen this man in person.

Tonight might be the night. Or maybe tomorrow. It would be up to Victor to decide when.

Their work was simple. They often received an assignment in the mail, telling them who their next visionary was for them to watch over. These visionaries were men and women who were struck by images of the future. Often these visions were of tremendous catastrophes. Murders. Accidents. Rapes. Some of the visionaries believed they were being given messages from God, others simply that they were going insane.

As "Facilitators," it was up to Adren, David and Victor to ensure these people didn't hurt themselves, and to watch over them until they were positive they could truly see the future. Once they were sure of this, and when the moment was right, they approached their visionary to talk.

This wasn't Adren's first time doing the job with David and Victor, though he always felt like the odd man out. The other two never told him as much as he wanted to know. He was newer at this than they were, but still, this man at the counter—this homeless looking, mentally troubled shell of a man—he was their seventh *job* since Adren was first recruited.

Eight months together and already their seventh visionary. A different city every time.

How could there be so many of them? Everywhere. These people were damn *everywhere*. They each knew things nobody else could predict, and it was up to people like Adren, David and Victor to facilitate them, help them sort through what they saw, urge them to prevent disasters from happening. The Facilitators thought of themselves as Angels from God whose job was to reach out to the messiahs of the present world.

Except, to Adren this whole thing started to feel like one big wasted effort. Sometimes he looked back at what they were doing, looked back and saw all the travesties that still happened despite their work, and started to doubt…

"Here ya' go," the waitress said, setting down their drinks. "Food'll be a minute."

"Can he do it?" David asked her.

"What?"

"The chef. Can he make my waffles and sausage tower?"

"Oh. He'll manage, but I wouldn't call him a 'chef' exactly."

The waitress walked away again. With a spoon, Victor dipped the whipped cream into his coffee, stirred, and took a long sip. He held the mug with both hands, as if trying to keep his hands warm, while fixing his eyes on the man at the bar.

"It's him, isn't it?" Adren asked.

"I don't know what you mean," Victor said, but never left his eyes.

David was looking at the man, too, now. He dumped spoonfuls of powdered sugar into his milk and stirred it until there was none left floating on top. Then he dumped some more. "Yep. Yep." he said between chugs of milk. By his third gulp the glass was empty.

They sat in silence for a long minute. The only noise was the chatter from the young couple; they seemed to be arguing over something, and yet the boy's voice sounded upbeat. Challenging. The waitress came back with their food. She had brought an extra dish of whipped cream for Victor, plus the bagel and the stacked tower of food for David.

"All good?" she asked.

David hadn't even waited, already stuffing his mouth with a brickful of food. He nodded. The other two thanked her, and she went back to the kitchen.

"Shall we?" Victor asked, nodding to the man at the bar who was now twisting from side to side on his swivel stool.

"What? *Now?*" Adren asked.

"At least let me finish my food," David said through a mouthful of syrup and bacon.

"Come on."

"*Here?*" Adren said, looking around. "You're serious."

Without answering, Victor stood up and flicked crumbs and lint off from his black coat. David slid off the booth and got up too, still holding the plate and fork with both hands. Victor gave him a look. David sighed in annoyance and put the plate down.

"Spit it out," Victor told him.

David opened his mouth and let the chewed-up food roll off his tongue and plop back onto the plate.

"Can't believe this," Adren murmured, getting up.

"In character," Victor said to him.

"I know, okay?"

They were silent now. Adren saw that the couple was just teenagers, seventeen or eighteen maybe. The boy and girl watched them move across the diner towards the man. Silence rung through the room like a hollowed heartbeat. Three overhanging fans spun, creating a draft around them. Victor stood behind the man at the bar, feet spread apart. David took the seat to the man's left and Adren to his right, both of them sitting erect, straight like statues, facing the man between them. He had nowhere to go.

"I thought you might come over to see me sooner or later," the man said without turning. There was a deep sadness in his voice, but no fear.

How old was this man? Adren tried to gauge him. He looked anywhere from sixty to eighty.

They said nothing. The trick was in keeping their silence. Keeping their silence helped the visionary do the talking. At times, this *did* make Adren feel like they were healers. In moments like this, while listening to the voice of a man who had become indebted to lost hours of sleep, he knew that there was *some* factor of healing to their silence. Adren could think of himself as a counselor or psychiatrist at times like this, soaking in the devastating stories of people who saw death in their sleep, in the faces of strangers and on the bleached walls of tall buildings. Visions of the future. Predictions. Calamities and destructions. From crumbling bridges to political assassinations, he and the rest of the Facilitators dedicated themselves to finding these messiahs and learning of the next big catastrophe.

Adren didn't know how these people received their visions. He just knew they were true. His first assignment on the job had been a small child named Elijah. Every time the boy was around water, he saw a grey figure drowning in the East River. The day after they had spoken to the child, a screenwriter named Spalding Gray had committed suicide.

Drowned.

Just a coincidence, Adren had thought at first. It was just small stuff. The vision had been so *vague* anyhow. Grey. Gray. It was dumb, he thought, to get swept away by such a simple coincidence. He began to think that joining the Facilitators had been a waste of his time. All they were doing was stalking random people who thought they could see the future. Except it wasn't until their fourth job that Adren realized these were no coincidences. The visions became more specific with each visionary; the predicted events became more and more painful to shake from his mind. The rape of a little boy who would be beaten and molested for a month before police eventually found his remains. The massacre by one office worker who grabbed a pair of scissors and slit the throats of four fellow employees. An entire street of houses burning up in flames like a torching snake.

Even 9/11…

The man at the bar finally spun around on his stool, facing Victor but looking down at his shoes. The lines on his thin face were like cracks in a desert. His hair was a bright gray, almost silver.

"I know you've been watching me." His pink lips barely moved as he spoke. "I know who you are."

The man looked up now. His eyes filled with quivering tears.

"Are you afraid of us?" Victor asked.

"You're them, aren't you?"

"We are."

"The Obsessors…" The man said the word as though he were unsure how it might sound once spoken. It seemed every one of their visionaries had a different nickname for them.

"Don't be afraid," Victor said.

"Only my mind scares me anymore."

Adren saw Victor smile. He had never done that before, not while on the job. They never smiled when performing their "healing." Sometimes they kept their eyes closed, opening them only when speaking, taking turns, one at a time. Other times they went for as long as possible without blinking. It was all a mind game. It was all to make themselves look more mysterious, to help their targets cope with their own estranged visions. If the Facilitators could appear omnipotent, then the visionary was usually more willing to talk. More willing to deal with the strangeness of his own thoughts. It was all an optical illusion of the mind. But Victor's smile…

It seemed to undermine his own mysteriousness.

The man laughed as he saw the smile. It seemed evoked out

of him.

"I'm Charles," he said.

"We know," all three said at once.

It was a lie. Adren didn't know the man's name was Charles before now. But this was their routine.

"Tell us what you know," Victor said.

"Tell us," said David.

"What you know," Adren finished. Everything was calculated. Everything they said was rehearsed. It was like a mathematical equation solved through the right order of cues. It worked. David and Adren just went off of Victor's cues. They had about a dozen or so different methods to make them talk, and it was up to Victor to decide which one would work best, depending on their target.

"The silver-haired woman," said Charles on the verge of tears. "She's going to get shot."

The three remained silent. They waited.

"I know when. I know where. I know how... But why me? Why the hell me?"

Adren could feel the two teenagers watching them, trying to listen in on what was going on here. He felt very uncomfortable doing this in public. They had never done it in the open, and it made him feel like something really bad might happen. But the thought was silly. They were just listening to some man talk. That was all. Why this feeling of dread lunging at his heart?

Charles went on. "I can't see her face, this silver-haired woman. But she's got the cure."

"The cure," said Victor.

"Some disease is coming. Some will think it's degenerative. Others will think it's a virus. It's not. None of those," Charles said. "This disease. It will be like a plague. It will eat people from the inside out. It will make people's faces look like raw meat. She knows the answer. She doesn't have the cure, yet. Not now… but she will once the disease goes out of control. It's all knotted up in my mind. I don't know. It doesn't make any sense. I just know she knows."

"She knows," Victor said.

"Yeah. The disease."

"Assassinated?" Adren asked. He wasn't supposed to speak or ask questions without Victor allowing him.

"No. Not assassinated. Just some random shooting. Some man at a gas station trying to rob the place. She gets killed for no reason. I just… Why do I know all this?" He looked to them, hoping they would tell him. "Why am I being tortured with this?"

"You're a visionary. You're supposed to know," Victor said, as if revealing the obvious.

"I just see this faceless woman get shot in the head, and from that, everything else goes. I don't even know this woman. I don't even see her face in my dreams. But I know she will have a cure. It's some simple answer everyone else will miss."

"What is the answer?" asked Victor, never moving, his hands fumbling with something in his pocket.

"*I don't know!*" Charles screamed. "I just know *she* does. Somehow she knows. And she'll solve it when it happens."

This was common among the visionaries they visited. They would know a story in chunks, but rarely be able to make connections between the pieces. It was as if they were looking at a picture through a metal sheet with holes in it, catching only random spots of the entire image behind the sheet.

"This gas station…" said Victor, trailing off.

"Yes?"

"You know where it is."

"I know."

"Where?"

He told them. It was a Circle K stationed off of Highway 35 on the way to Austin, Texas. He even knew which town it was closest to. Georgetown. He knew the date, and roughly the time.

"Just before midnight tomorrow. Just before Easter," he said, as if in awe by this thought. "It's as if..." but he didn't finish the sentence.

"As if... ?" Victor pressed.

Charles sighed through his nostrils, lips pressed shut, unsure if he should say it or not.

"As if what?" Victor pressed again.

"As if I'm the one who's supposed to do something about it, *okay?*" He was angry now, but not shouting. "As if this old, wrinkled man is supposed to save this faceless woman. I don't even know what the hell she looks like. Silver hair. That's all. Silver hair. What am I supposed to do with that?"

Charles looked up at Victor now. Then he turned to his sides, first looking at David and then at Adren. He was looking at each one of them as if he expected them to tell him the answers to his questions. As if they could fill in the gaps or connect the random chunks of his images. But they could not. He was the one who was supposed to tell them, not the other way around. They knew nothing other than what he told them.

Charles shook his head, heavy as a stone, bringing it back down on his chest.

"You're going to save her," Victor said, his voice balanced between a question and a statement.

"I have to," he said. "I saw the way this plague devours people. Children even."

"Are you sure?" Victor asked.

"I'm doing it," Charles said, convinced, tightening his hands into fists on his knees.

The man's words brought a ringing inside Adren's chest. He couldn't contain it. The man's words excited him. This was a first. In eight months, this was the first time one of their visionaries had been determined to do something about his visions. *There is hope,* he thought. Every other time, the visionary would beg *them*—beg the Facilitators—to help him. He would beg *them* to do something about his visions because he was too afraid or weak or unable. Every time they begged, Victor would explain that this was not their job. He would explain, as calm as a spring rain, that their job was to facilitate the visionary in making a decision about his images. Every time—until *now*—the visionary had broken down crying, admitting his own weakness, saying there was no way he could stop a street full of houses from burning down, no way he could prevent the bridge from crumbling, or save a U.S. Senator from being assassinated. *They would never believe me,* was always the excuse. Often this was because the visionary had tried to stop a previous catastrophe from happening and nobody had believed him *then,* so how should anyone believe him this time?

But this was different. Charles was different. This old man. He was actually going to try and save this silver-haired woman. There was hope. Adren felt it like a tender touch. He could feel the determination in the man's voice despite his own sadness and pain. Despite having seen the woman getting shot in the head countless of times in his dreams. Or the disease devouring people.

Healers, Adren thought. Maybe that word was true after all. Maybe they were not leeches. *Healers.* He repeated the word in his mind. They were healing the world. They were—

A gunshot rung inside the diner like an explosion.

Adren jumped at the sound. He had come to his feet without realizing it. The teenage girl behind him screamed. The boy sitting across from her shuddered.

Victor was holding a gun; he had shot Charles in the face, making it blow like a ripe pumpkin into a burst of blood. The blood was all over David and Victor, but somehow, not even a drop had splashed onto Adren's black coat. He was clean.

The teenage girl ran for the door, but Victor turned and shot her. She dropped straight to the floor, half-in half-out of the diner, keeping the door open. The boy held up his arms, seeing there was nowhere to run, and Victor's bullet went straight through the boy's ear, through his skull, ending his life.

Adren was trying to catch his breath, struggling to do so. He wanted to scream but couldn't. The waitress had just stepped into the dining room when Victor fired his first shot, which had killed Charles, and now she was turning to run back into the kitchen.

What had she called them earlier? Gunmen?

David already had a gun out and shot her in the back, she fell screaming, and he shot her again in the back of her neck. Her screaming turned into a gargling now. Victor looked at David, seeming disappointed at the kid for needing a second shot.

"Open the register," Victor ordered Adren.

"We're robbing the place?" He didn't know how he had managed to say this.

"No. We're going to make it look like we are."

Adren couldn't move. His bones were twitching. David saw this, so he went over to the register and opened it himself. He pulled out some of the bills, there weren't many, and stuffed them in his back pocket.

Things clicked inside Adren's mind. Somehow the chunks of his own mental images started to come together.

He and these two men were not facilitators at all.

"You lied to me," he said to Victor. "You people lied to me." He was angry, scared, incredulous.

"I don't know what you mean," Victor said, his eyes narrowing and his lips smiling. That smile. It made things even clearer. It destroyed the illusion of everything they had tried to make Adren believe. They had made him believe he was helping them heal the world of catastrophes by chasing after visionaries. That order might be restored eventually in this world if they persevered. The very opposite was true, and Adren could see it on Victor's lips. He could see it in his smile.

Their job hadn't been to prevent disasters, but to *ensure* no one would ever tamper with them. They had watched and stalked these visionaries to make sure they would never interfere with whatever they saw in their heads. That's why in the past eight months on the job, none of them had ever tried to stop anything. Not *despite* of the Facilitator's efforts, but *because* of them. Their visit had actually intimidated these distraught men and women with the images they couldn't stop, not *healed* them. He now felt responsible for countless of deaths. All of these thoughts sparked inside Adren's mind like a box of matches catching fire, one match lighting another, lighting the next and the next and the next until the whole thing was aflame.

That fast.

Everything was made visible to him.

"Come on now," Victor said, with that same old-man smile, trying to soothe Adren's tumbling mind, as if he could read every one of his thoughts.

How many Facilitators existed across the country? Adren tried to think. A few dozen? A couple hundred? He wasn't sure. There were cells planted in every state. They would all turn against him soon. The whole organization was like an underground cult, with tentacles in everything. It was like a tumor that held a grip on the vital organs, every pulse of the country.

"Okay," Victor said. "You know now."

David grinned. All teeth.

Victor raised his gun. Adren took off running towards the door. The gunshot zinged against the doorframe, the glass splintering into shards. Adren stumbled over the girl's body, tripping through the doorframe. He was out of the diner and got back to his feet. Into the isolated night under the Oklahoma sky. He was miles from anything, and he ran as if the ground beneath his feet were crumbling behind his every step.

Georgetown, Texas, he kept repeating in his mind as he ran. *Circle K. Midnight. Georgetown, Texas. Circle K. Midnight…*

He had one day to get there…

To get there before Midnight.

Small Pleasures

Victor sat on the wall of the concrete bridge high above the mall's parking lot, kicking his feet one at a time, drumming a beat that was familiar only to himself. It was closing time for the mall. In a few minutes, the doors would be locked up and no one left inside.

The ledge Victor sat on hovered sixty feet above the ground below. He spat down, aiming for a rusted gutter, but the breeze took the shot away from his target. He wore a black T-shirt that read: "Screw the world, but do it nicely." His hands gripped the edge of the wall, making sure he wouldn't fall off.

At least not yet.

Thick veins ran up his arms, bulging out like cable wires. His hair was bleach blond and spiked. His face was slim and hard with youth and displaced anger. It was a hardness that came and went.

"Nice night out," a voice said from beside him.

Victor turned his neck and saw a middle-aged mall security

guard leaning on the ledge with his elbows. The top button of his uniform was undone, showing that he was ready for this night to end. The man's eyes searched the sky in wonder, looking at the hazy clouds that were slowly disappearing. His face was worn, deep with lines that ran down to the far ends of his chin, searching for his neck. His hair was clean cut, short and combed to one side.

Victor spun his legs around and sat with his back to the parking lot below. "It's nice, but there just aren't enough stars in the sky."

The man was surprised that he had received a response from the kid. He had said it more to himself than to Victor. He wasn't expecting the start of a conversation by it. He was, after all, a mall security guard, and mall rats like Victor never really engaged in conversations with security. But now they had spoken, and he didn't mind the idea so much.

"There's enough stars to keep me satisfied, I guess," the guard said while sticking a Marlboro between his lips. Then he tilted the pack towards Victor, offering him one.

"No thanks, I'm only fifteen," he said with a charming smile.

"So's my son, but that doesn't seem to stop him."

"There are more effective ways to kill yourself, I guess."

A silence hung between the two.

"I'm Victor by the way," the boy said.

"Nice to meet you, Victor. I'm Eric. So what are you doing out here? You waiting on someone?"

"You could say that."

"How long have you been waiting?"

"A few hours," Victor said indifferently, holding his hands together between his knees.

"You sure they're going to show?"

"They might."

"They *might?*"

"We'll see."

"You need to call your parents? I can let you inside to use the phone."

"Naw," Victor said. "If they don't show, I'll walk."

"When were they supposed to get here?"

"There's no set time. If they show, they show. If they don't, I walk."

"Okay then," Eric said.

"I have patience."

Victor and Eric both watched the last person of the day walk out of the mall's entrance holding onto two large shopping bags. A soft pretzel was stuffed in his mouth, which he tried to chew without dropping it or using his hands. Moments later, a man in a suit came to the door and locked it using one of the many keys on his ring.

"You know what I've never been able to understand?" Victor offered with a tone of curiosity.

"What's that?"

"How our world revolves on set schedules."

"What do you mean?"

"Set hours. Set time. We're so dependant on it."

"Well, yeah. What's so weird about that?"

"I don't know. A person decides to set a schedule—an arbitrary time on a clock—and the world commits to abide by the schedule's rule. I find that strange. That we are so obedient to the rules of time. So orderly, so obedient."

The kid didn't sound like a teenager when he spoke. He

sounded like a philosopher or a deep thinker.

"What do you think makes people so subservient?" Victor asked. "Why so willing to abide by the malls' closing schedule, for instance?"

"Well for one, security."

"Sure, security. But I'm talking about something besides a physical force. It has to do with something inside of us. A sort of structure or need for order. Why are we like that?"

"Maybe they have no reason to stay longer because all the stores close at the same time."

"I find it strange that we're all so easily synchronized. Everything orderly and pre-conceived. It's awful, really."

"What do you mean *awful?*" He was taken aback.

"I mean just that. There's no excitement in the structured. No real surprises. There's no trust in chaos."

"But is chaos something we should trust?"

The guard never thought he'd become immersed in such a conversation tonight.

"Chaos is the only liberty we have. The only chance to break free of the sovereignty of law."

"I don't think you can equate chaos to freedom, exactly," Eric said.

"Well what do you call your job? Do you call that freedom? Your regular hours. Your regular duties of *regulating* others inside a mall?"

Eric thought about this for a moment. Thought about his job. How even his uniform had to be pressed and worn a certain way. Everything was dictated. Perhaps the boy had a point. But there was also comfort in the predictable. There was much to gain from a steady life. A paycheck, for example.

Victor gave the man a smile. There was a hint of mischievousness to that grin, but man, was it ever charming. It made you want to be on the boy's side. It made you want to agree with everything he said. It was *that* compelling.

"We're not *completely* organized," Eric said. "There are still disasters and violence. It's all around us, in fact."

"Very true," Victor said. "But it's funny."

"What is?"

"It's funny how there's killers and rapists and robbers out there, and nobody's ever really going to put them completely in order, but when it comes to closing time, it's never too hard to get the last person out by eight-fifty-nine."

Funny was not exactly the word Eric would have chosen to describe that dichotomy. It was a troublesome reality. How the human race happened to be so easily organized and yet so lawless, all in the same existence.

"I wonder if there's a way to harbor those disasters. A way of making them serve a larger purpose. I think it would be fun to disrupt our daily order. To fill life with a little chaos. Maybe it would bring back some excitement into our lives."

"I like your spirit," Eric reassured him, "But it sounds a little dangerous."

For a moment, Eric wished he hadn't said that. Dangerous. He wasn't sure if that's how he actually meant to describe the boy. He was just a kid. Not even old enough to drive. He wasn't a *bad* kid really. He probably didn't have a set of parents to teach him right. What kind of parents would forget to pick him up in the middle of the mall's closing hours?

"Yeah, I know. I'm odd."

"No, not odd. You look at things differently. Time. Order. Chaos. Who knows, man. Who knows why we gravitate to firm schedules so easily, and yet we're capable of such disorderly things."

More silence. A breeze gathered around them, and they took pleasure in that for a moment.

"You're a good kid, Victor."

"Am I?"

They looked into each others' eyes. For a moment, Eric thought that the boy's eyes held a challenge. *I dare you to call me good again.* But perhaps he was misreading the look. Perhaps the look was more of yearning. A desire for an affirmation.

Eric *wanted* the boy to be good. But he couldn't say for sure.

"You've known me five minutes, how do you know if I'm a good kid or not?"

A hardness came over the boys face. It came and went.

Victor was right. He *didn't* know. He didn't know the boy at all. Maybe it was wishful thinking. The boy could be capable of anything for all he knew.

In that instant, Eric wanted to walk away. He wanted to just leave the boy behind and go back home to his bedtime whiskey and coke.

Man. The boy was right. His life was ruled by routine.

Was he free at all? Did he freely create these routines, or did those routines entrap him into an ordinary life—a life without surprise or real excitement.

It was because of that question that Eric decided to stay a little longer.

"You know," Victor said, "every time I come here I have the

strangest urge to leap off this bridge."

This time the boy's voice was not filled with viciousness. He didn't say this as an urge to defy life nor living. He said it more as a conversational topic. It was a casual statement that simply rolled off his tongue and went out into the air.

"Really?" Eric said, surprised. He took a long drag of his cigarette, and as he spoke, wisps of smoke danced out of from his mouth and nostrils. "Me too, actually. And not because I want to commit suicide or anything. This ledge draws me in. I come here almost every night to look down below, and every night the thought comes up just to tease my mind a little. That's why I look for the stars, because I think if there were no stars, the pull of this ledge might be too much." He sighed heavily. He felt dazed by his sudden confession. It made him feel connected with this strange boy, somehow.

"But what I want to do most," said Victor, "is wait for an expensive, luxurious car to drive by, like a Lexus or a BMW. Then I'd dive off and crash right on top of it. I'd do it just to screw some rich prick's day over."

Victor's feistiness forced Eric to laugh. It was a nervous laugh that took him by surprise. More smoke flowed out in curls. "Now *that's* something! Isn't that going a little out of your way just to pull a prank on some guy you don't even know?"

"No, not really. If you're going to do something, might as well do it right. Maybe that's my contribution to the chaos we all need."

Eric could sense the hatred harbored inside the boy. Victor was only fifteen, and even though he sounded philosophical when he spoke, there was still an immature sense of recklessness in him. The thing he feared most was what would happen if Victor were older and wiser? What if nobody intervened and stopped him from causing havoc on the world?

"You know, most people try to *avoid* car crashes." Eric pressed the end of his cigarette into the wall, snuffing it out. Then he flicked the butt onto the parking lot below and watched it fall to the ground.

"Do you think he would care?" Victor asked.

"Who?"

"The driver."

"Well I think he'd be pretty ticked if someone crashed into his car, yeah."

"What about me?"

"I guess. I mean... *I* would. I'd probably rush you to the hospital or do whatever I could."

"But we're not talking about you. We're talking about some rich jerk who drops money whenever he goes to the toilet and worships materialism as one of his gods."

"How do we know that he's a jerk?"

"The world is filled with jerks, Eric. The rich just happen to be the worst of them."

"I think he *would* care about you. I mean, come on. How *couldn't* he?"

"I'm not so sure," Victor said pensively.

Eric laughed to himself, silently, because it was more sad than funny. He shook his head slowly. He pulled out another cigarette from his pack, paused, then pushed it back in, remembering he'd just finished one.

"Why'd you put it back?" Victor asked, testing him with the question.

"I just finished smoking one."

"Are you afraid of becoming a chain smoker?"

"Yes actually," he admitted. He had never admitted that fear to anyone else before. His father had died from smoking. He would die from smoking. His son, too, some day.

This was his schedule.

"Well, if you're afraid of becoming one, maybe you already are. You *did* have the impulse of taking it out."

"Yeah, but I put it back."

"True, but the urge was there."

"So what does that mean?" Eric asked.

"That means we should do whatever pleases us in life. Maybe the only way to get rid of temptation is to give into it. If that second cigarette is what makes you happy, then there's no reason for you not to enjoy it. Go ahead and light it. Smoke the hell out of it. Give in to your impulse."

Eric hesitated, fingering the corners of his pack for a second. *Oh what the hell.* He flipped the tab with his thumb and pinched the same cigarette he had reached for before.

"So this is the key to life?" Eric asked, holding out the cigarette in front of his face.

"Small pleasures? No, not exactly the key, but they are what make life more bearable. I don't know what the key is. Maybe there isn't one. Or maybe there is a key, but not a door it matches to."

"There's gotta be a door," Eric said, lighting up and sucking in the smoke. How he loved tobacco. How he loved to smoke in the breeze.

"How can you be so sure?"

"If there isn't one, what does that leave us with?" Eric asked.

"Escape."

Eric thought this over.

"And how do we escape?"

"We escape this preplanned, preconceived order of life through chaos. By controlling our own life and death. By setting our own schedule. By telling God we're ready to die when we please."

Eric waited a moment, giving himself time to take in what he was being told. He didn't know what to say. He did not like so much where this conversation was going. Not because of what it revealed about the kid, but because of what it revealed about himself.

"I don't know," he said. "Even escape puts you someplace."

Just then, a Mercedes-Benz pulled into the lot below. The silver paint job was slick and waxed smooth. Everything reflected off that paint job, gliding along like streams of liquid silver. The Mercedes took a wide turn, driving right beneath the bridge. Victor's eyes exploded with joy.

His wait was over.

"The small pleasures of life," Victor said with a broad smile that bubbled with laughter. But really, it was only a whisper. Then he let himself go, free falling backwards. Like a dove in mid-air that decides to let go of flying and just lets itself drop to the ground by the pull of gravity.

Victor could see himself falling. He counted the seconds of that fall. The timing and the destruction of timing because there was no schedule to this. There was only falling. Sixty feet of chaos, all under his control. He heard the crashing of his own body smacking the hood of the car, glass cracking and the squeal of tires rubbing on asphalt. He wanted to hear the words of the driver, angry and shouting and blubbering about his car having just been detailed.

That would make him happy. That would give him pleasure.

A hand grabbed his shoulder. Victor twitched. He was still sitting on the ledge. The Mercedes drove on, perhaps returning home to a family where children expected their father home with gifts and hugs.

"Why'd you do that?" Victor shouted. His anger. His hardness. It came.

"You were about to fall," Eric said, his eyes narrow and even with the boy.

"*Was I?*" Victor said. The anger in his voice could have dented metal. As an impulse, the boy's hand swatted the cigarette from Eric's lips. They both watched as the burning cherry dropped to the ground below. Sixty feet and yet they could still see the orange flicker burst in tiny fireworks as it hit the ground. A last flicker of orange light, and then it died.

Victor expected the security guard to slap him.

"I guess we're even then," is all he said instead.

Victor glared at the middle-aged man. His eyeballs could have popped with hatred. Just a minute ago they were philosophers discussing the matters of chaos and order on friendly terms.

"You're just like the rest of them," Victor said. "Having to set order to things. Can't let a little chaos go on. Why don't you go on with your predictable, miserable life?"

"Maybe some pleasures aren't worth consuming our lives," Eric said.

He pulled out his pack of cigarettes from his shirt pocket, held it upside down over the ledge and shook the pack until every single cigarette scattered into the breeze. They both watched the little white sticks fall. Then he tossed the pack, as if holding onto it was too much of a temptation, too.

For a long, hard moment they said nothing. They only stared.

"Do you want a ride home?" Eric asked.

"I don't need a ride from you."

"No. I guess you don't."

Eric stepped away, walking backward a few paces, making sure to keep his eyes on the kid, but then the boy's shoulders slumped— the hardness went—and Eric knew he wasn't going to jump. The boy walked away. Eric returned to his car and drove home. Some semblance of order had been maintained for tonight.

The Follower

Zephan was alone in the car, out for a joy ride in his dad's Explorer. He loved how the old engine revved. Loved the feeling of air rushing in through the window and whipping his hair back. Loved to blast punk rock music until the speakers nearly exploded.

The road stretched out as wide as a grin. No cars in the way. He had the road all to himself. In the midst of the night, it felt like his high beams would never reach the end.

This was his third time taking out the car in the middle of the night without his dad knowing it. He loved the thrill of it.

He was thirteen.

He was a hard kid to control.

He egged cars at night with his friends. Smashed mailboxes with baseball bats while driving around neighborhoods forty miles an hour. Created homemade explosives with Drano and aluminum foil, and set them off in public places. All the stupid, destructive things kids found hilarious.

Already he had needled his first tattoo on his body using a tattoo gun a friend had bought online. He had borrowed the gun for a few days.

He tattooed a picture of a face with a piece of duct tape over his mouth. He wasn't sure why. Maybe it was the sense of control he liked about the image. Being able to force silence.

He inked the face on his left shoulder where he could cover it easily with a T-shirt.

But then his mom found the tattoo gun, and one day she just "happened" to stumble into the bathroom while he was taking a shower. She saw the tattoo through the glass door.

"Why would you tattoo that on your body?" she asked.

"You're one to talk," was all he said. He covered himself in a towel and went to his room.

Zephan's mother was not one to lecture anyone about the purity of ink-free skin. Her body was covered in tattoos. Small phrases, dates, poetic lines were etched everywhere on her body. She was ashamed of them now, always wearing clothes that could hide them.

She followed Zephan to his room.

"Mom, I'm getting dressed."

"I don't care. You listen," she told him.

She rolled up her long sleeves to reveal her arms.

"These are my past, okay?" she told him. "Your dad and I, we put our past behind us. We left our home and came here to try and start fresh. For you, okay?"

Zephan was five when they left Chicago. They moved to Pittsburgh, a place where they intentionally knew no one so they wouldn't be tempted to go back to their old habits, and they both began rehab. Zephan still had a vague memory of his father taking him to a back alley one day to complete a drug deal when he was just a boy.

What kind of dad does that?

But was that even a real memory, or was it something he just imagined, like the weird dreams he sometimes got in the middle of the day? Coal mines caving in with workers trapped inside. Buildings collapsing. Industrial plants catching fire. Sometimes he wished the images would stop. They were like voices, these daydreams, pulling him in.

"Why would you even tattoo that?" his mom asked. "What does it mean?"

She always had questions. Always. Never-ending questions.

Why did you do that?

What were you thinking?

Why are you staring off into space like that?

Did you have nightmares again last night?

Why do you talk to yourself sometimes?

Do you need to talk to someone?

Why are you so destructive?

Because he felt like it, that's why. There was no reason to it. He just wanted to.

His eyes caught sight of the time on the dashboard. One in the morning. He better get back before a cop decided to pull him over. He'd driven twenty or thirty miles around Pittsburgh, and already he'd seen four or five cops cruising around. Maybe it was true what they said, how there's more cops out at the end of the month to meet their quota.

He moved over into the left lane and hugged the median that separated one direction of traffic from the other. That median was shooting fast. It reminded him of the belt sander in his woodworking class. That machine both mesmerized and terrified him.

The sight of the median, the thought of the belt sander, they brought the smell of burnt wood to his nostrils. He loved the smell of sanded wood. He loved especially touching the smooth wood after it was polished down with fine sandpaper.

He inched the car closer to the Jersey barrier.

Then closer still.

He could easily reach out and touch it if he wanted to.

The thought both frightened and attracted him.

He inched a little closer.

You're not going to try and touch it, are you?

Maybe he would. Who knows? Maybe he would scrape just his fingernails off the barrier. Sand them down a little.

"It's only sandpaper, that's all," Zephan said to himself without even realizing he had spoken. A hypnotic tone stained his words.

He kept one eye on the road while the other one on the strip of concrete shooting past him. He pushed his arm out of the window and had to force it steady against the rushing wind. He opened his left palm and drifted it a foot above the barrier.

In his mind, he pretended his hand was a plane and the barrier was a landing strip.

He was going about fifty miles an hour.

He nudged the hand closer.

It was hard to keep his arm steady against the wind's turbulence. His hand kept wanting to wave, but he held it there best he could. He brought the hand lower. Maybe ten inches. Maybe eight.

He pictured a plane crashing down hard as it tried to land. He envisioned the metal body busting open. Luggage and magazines and personal items scattering out like confetti. People remained buckled to their seats, but their heads and torsos whipped around and smacked into each other, smacked into the walls of the cabin and headrests.

Six inches now.

That's how far his hand was from the landing strip.

His eye caught sight of the speedometer. He was going close to sixty. A speed limit sign shot past him on the far side of the two-lane road. Forty-five.

Something else caught his attention.

A car was behind him.

You're being followed.

Stop it. Now he was just being paranoid.

"You're just paranoid," he told himself, as though he needed to keep repeating the word to snap himself out of it.

He pulled his hand inside—both hands on the wheel now—and closed the window. He eased the car away from the median.

How long had that car been driving behind him?

He didn't know. That was bad. He wasn't sure how long he'd had that hand out. Felt just a few seconds. On the dashboard, ten minutes had passed. Could he have had his hand out that long? No. That was impossible. But how long had the car been following him?

You can't get pulled over man. You can't.

"I know!" he shouted.

Who was he shouting at? Himself? Was there another voice inside the car with him? No. He was alone. He was all alone. With someone following behind him.

Was it a cop?

"Shut up! I don't know, okay?"

Zephan eased on the gas. Turned down his music. If it were a cop, he would have pulled Zephan over by now. Wouldn't he?

He tried to make out the shape of the car and the headlights. It looked like an old Crown Victoria. Some cops used Crown Vics as their undercover ride in this area, but most departments had switched to a newer car by now.

The median had ended a while back now, but Zephan barely noticed. His thoughts were consumed by the headlights behind him and what they might mean. So far, that's all he could really make out. He was just guessing as far as the make and model of the car was concerned.

He approached a red light. He slowed down to a stop. He did it carefully, calculating every aspect of his driving.

Slow down now. Steady.

Don't hit the brakes too hard.

Keep those hands on the wheel.

Put your turn signal on.

The red light beamed on for what seemed like forever. The car behind him approached closer. It was close enough to make out the outline of a head. The driver's head then came slightly more into focus. One of the street lights grazed the side of the follower's face.

Zephan's eyes kept jumping back from the red light to the rear view mirror. The red light seemed impossibly long. The man behind looked like he had a head full of hair. Thin face, it seemed. Wrinkles, maybe. It was hard to tell.

He stared at that face for a while, trying to make it out as best he could.

There was an incessant clicking sound.

What was that?

Calm down. Just your turn signal.

That noise wasn't going to stop until the light turned green.

The driver behind him seemed to be wearing a uniform, or at least a suit and tie. But that could just be Zephan's eyes playing tricks on him. He'd like to believe that, too.

The man pulled out some sort of block and rested it on his steering wheel. Zephan couldn't see it clearly, but noticed that he… Was he writing on it? He was. The follower's eyes kept looking at Zephan's license plate.

He's writing down your plate number.

"Come on now, that's crazy. I haven't even done anything."

You tried to rip your hand off your wrist by pretending it was a plane on a landing strip.

Zephan wondered if the follower had seen that.

No, the suggestion was crazy. Why would he be taking down his plate if he hadn't done anything wrong? He rambled between thoughts, his mind consumed by chaos.

The man put the pad and pen away and took a warm chug from his mug. Looking at the follower more closely, Zephan noticed his eyes jump up. They stared directly at Zephan now. The man squinted his eyes to tiny slits, glaring at him.

It was impossible for the traffic light to still be red after this long. But it was. Still red.

Just run the light. Run it. Get away from him.

"Please shut up," he said. He held a hand over his mouth.

He's watching you. He's coming for you. You're not safe.

Zephan's eyes felt warm. They stung for a moment. Tears. He wiped them with his fingertips, then returned both hands on the wheel.

When is that damn light going to turn gree—

Before he could finish his thought, the light turned. A green arrow pointed left. He pressed the gas and turned the wheel.

His treads were bare, and the tires tended to screech if he took a turn too sharply or fast. He waited for the screech, expected it to come, even held his breath, but when he spun the wheel back and made the turn, he knew it wasn't going to come.

As he made the turn he caught a glimpse of the car. He was right. It was a Crown Vic. But this one looked blue, and most of the undercover cars he'd seen were black or white. Maybe it was black. It was hard to tell at night.

He drove down a hill and the follower followed.

His car rolled faster, so he tapped the brakes to slow down to the speed limit. He couldn't chance a stupid mistake.

As he made it down the hill, he saw another pair of headlights ahead. This time it was an actual, marked cop car.

They're everywhere.

He shot his eyes back at the rear view mirror. The follower hadn't turned. He was still there. He could hear his thoughts.

I'm coming for you. I'm going to getcha.

He imagined the follower whispering those words. He pictured a pair of green eyes and a malevolent grin.

But the face behind him remained dark and expressionless. He couldn't make out anything about it.

Zephan turned the volume up again. His own thoughts were becoming too much to listen to. System of a Down blared incoherently through the speakers.

At the next intersection, Zephan looked both ways then turned right on red.

He wondered for an instant if that was an illegal turn, but no sirens whaled to indicate he was being pulled over.

How long had this chase been going for? *It's only a coincidence. He's not following you. It's just a coincidence,* he told himself, taking a stab at reassurance.

But he couldn't let himself be reassured. Not until the follower took a different turn and left him.

Another intersection. He made a left and so did the car behind him.

"What do you want?" he screamed at the reflection in the mirror. "Get the hell away from me!"

This time, he paid no attention to the road in front of him. His eyes were fixed on his follower. Could he see his face? Could he see him grinning?

The hell with him. Just go. Hit the gas and lose him.

Zephan didn't like listening to that voice, but this time he obeyed. He jammed the gas pedal. The engine revved for a moment before the transmission caught and lurched him forward. He gained speed and saw the other car lag behind.

He wasn't paying attention when a deer jumped on the road in front of him. He saw the deer at the last instant. He cut the wheel to the right, almost tumbled off the side of the hill, then readjusted, only to smack against a tree trunk instead. His body flung forward for a moment before the airbag exploded and shot him back in his seat.

He lay limp there for a while. The front of the car had crunched like an accordion. It stood there motionless and silent. But his body felt like the tossing of bodies and metal parts. Like that airplane he had imagined while trying to scrape his hand off of the median. He pictured that airplane tumble and break apart. Bad landing. Numbers flashed in his head. Atlanta. Why did he think of Atlanta? He had never been to Atlanta. Screaming. That sound.

It warped and bended. It wasn't screaming. It was his head. It was the sound your head filled with when you were in a bad car crash. The sound of ear drums bursting.

His window had shattered. Broken glass lay on his lap.

A foggy voice called to him.

"Are you okay?"

For a moment Zephan couldn't make anything out. He saw broken glass and felt a lot of pain. His vision was blurred. Slowly things took shape.

"Hey! Are you alright? Don't move."

Don't move. That's funny.

"Who are you?" Zephan asked.

Up ahead, Zephan could see the Crown Victoria pulled over with the blinkers on. The man standing by his window talking to him had blond hair. Bleached almost. He looked like he was in his mid-forties. He was wearing a black suit and tie.

"You're not a cop," Zephan said.

"No. I'm not."

For a moment, Zephan felt relief. But only for a moment. That feeling left when he realized he had blood on his face.

"Am I okay? Am I alive?"

"You're going to be fine. Let me help you out," the man said.

"I don't think I should move. I don't think that's a good idea."

"Nonsense. You're going to be okay. Let me help you out. I can give you a ride home."

"I think we should wait for the cops," Zephan said.

That fogginess hung over him. It was hard to think. Why did he think he was in a plane crash? It was a car crash. His dad's car. Damnit. His dad would be furious.

"Listen, I'm only thirteen. I can't go to jail for this."

"You're not going to jail. You're going to be fine. Let me take you home."

The man was working the door to try and pry it open. He couldn't get it budged.

"Were you following me?" Zephan said.

At that point, the two looked at each other. It was hard for Zephan to keep his eyes open. It was hard for him to see clearly then, but he was sure that the man's eyes were green. His breath smelled of garlic. He didn't know why those details were significant. Green eyes. Garlic breath.

Paranoid or not, he did not trust the man.

When the Knife Opened

I came to New York City to visit a friend who returned from Iraq. His marriage was falling apart. We met at a coffee shop in Manhattan and talked most of the evening. There was a lot of silence too, and even that seemed to speak volumes. I told him to remain faithful. I reminded him of the Ephesians Five model of marriage.

"Love your wife the way Christ loved us," I told him.

"Right, yeah. I know that verse. I must die for my wife, right?"

"In a way, yes," I said.

The longest silence of the night took place then. Which told me that maybe he didn't understand the verse. And because I let the silence linger, it told me that maybe I didn't understand it well enough to bring context to it further.

"In a way I've already died for her," he said. "Can't she see everything I've done for her? I mean—I deployed for a year. I gave her a son. I..." he stammered, trying to find more reasons why his wife should stay.

She had said she wanted to leave. The worst part was she wanted to take their son.

"She is so ungrateful," he said. "So ungrateful. And I feel so powerless."

Could he hear himself now? How desperate he sounded?

For some reason, I thought he was describing everything much worse than what it actually was. Not that he was intentionally exaggerating his trouble, but that he was disconnected from reality. Maybe there was hope, a simple answer, but he couldn't see it because he was too emotionally wrapped up in the moment. He was too close to his own fears of losing his wife and son.

It reminded me of a passage from Isaiah.

"Fear not, for I am with you; be not dismayed, for I am your God. I will strengthen you. Yes, I will help you. I will uphold you with my righteous right hand."

This was from the same God who again and again commands us to fear *Him*.

I tried to reassure Myron. To remind him of hope and of God's providence.

"Fear not," I told him. I recited the passage from Isaiah 41 to him.

We talked until around ten that night and finally we came to the realization that no matter how many more words we spoke, none of them would fix his marriage from inside that coffee house. Any more talk, and it would only make us armchair theologians at best. Sleep might do him more good.

"Want to go for a drink? It's only ten," he said.

To him, a New Yorker, it was only ten. To me, a Pittsburgher who was used to putting two boys in bed by seven, ten was a late night.

I shook my paper cup, rattling what little coffee was left inside. It was my third of the night.

"I thought we already had a drink," I said, joking.

"I mean a guy's drink. A beer? A shot? Maybe both." He said this as if he were half joking.

"I'm good. I should get back to the hotel," I said. I felt edgy and tired.

My room was in Queens, a shuttle ride away from the La Guardia Airport. It would take me an hour by subway and bus to get back from Manhattan. If I got lucky, I would be in bed by eleven. Probably later.

We said our goodbyes as I waited for my first train. We hugged. I told him it would be okay. To not be afraid. That I would pray for him.

My first train took me into the Times Square station. I walked through the subway tunnels looking for my connecting train. In my jacket pocket I held a knife in my hand. New York wasn't my city. I had navigated my way into and around Manhattan with a subway map sticking out of my back pocket. I was clearly a tourist, and I knew people around me could see that, so I gripped the knife for extra precaution. I didn't want to be a target.

Maybe my fears were overly fabricated by TV news stories that revolved around bleeding headlines. The movies and TV dramas I'd watched didn't help, either. Anybody who sat next to me on a subway train, or walked too closely behind me was a potential robber or murderer.

I had come to New York to talk to Myron face to face because I knew he was in a bad place with his marriage. I knew a phone call or email or Facebook message wasn't going to solve any of his worries. He had served our country, and I wanted him to know I appreciated it by coming to see him in a time of need.

But now, as I walked through the subway tunnels looking for my connecting train, I felt silly and paranoid with my fingers tightly gripping a knife. It wasn't even a switchblade. Just a knife that folded shut into a plastic handle. I wasn't sure that I could even open it fast enough if the time came to use it. To defend myself.

Up ahead, a man played a violin. He leaned up against the tiled wall, making long, swaying motions with his playing arm. His whole body rocked gently with that motion. The violin case on the ground was sprinkled with spilled coins and dollar bills.

I didn't trust the way he played, as though his instrument were just a gimmick. As though the real music was coming from a set of hidden speakers, and he was just pretending.

I stepped on the far side of the tunnel to avoid walking by him.

Somehow, in that moment, I thought of Christ's command to "Love thy neighbor," right as I scurried past a stranger in need of change who was willing to share his music in return.

A black man in a leather jacket and dark hoodie dashed past me. I gripped the knife tighter. It made me feel safe. I didn't feel panicked or rushed or terribly afraid. I was just cautious. Prepared. The tightness in my shoulders eased once I reached open space.

I boarded the Seven train. For a long time the doors didn't shut. I found a seat in an empty row, but as the seconds passed, the seats filled up. The lack of personal space didn't bother me. I tried to embrace the closed-in environment. I touched shoulder-to-shoulder and hip-to-hip with strangers, and I let it go. But still I gripped the knife as a precaution.

Once we got moving, our bodies swayed to the gentle rocking

of the train. Minutes passed. I listened to the sound of the train moving through a tunnel of air. More people filled into the train with each stop. I was amazed by the mix of people in such a small space. Asians. Blacks. Hispanics. Middle Eastern. I felt like I was the minority suddenly. As the bodies filled the car, I began to feel warm.

At first, their warmth was a comforting escape from New York's October chill. I tried to find something philosophical about it: The idea that the presence of people could keep you warm. But soon I felt hot and crowded. I felt outnumbered.

I took the jacket off my shoulders, bumping an elbow into the guy next to me.

"Sorry," I said.

He didn't notice me. He kept his eyes ahead.

I slipped the knife out of the pocket and folded the jacket over my hand on my lap to keep the blade hidden.

It was then that I noticed the man in front of me.

He was the only other white guy in the car.

His eyes had caught sight of the knife, and now he was staring at my lap. I moved my jacket to better cover my hand, and the man lifted his eyes to look up at me.

I tried a friendly nod to let him know I meant him no harm. But he just stared.

And I couldn't help but stare back.

What was he going to do?

His eyes were round and wide and alert. Not scared or alarmed, but aware. Like he had no intention of taking his eyes off me. His face was worn and grizzled. He must have been at least forty if not older. His hair was dark and ragged and long and fell down to his jaw line. He had a square jaw and long chin covered in grey stubble. He looked like a man who had been in jail several times.

"You better put that away if you don't intend to use it," he said. His voice carried through gruff and even.

I took my eyes off him, pretending to ignore him, pretending not to know what he was talking about. I swallowed and found my mouth dry. I tried to produce some saliva in my mouth and swallowed again.

Nobody else was looking at me or him. The train was full, but it felt like it was just the two of us there. Like any moment he might do something and there would be no witnesses.

"I said put that away," the man said. His tone was low.

I ignored him again. Two girls sitting further down the train car were arguing over something.

"Hey," he said, in a low, directed voice.

I looked at him.

"I'm not trying to hurt anyone," I said.

"Then put it away, or I'll *make* you use it."

The words brought a shiver to my neck. I had no intention to use the knife. I had no intention of sinking the blade into another man's flesh. But now it felt like an inevitable outcome. Like I had cornered my way into this position.

For the first time, I could feel people paying attention to us. A few shifted uncomfortably in their seats, in their stances. An older black lady with a perm looked at the man, then at me. Our eyes caught and she looked away. Her lips pressed.

"Listen," I said, hoping only he would hear me and nobody else. "Leave me alone."

I could tell my knife was making him paranoid, but now I feared that putting the blade away wasn't an option. Doing so would leave me vulnerable. He could jump me at any minute, and

I could do nothing to stop him.

The knife was closed, held in my fist. It was barely a weapon. It was only an implied weapon. It would do me no good to protect me the way it was. I felt an urge to open it. If this man suddenly jumped on me or attacked me, I would have nothing but a plastic handle to defend myself. I would have been safer holding a pencil.

I watched his body tense up. He placed his hands on his knees. Like he was getting ready to do something. Fight or flee? I had no idea what his intentions were. Worse yet, I had no idea what mine were either. I had no clue what I was made of in a situation like this.

I had never been in combat. I had never deployed. Never in a fight.

I had brought the knife along to defend myself in case of a situation like this, and now here I was, without any clue of what I might do.

The only real thing I wanted then was to feel safe. I wanted the next stop to be my stop. Or better, to be his. I wanted to be back at the hotel. Anywhere but in here with this man who might do something. I would rather be back in the coffee shop with Myron talking about his failing marriage, listening to his world described in ruins.

The train hit another stop. A few people stepped off the train, but even more boarded.

I thought that being in public would make me feel safe. But instead, the fullness of this crowd reminded me of a story I had heard of a woman who had been robbed in public, surrounded by people, and nobody had done anything to stop it. Where did I hear that story? It felt so real and applicable now.

This man was going to jump me, grab the knife from my

hands, and stab me with it and nobody would do anything at all. They would just let it happen.

Everything felt so alien. I was the one with the knife, and yet I felt unarmed, threatened and unable to defend myself. Nothing had happened yet. No violence had taken place. But I felt its imminence.

My desire for safety overwhelmed my sense of reason.

Only one thing would make me feel safer.

Open the blade, I thought. *Open the damn blade. Otherwise it will be too late. Open the blade or you might as well be dead.*

I was convinced of this. And now, as I think back to it, removed from the here and now of that moment, I knew the thought was a mistake. But then and there it was the only thing.

I thought of Ayden and Roman, my two boys. Ages two and four. The headlines would read, "Father of two stabbed to death by own knife." *I should have brought a gun, instead,* I thought. The thought of a gun made me feel safer. I didn't even own a gun, yet this alternative seemed reasonable when compared to the knife I held now.

A knife was too close-quarters combat for my taste. Too savage now that I might have to use it. If he came at me, I would be forced to stab him in the chest. Or perhaps go for his throat. I didn't like either option. I didn't like the visuals it presented.

I had simply wanted the *threat* of a knife. As though the threat itself would be enough to avoid this type of situation altogether. Instead, the knife had created the situation. *Caused* this tension to happen.

Open the blade and show it to him and he will leave you alone. Then maybe you won't have to use it.

The man leaned forward some in his seat. His fingers clutched his stained jeans at the knee.

"What are you going to do?" I said, maybe a little too loud because more eyes looked at us. They looked at us two crazy white folks and knew something was going down.

"I told you. Put it away."

He was threatening me. I believed those words as threats. If I put the blade away now, he would jump on top of me, choke me out, grab my knife and stab me to death. He looked old and worn, but in my mind he was capable of speed and violence.

Was anybody going to do anything? Would anyone save me from this maniac? I couldn't believe that nobody said or did anything to stop what was going on.

I reached below the fold of my jacket with my free hand and opened the blade.

When the knife opened, there was a small click.

And that click felt irreversible. Like a lock catching.

The old woman with the perm moved away from us. I recognized it as panic, but the people she bumped into mistook it for impatience.

The train stopped. The doors opened. The woman left.

And I had my chance to leave this place, to run for safety, but more people spilled in. There were more bodies now than there was air left to breathe for all of us.

So I felt stuck. Stuck with an opened blade in my hand with no intention to use it, but unable to put it away either. And I felt powerless, too. I was the one with the weapon, but the object offered no strength. In fact, I felt weakened by its possession.

I remember thinking the words, *I did this. I did this.*

What *did* I do? I had done almost nothing. I had opened a knife and held it underneath my coat and stared at a man in the eyes and asked him to leave me alone. Nothing had happened, and yet the knife had opened up everything. Every bad possible outcome was on the brink. The fears exploded and multiplied in my brain.

"When is your stop?" I asked the man.

The man didn't say anything. His eyes bounced from my face to my lap and back up. His fingers released the grip on his knees.

"Which one's your stop?" I asked him again, more forcefully.

"Vermont Boulevard," he said with caution.

I looked up at the subway map on the wall behind him. It was just a mesh of colored lines drawn in every direction. It was too far to make out any of the words. I had no clue which station we had just passed.

"It was two stops ago," he said.

"Why didn't you get off?"

"You were going to follow me," the man said.

This man was paranoid.

"Follow you? *You're* the one who threatened me," I said.

I can't recall how loudly I said this. I don't remember if anyone thought I was shouting. Nobody told me to hush.

"I don't know what's going through your mind, kid. But you're crazy," he said.

He nodded at my hidden knife with his eyes.

"Calm, your crazy self," he said. "Nobody threatened you. I just asked you to put the knife away." For the first time I noticed a quiver in his words.

"I don't mean you any harm, okay," he said.

He meant to harm me. I was sure of this.

His hands shook, but then he steadied them. He was going to do something.

"You told me you were going to make me use this," I said, and I pulled the blade out of the jacket and held it in full view.

"Woah, woah, woah," he said rapidly, and held his palms up, like an innocent man.

He stood slowly, palms facing me. I didn't trust him. He was going to jump me now. Or any moment. I stood up also and held the knife in the space between us, pointing it at his body.

Then it felt like the train had crashed into a wall. But it was one of the passengers who tackled me to the floor.

"You crazy white dude. What the hell was you thinkin'?" someone said.

"I told you!" someone else shouted to the whole train. "I told you, you can't trust none of them white people!"

My arm was being twisted by two or three different passengers behind my back. People were shouting at me to drop it. Drop the knife. *What knife?* I thought. *Aren't you going to save me from this crazy old man who wants to stab me?*

But the pain in my shoulder, elbow and wrist was too much, and my hand let go, and I remembered it was me holding the knife, not the other.

They stood me up. Call it providence or call it luck, but right then the train stopped, a rush of momentum coming to a halt. A hard stop. And most of the people fell or reached for things to keep their balance. I caught a handrail, then bolted. The door opened, slowly, too slowly, but somehow I made it through and ran. I left the jacket and knife behind, but I didn't turn back. I didn't even know which stop this was, but I didn't care. I thought someone might follow me. For sure at least the old man would chase me. But as I made it up a flight of stairs and turned a corner, I didn't see anyone come after me so I stopped. I caught my breath.

I found a bench and sat down. I felt so embarrassed. So stupid for being so impulsive.

I replayed the whole scene in my mind. How quickly it had escalated. How quickly I turned to a knife I didn't know how to use.

To this day I still can't reason with why I opened that blade. It was fear and a desire for safety and self-preservation. I don't know what motivated my fear. I wish it were as simple as blaming it on news stories or television. I wish it were as easy as blaming it on drinking too much coffee, or staying up too late at night or dealing with the stress of a friend's failing marriage. Or the fact that I felt threatened by the only other white man on a train full of blacks, Hispanics and Asians. A man who looked like he had been in jail several times.

The man sitting in front of me tried to kill me, I reasoned. *He told me he would force me to use the knife.* I made excuses for my reaction.

What would my wife tell my boys if that man had killed me?

I asked myself that question as a defense for pulling out the knife. Because I couldn't bear the though of my wife having to deal with my death. Or my sons growing up fatherless.

All of these fears. They clung to me like roots to a pot of soil.

Looking back, now that those weeds have died and the immediacy of those moments have passed, I ask myself different questions.

What would I have told my wife after killing a man on a subway for no reason at all? What would she have told my sons? How would the news reporters have written that story? What would the passengers on the train have said about me?

To this day, I have never told what happened to anyone. Not

my friend in New York. Not my wife. Not my children. And, fortunately, not the police.

That evening, I returned to my hotel and never slept. I felt consumed by the fear that any moment the police would come to my door and arrest me.

I caught my flight the next day, fearful that maybe some crazy passenger like me made it on the plane with a knife.

I hugged my wife when she picked me up at the airport, thinking that maybe if I didn't start loving her more she would take my children and leave.

How many fears would rule my decisions?

Every time I pray, I thank God that a passenger tackled me to the ground on that train. I thank God the train stopped and He allowed me to escape. Most of all, I thank Him for not allowing me to hurt anyone or myself. I don't know what might have happened, otherwise. Fortunately, those are fears and uncertainties I didn't have to face.

Sometimes, I try to picture myself on that train the way the other passengers saw me. A scared, scattered young man holding a knife to some old man. That wasn't me. It couldn't have been me. That was someone else with the knife. I would never do something so stupid. So irrational.

Eventually, Myron's wife did leave him. She took their son. His fears became reality. I had met his wife several times before. She had seemed like a sweet, reasonable woman who would cause no harm to anyone. I never imagined her to be someone to leave a husband. To take a son.

It took them a while to recollect the pieces and get back together.

But when she had first left him, I thought of how Myron's

fears—the ones he had unveiled to me over coffee in New York—had transformed into prophecies.

My knife, too, had been a prophecy. I just thank God, that in the end, that prophecy was interrupted.

I wonder if our fears are inevitable, or if they cause things to *become* inevitable.

I wonder, in part, if the passage in Isaiah not to fear is more a commandment than a suggestion. A commandment against our stronger tendencies.

It's funny.

God tells us not to fear the world in which we live—a world we can smell and touch and see full of scary things—and in the same book, God *commands* us to fear Him, a God most of us don't fear at all. And it's not because we can't see him. Every day, we fear things we don't see or know. So is fear itself a great evil? Can fear save us? Can it condemn us? Can fear kill us and other people, too?

That same image of me on the train holding a knife keeps coming back. I try to put it away, fold it shut, but it always returns. I see myself pointing the blade of a self-fulfilling prophecy at a man who was just as scared as me. Look at that blade. Just look how small it is compared to the size of this world. Just a few inches of steel, in the shape of a sharpened tongue. Short enough to fit inside a palm, and yet… long enough to penetrate a heart. Sharp enough to make a person bleed.

Trailing

Devin and his father rode south on Highway 35 in the still of night. The mover's truck dragged the twenty-foot trailer behind them, packed with furniture and books. His father, white-bearded and round-bellied, slept beside him on the lumpy seat, snoring quietly. The truck's high beams pierced through the night, the road slipping past them at sixty miles an hour and grinding.

Devin kept snatching looks at his father. Sound asleep. Eyes dreaming. He thought of all of his father's sacrifices. This was their third move in the past two years. College professors who taught theology didn't stay in one place very long, especially if universities had to shave off faculty to save budgets. Austin lay ahead somewhere, and Devin wondered if this next stop would help his father provide for the six of them.

At twenty-one, Devin had already changed schools three times, living at home to afford classes, and falling behind because most credits didn't transfer. He stayed away from the house when he could. It bothered him to see all those unopened boxes. They reminded him of how temporary their efforts were. He avoided conversations with his father when he could because too often the words came out wrong.

He looked at his father again, sitting beside him. Every day, the old man seemed to be getting older—his beard becoming grayer, the bags under his eyes more lined with grooves, little crusties forming at the corners. Devin wanted to tell his father how much he loved him right now. Wanted to tell him how much he admired his passion for teaching despite the low wages. Wanted to express in words what he felt in his heart every night he saw his father up in the late hours, correcting papers under the glow of a desk lamp with his hand cramping from writing so much. But as Devin looked at the old man's sleeping face now, he decided he should let him rest.

He would find the words some other—

Devin's eyes jumped up to the road and saw the traffic coming to a halt. As he slammed the brakes, every hinge in the truck screeched, tires scraping across asphalt. His father awoke, startled by the force and sound of the truck braking suddenly. His lips murmured in mixed panic and confusion.

"What's going on?"

"Damnit! Sorry, okay? Damn!" Devin screamed.

The truck stopped just in time before crashing into the cars ahead. Blue and red police lights flashed in the distance, coming from a Circle-K station at the next exit.

"You scared me, son."

"I didn't mean to, okay?"

"No—I mean... Okay."

"Say it."

He waited for his father to say something. He was furious at himself for disturbing his dad's sleep. His father looked so old now—looked in so much need of rest. Devin felt angry and stupid with himself. His father remained silent.

"Say it!"

"Maybe you should let me drive."

"I'm fine."

"Do you want to rest?"

"No I don't want to rest. You rest. You should rest, dad, okay?"

"You sure?"

"I'm sure."

"Okay, then. I'll rest."

"Rest then."

"All right."

"Okay," Devin said, fumbling for anything else to say. He couldn't find the right words. A bitterness grew inside him. What were the words he had wanted to find a moment ago? He didn't know. He felt too angry with himself to want to look for them now.

"Damn," he muttered again.

The traffic seemed to stretch for miles ahead of them. It would take them hours to unload the trailer in the morning. Maybe longer. He didn't know anymore. He just stared at the blue and red police lights flashing in the distance, wondering what the hell had happened at that gas station, hoping his words might come to him some other time.

Author

Some would die tonight, but not because I do not love them. To allow someone to die is painful enough. Even more so if it's someone you've created.

June twirled the straw in her tall glass. Thomas didn't let their conversation distract him from his appetite. He sucked down another gulp of his root beer float. He already devoured his burger, so he picked at his fries between gulps of his drink.

"How?" Thomas asked after he swallowed. He had a tendency of getting engulfed by these discussions. He wasn't angry, but charged. "How can you say that?"

"Because," she said.

A moment ago they were immersed in their flirting. Immersed in a perfect moment of immortal joy. Now she was almost sorry she had brought it up.

"That's not even close to an answer. Give me your reasons."

Thomas was all smiles, even as he said this. He actually found the topic fascinating, but he became so intense that June often retreated rather than feed into his gluttony for debate.

Thomas gestured to the waitress for another float. June thought he could have hers, but if she offered, then he would think she was slipping back into her anorexia, and at this moment she wanted to deal with that less than him questioning her beliefs.

"Fine," she said, finally giving in to his demands. "I want to believe there's something greater than just us driving around for miles every Friday night to find whatever diner has the best root beer float in the state of Oklahoma."

June and Thomas were both seventeen. Highschoolers who made nights like these into dates. For them, it was all true about negatives attracting each other. June was a sweet, tended-hearted girl who came from a well-off family. Thomas was brash. Or he could be at least. And Thomas, at seventeen, was basically the main source of income for his mother and her boyfriend.

This diner was dingier than most others they had visited. Most of the other diners looked like they were modeled after the fifties to revive a retro yet modern feel. This diner looked like it had been *constructed* in the fifties and hadn't been retouched since.

There were a few colorful, paper bunnies and Easter eggs taped to the windows. It was just enough to make the place look tacky.

June remembered it was Good Friday.

Easter was coming up, and she would spend the day at church and at home with her family. She wasn't sure what Thomas would be doing for Easter, and had thought of inviting him to spend time with her family.

"Just because you *want* him to exist, it doesn't mean he does."

"Well the same goes to you then. Just because you don't want

Him to exist, it doesn't mean He doesn't."

"First of all, it's not that I don't *want* him to exist. It's just that he *can't*."

"Why?" June asked, and realized it wasn't often that she reversed the table to question him. Now she expected him to get defensive, but it didn't happen.

His eyes narrowed, but his voice remained even from start to finish.

"It's simple. First of all if he is our loving creator, then where has he been my whole life? Where is he while my mother takes money from my checking account every month to feed her boyfriend's fix, like I don't even notice?"

"Sorry, but that's just silly."

"What's silly about it?"

"That doesn't deny his existence."

"Sure it does."

"How?"

"If we are to believe in this so-called author, this omnipotent, all-knowing figure, then it means he is ever present in everything we do. What's that word you used?"

"Sovereign," she said.

"Sovereign, right. So if that's what he is, then it means he is in charge of everything that goes on around us, right?"

"Right."

"The good, sure. But the bad, too. He's in charge of everything awful around us. And that defeats any notion of his goodness," Thomas said.

He allowed this thought to settle in, like smoke filling the air, before he resumed.

"So he's there when my own mother takes money from me and

tells me she's going to use the cash to get groceries, except when I come home from my minimum-wage job, it's still the same carton of eggs in the fridge, only a day older, and the mold on the bread is so green you'd think it was grass."

"So?"

"So that's not a creative authority I can respect or even accept. Not only that, but does that mean he's here with us now? Listening to us talk? Watching you stir your float while we wait for the waitress to grab me another? If that's the case, then who the hell are we? What kind of freedom is that? We're just a bunch of puppets on strings."

June exhaled before she answered. She didn't want to play into his emotions. Didn't want to get sucked into the heat of the conversation.

"We're not puppets," she objected. "We're His creation."

Just then, a man from a table in another booth blurted out a word. June and Thomas both turned to look. It sounded like the man had shouted either "peaches" or "leaches." It was hard to tell. There were two others sitting with the man, all wearing dark business suits.

"What about them over there then?" Thomas pointed at three men huddled over their table and talking more quietly now. "Look how secretive those three look. Is our creator listening in on *their* conversation at the same time as he is listening to ours? Doesn't that seem a little improbable? What about the cook in the back who grilled my burger and mixed your salad you haven't even touched? And that man at the bar, mumbling to himself? Does this creator watch us all at the same time?"

"Maybe He does. He has to care about all of us personally, I imagine," she said.

"Why?"

"Because He created us."

"Except, you make him sound more like he's controlling us if he is so omnipotent. If he is in charge like you say he is."

"I don't know that controlling is the right word," she said.

"Then how sovereign could this author really be?"

"I look at it like a mystery. He created us; He's in charge of our lives, and yet we have the freedom to make the choices *we* want," she said. And even though she was convinced of this truth, as soon as she spoke it all out, the explanation sounded faulty to her. She started to see the hole in that theory. Started feeling paranoid, too, maybe. Was that the right word? Paranoid? Is that what she felt? She felt watched. She didn't like it.

She shut the thought out.

"Does he know our end from the beginning?" he asked.

She thought carefully. Had to make sure that whatever answer she gave fit with her understanding of the author.

"Yes. I believe He does."

"So he knows the day we are going to die? He knows the moment we make the one decision we will regret forever. For the rest of our lives?"

"I…" she stammered. "I guess He would have to."

She felt Thomas peering at her. She felt his mind working over her every answer as a weakness to attack. As though he were trying to corner her, force her to admit to the creator's inexistence. Or at least admit to her doubts.

"So where is his love for his so-called children if he lets us slaughter one another so easily?"

"Freedom has consequences," she said. It was the only thing she could think of at the moment. She had always imagined she would be better prepared to rebuff his attacks more convincingly than this. Instead, all she was offering was non-answers or distractions from the problem at hand.

"He's sovereign, and yet we're free," he said, as though reflecting this over like some mathematical equation. He gave it a chance, pretending for a moment that a positive and a negative could actually be connected by an equal sign.

It didn't fit.

"I think it's like this," she said, and had to pause for a moment. "I think we are free to do whatever it is that we want, and the Author can intervene in any way He wants, and no matter what we decide, there is no action that we can take that can undermine His control. Nothing we do can defeat his sovereignty."

"You're the one always talking about our lives having a greater meaning, but how is there meaning in that?" Thomas said. "I refuse to believe in that kind of creator, one who is always in charge no matter what we do."

"Then you refuse what He is, except you make Him sound like a neurotic and demented puppet master, and that's not it at all."

"What is he then?"

"Our loving, dedicated, thoughtful creator."

"You're too kind. What if we died tonight in a car crash on our way home? Some drunk driver or a tired businessman falling asleep at the wheel. Is that love?"

"If that happens, you can't just pin it on Him."

"But you just stood by his sovereignty. You can't backpedal your way out of it now."

"Like I said, there's still freedom under His will. We still have choices we make. We still have our own desires. Our own characteristics. Our own faults and our own strengths. His sovereignty doesn't deny any of those. If anything, it further shines on His love."

"How?"

She cherished this question for a moment. This one was different than his regular inquisitions. There was a tone to the question that exposed Thomas. That exposed his curiosity and his desire to want to fit it all together. To make sense of it all.

"He loves us in spite of our sin," she said. "He loves us in spite of our wicked hearts. Even in spite of our hatred for Him. He plucks us out of our deadened nature."

Now she had hit a string that resonated with truth. It sounded right to her ears.

"But he created us. So what you're saying is that he loves us in spite of how he made us?"

"The fact He created us in the first place in spite of knowing how we would turn out should speak for itself."

"You lost me just then. Say that again."

"He loves us even though He knew we would turn against Him," she said, slowly.

"Come on. That's just a bunch of rhetoric. Listen to yourself. You make it sound like we're some evil little creatures just chomping at the bit to destroy everything we see."

Her eyes stared back at him, her gaze hung as an accusation.

"We're not all like my mother and her boyfriend, okay?" Thomas interjected, reading the expression in her eyes. For the first time, he sounded defensive. "We're not all sucking up blood from society through welfare and still managing to steal from our own kids. We're not all drug addicts, pedophiles, rapists, murderers, gluttons..." he trailed off.

"Anorexics," she cut in, as if to finish his sentence.

"Hey, I never said that was a sin. I never *called* you a sinner."

"Porn addicts," she cut in again, like a jab.

At this he became silent. His eyes narrowed, and he folded his own arms. For several moments neither of them talked. The waitress arrived and set down his second root beer float.

"Will there be anything else for y'all?" she asked.

Neither of the two looked at her.

"Alright, then," she said, left the check and walked away.

Thomas pushed the tall glass across the table.

"Listen," June said, and breathed deeply. There was kindness in her voice. She wanted to reach over and touch him, to let him know she meant no harm.

"Drink it," he said. There was no kindness in his tone.

"We're all guilty of something, Thomas. That's why we need to accept His plan. His forgiveness. His salvation."

"Drink the stupid float," he said. "Listen to you talk of salvation, when you can't even save yourself from your own disease."

Any other day, that comment might have stopped her in her tracks. Offended her and sent her away. But tonight was an opportunity for grace.

"Can *you?*" she asked. She matched his every mean-spirited sentence with her own tender words.

"I'm perfectly happy with the way I am."

"How do you think we got here Thomas?" she said, now trying a new approach in the debate. It was a question that always stumped him. It was one of several factors that convicted June of her beliefs.

"We drove," he said. "Same way we'll leave here."

"No. You know what I'm asking. How did we get here? How did we come into this existence?"

"There are other ways."

"We didn't just develop our way onto the page. We didn't just *write* ourselves into existence."

"So maybe we were created. That's fine by me. It's the point of sovereignty I take issue with."

"So you want a Creator who doesn't care? Someone who will let you live your own life into self-destruction all the while you force-feed yourself a make-believe happiness?"

"Better than one who needs to *'save'* me after the way he's already made me."

Just then, the three men at the booth stood up. They walked over to the old man hunkered at the bar. All of it seemed strange. The men walked slowly, as if calculating their steps. They began talking with the man in turns, one after the other as if finishing one another's sentences. June and Thomas watched, putting aside their conversation for now.

Watching the three men, June felt uneasy.

The three dark-suited men stood while the old man looked up at their faces as if in pain. He seemed close to tears, his voice rising and falling in uncontrolled bursts. The three men looked identical except for their hair: one blonde, another red-haired and the third with hair so black it could swallow the moon.

June had the sense that something bad was about to happen. She didn't like the way the three men stood over the old guy at the bar. Surrounded him.

Thomas was too frustrated to talk anymore, so he welcomed the distraction.

The two of them couldn't make out what was going on. They tried to listen in on their conversation without getting caught.

As the old man spoke, the word "disease" kept coming up

again and again. It's the only thing June could pick out from his ramblings. Thomas mistook this moment as yet another glimpse of life's senselessness. There was nobody in control over this. Stuff like this, random men talking to other random men about disease… it just *happened*. There was no explanation. There was no purpose. No plan.

June and Thomas remained quiet as they tried to listen carefully. The old man spoke of an old woman getting shot in the head. The image brought a pulse of anxiety to June's chest. She reached across the table to touch Thomas's hand.

"We have to leave," she whispered. "We have to leave now."

He didn't even feel her touch. He never heard her voice, being so immersed in this strange, random event.

"I don't know!" The man screamed.

"Thomas, let's get out of here," June whispered more forcefully now. "Something bad's going to happen. Something really bad is going to happen."

"Nothing will happen," he told her, and turned back to watch.

The men's conversation continued. There was something very calculated and rehearsed about the way the three suited men spoke. Then, even though they couldn't hear exactly what the old man was saying, both June and Thomas heard relief in his voice. Thomas relaxed at this, but June tensed even more.

"Let's go," she hissed. "Now!"

Thomas turned to shoosh her. Here was the evidence to defend his case, right before their eyes in this randomly selected diner along a forgotten highway, and she was doing everything she could to reject it. Nobody was in control. Nobody was watching them. Things just happened because the world was what it was, untamed and untamable. It was up to them to survive. There was no divine providence. Just acts of sheer randomness.

A gunshot blasted. The gun flash brought a spark of light to the dimly lit diner. June screamed. Thomas shuddered. The blond man held a gun, and now the old man sat with a hole in his face the size of a fist.

June ran for the door. The little bell jangled as she swung it open, but before she could make it through, the blond man shot her dead in the spot. She dropped straight to the floor, half-in, half-out of the diner, keeping the door open.

Thomas held up his arms. All of this was too much. He didn't understand, and this scared him. It scared him not to believe as June believed. It scared him for the first time to witness madness like this and think nobody was watching. Nobody cared.

Eyes filled with tears, but they weren't those of Thomas. They weren't the eyes of June, not those of the waitress, nor the men in suits, especially not the eyes of the man holding up the gun. There is always pain in killing something you create. There is pain for being rejected by those you love. The blond man fired the gun once more.

The bullet moved through the air.

Time is relative if you decide to slow it down. The time it took the bullet to travel from the gun, through the space inside the diner, into Thomas's ear and skull was faster than anyone in the restaurant could control. But anything could have happened. Anything unexplainable or illogic to prevent the bullet from following its path. A cheap, 1950s style ceiling fan, badly-bolted to the ceiling, could have fallen down and redirected the bullet elsewhere. A mysterious gust of air could have traveled through the doorway and evaporated the bullet into dust. Maybe Thomas might have slipped and fallen just in time for the round to miss his head completely.

Those things did not happen.

The bullet moved through the air as the shooter intended. It pierced through the cartilage of the boy's ear, punctured through the skin and ripped through his skull. It grazed the outer tissue of his brain.

It is written elsewhere that this bullet ended Thomas's life. There was no time at that moment to explain what this really meant. The bullet ended the life he knew to live. A life of contempt. Of resentful doubt.

Paramedics rushed to the scene after someone dialed in a tip to the police. At first they thought Thomas was dead. Everyone was. The waitress. The old man at the bar. The girl in the doorway. There was so much blood over the boy's body. And the skull had caved in like it had been struck with the edge of a shovel. And no pulse, poor boy. No pulse or breathing or anything else to indicate to a man of science that life was still within this boy.

They brought the bodies to a nearby morgue that was not used to handling such a heavy volume at once. Four bodies. The boy. The girl. The waitress and the old man. Police were still looking for the cook. Still investigating.

On Sunday morning, when the coroner finally got to Thomas, the boy's body jolted and sat up. He gasped for air and inhaled for a long time. The coroner and his assistant watched the body rasp, eyes still shut from the swelling, head still as concave as a cavern, and they were terrified.

Both the coroner and the assistant shuttered. They looked at each other. Look at the boy. Back at each other.

"Where's June?" the boy asked, but his voice was garbled and hard to make out. "Where is she?" he asked.

"She's in the other room," the coroner said.

Thomas made a move to get off the table, but as his feet touched the ground and he put weight on his legs, his body dropped. He stumbled on his four limbs, trying to get out of the room.

The assistant coroner tried to get a hold of the boy and help him up.

"Young man…" The coroner said, but stopped. What do you say to a boy you thought was dead and you were about to dissect? No. Not *thought*. You were *sure* he was dead. He'd been dead since Friday.

"You can't see her. Not the way she is," the man in the coat said. He realized he was holding a scalpel. He couldn't remember how long he had been holding it. He set it down, gently.

"Dr. Rupert is right," the assistant said. He lowered Thomas's body back down. "You need to stay calm. Sit down. Relax."

"I want to see her," Thomas said. His jaw felt loose. It was hard to talk without slurring his words. It was a miracle he was talking at all given the damage done to his brain.

"You'll see her. You will. But first you need to be looked at."

They called in an ambulance and had him escorted to the nearest trauma center.

When the coroner later spoke to the media about the event, this man of science, this man who lived within the boundaries of reasonable explanations only, used the word "rose" to describe the way Thomas's body jolted and sat up. He gave no explanation. The boy had been dead. He was sure of it.

That's all the reporters needed to make the news into a media firestorm. They called the event, "The Easter Morning Miracle." They called Thomas, "The boy who rose on Easter Sunday"

And I'd be lying if I said I hadn't planned it this way. I'd be lying.

A medical team began operating on Thomas right away.

The boy spent a month at the hospital recovering. Due to the amount of work they had to perform on his skull and brain tissue, they couldn't release him to see June's body. He never made it to her funeral. It took months and months of physical therapy, as he gradually regained control of his motor skills.

His mother came to visit him sparingly. When she did visit, she asked how long before he could go back to work. They were running low on food and needed the money.

"I'm not giving you any more of my money," he told her.

She glared at him.

"I'm dead to you," he said.

So she left.

After that, she didn't come visit him again until he was released from the hospital.

I can't say Thomas lived happily ever after. I can't even say that after the shooting life was somehow more vibrant, or colorful or glamorous. His girlfriend, June was dead. His mother and her boyfriend still addicts. And now they tried to exploit every media opportunity they could. From local TV interviews to national media attention. Thomas couldn't move out on his own because he was still a minor. Legally, they were still his guardians. They pushed him into every microphone and camera and journalist that came to the house.

Everyone wanted to interview the boy who survived the bullet.

Thomas refused to appear on TV unless he wore a hat to cover his head.

It took several more surgeries before they could restructure his skull back into a normal shape. A terrible, crisscrossed scar still remained where his hair would not grow again.

He touched the scar at night, when he couldn't sleep or when he thought back to the shooting and couldn't believe it actually happened. It was only by touching the scar that Thomas believed. That he was still alive. That a bullet had penetrated his skull. That June was truly gone.

He was jealous of reporters and national audiences who believed his story as he told it. Such faith on their part. He didn't show the scar to anyone in the general public. He received hundreds of emails and letters from people who said they were praying for him, and that his story had touched their lives. He resented them for their easy belief, when it was so difficult for him to do the same.

Yet, difficult belief was still belief.

He secretly felt a compassion for skeptic reporters who tried to hide their scoffing disbelief during interviews.

Thomas's own resentful doubt was gone. His old self was dead, and he had been born again inside the coroner's office. He often ran his fingertips across the scar as if it were a Braille message he could read.

And yet, he wondered if it was all worth it. For three people to be killed randomly—four if you counted him—just so he could live in belief. Why such drastic measures? His biggest hope was that maybe the shooting had served a bigger purpose. Evaded some larger disaster. Though he could think of no reasonable possibility for that. How could this one reckless, random and violent shooting somehow fit into a larger scheme of orderly purpose?

All the same, Thomas felt small and humbled. Because maybe he had been a survivor of some greater work. Maybe he was part of something he was not able to see with his eyes or touch with his hands. Something big and lofty and too complicated for his own mind to comprehend.

He wasn't a guy to watch the news often, but when he caught the headlines, he realized that shootings happened all the time. Some more violent than others. All of them senseless in their own way.

Shootings happened so often that it made him think that June was right. That people are not so good on their own, left to their own devices. What had she called it? There was a word or a phrase she used to describe the human condition...

Depraved. That's what it was. They were all depraved.

And all these shootings, not even counting the rest of the tragedies but the shootings *alone*, were so frequent and each so violent, that it made *his* shooting feel both insignificant and extremely powerful. Insignificant because it was one of many. A grain of sand on the beach. Powerful because he was the only person he knew who died from the shooting and came back to life.

The years passed.

The scar never faded.

He attended the University of Pittsburgh because that was the farthest school from home that accepted his application.

The event and June's death didn't bring about all of the answers he wanted. The shooting never balanced out the equation of freedom and sovereignty. If anything, it made that equation even harder to resolve.

Thomas had been the one who picked the diner at random out of dozens. They could have gone anywhere, but on that Friday night *he* had chosen that diner. *He* did. And yet he felt a sense that it had been chosen for him. He got the sense that the bullet was always meant to go through his brain and kill him so he could come back to life again.

Why wasn't he simply born a believer?

Why go through this entire process and shed June's blood?

None of the answers he came up with felt certain.

It was only the scar that he knew was certain. That, and that the Author existed.

ACKNOWLEDGMENTS

I want to thank my wife, Heather, who has constantly encouraged me to return to writing after several years of near abandonment. But I want to thank her even more for putting up with me when I decided to set a rather ambitious deadline to publish this book, which forced me to sacrifice valuable family time with her and our son, Phoenix. My wife has also served as the source of inspiration for numerous stories included in this collection.

An enormous thank you goes out to my parents, Alain and Chiara, who made tremendous sacrifices to bring our family to the U.S. from Italy. English was obviously not our first language, and yet, they took on jobs as teachers and professors to provide for our family. I can't thank them enough for everything they have done for us. They brought us to Pittsburgh, a city that will forever hold a place in my heart.

I also want to acknowledge the University of Pittsburgh, a fine institution with an even finer English Writing Department. All of my writing professors at Pitt have in some way shaped my style and writing voice. A few of these stories have gone before their red pens first before landing on these pages.

Speaking of firsts, there were anthologies and literary publications that printed my stories before I ever had the bright idea of putting them together in this book. "Ampersand Review" was the first to publish, "Amidst Traffic." "Wet Ink"—which is an Australian literary magazine—published, "Midnight." "Brand"—a British literary publication—published, "A Tin Can Mind." "Writers Journal" published, "The Duct Tape People." "Best New Writing (2008)" published, "Lost in the Night." Some of the other stories, such as "Black Coats at the Cheyenne Diner" and "The Problem with My Shoes" have appeared in online publications. Thank you all for believing in my writing and giving it a place where people could read my stories.

I would be a tremendous jerk if I didn't thank my friend, Matthew Kovalcik, who helped me shoot the cover of this book. As a photographer, I had a very specific idea in mind for the cover, and he helped me execute it just as I had hoped. We went out in the middle of traffic one Friday morning before the sun came up and shot more than six hundred images of me in a suit and tie. We had actually tried some photos of me on the road in bumper-to-bumper traffic, but in the end I decided to go with the shot seen on the cover. It was hard directing someone else with the camera to execute an image that looked a certain way in my mind. I could never work as an art director, that's for sure.

Additionally, a well-deserved thank you goes out to Mike O'Brien, who reviewed this book under a demanding timeline to edit its content. It is thanks to his work and effort that I felt *relief,* not angst, in publishing the final version of this book.

Without question, many of these stories have a deep theological undertone. My friend, James Samreny, deserves all of my love for bringing me to Christ. But the Glory and credit (James would agree), goes to God, Himself. We do have a magnificent Creator— or "Author," if you will. My prayer and hope is that maybe some of these stories have paused you to reflect on His existence and impact in your own life. When we are in the midst of our chaotic lives, it's hard to see His hand leading our path. Thank you, God, for Your Providence, which steers me safely through the traffic of my own life.

—Michel Sauret

CPSIA information can be obtained at www.ICGtesting.com
Printed in the USA
LVOW071554210113

316592LV00015B/770/P